MacIntosh
Mountain

MacIntosh
Mountain

VICTOR J. KELLY

ZONDERVAN PUBLISHING HOUSE
OF THE ZONDERVAN CORPORATION
GRAND RAPIDS, MICHIGAN

MacIntosh Mountain
© 1983 by Victor J. Kelly

Library of Congress Cataloging in Publication Data

Kelly, Victor J.
  MacIntosh mountain.

  I. Title.
PS3561.E3972M3 1983   813'.54   83-6497
ISBN 0-310-35181-2

Book Designer: Kim Koning
Copy Editor: Penelope J. Stokes
Editor: Judith E. Markham

Printed in the United States of America

83 84 85 86 87 88 — 10 9 8 7 6 5 4 3 2 1

for Joyce

Each of us potentially can see one unique glimpse of the beauty of God that no man can see entire. It is for us, first, to see, then to communicate.

—Sheldon Vanauken

Prologue

The couple wandered out of the pines and through the brush and stopped for a moment to gaze across the open slope tilting gently away from them. It had once been a pasture, and before that an ancient farm; but that was when the soil was still good, and neither it nor the people had become tired.

Now, with little sustenance left to give, it lay forsaken. Year by year it brought forth a new crop of winter stones, and each summer yielded a little more of itself back to the woods. The center basked sunny, fragrant with sweet grasses in the early June dampness; but as the field stretched towards the surrounding trees, daisies appeared, pungent white and yellow patches. These yielded to coarser wild flowers and grasses seeking such shade as the bushy gray birch and the poplar afforded. Like young adolescents the poplar rustled in the spring breeze, wriggling, ceaselessly urgent to be free. The older pines, oaks, and maples, their dark-visaged forebears, stood behind them, frowning at their impatience to move out into the open spaces.

Traces of an old wagon track brought the couple to a declivity, a little longer than it was wide. Before the war it had been the start of a shallow cellar, but over the years the sides had collapsed; unless one knew how to look, the land gave little hint of the abandoned dream.

"I don't think Edwin ever meant to finish it." The young man's thin, straight lips hardly seemed to move. The uniform he wore, the straight black hair, grown long on top and cut close at the sides, made him seem young. The troubled brown eyes, and the sad, clipped consonants of his speech made him seem old.

"After you left, your Pa saw Edwin was ruinin' the place. He just sort of closed his eyes to it." Her voice was quiet.

"Just can't believe Edwin used up all the money I sent home." He thrust one hand into a pocket and stood, tall and knotty like one of the nearby trees. Only his eyes, nervously blinking, betrayed his pain.

"It'll work out." Her gaze was steady and blue.

"Could lose the farm." The kuckles on his free hand turned white as he clenched his fist. "With Pa still half-paralyzed from that stroke, and Ma most the time in a place I can't reach—we dreamed better'n this." He extended his fingers and the skin over his large knuckles darkened.

"You're back." Her voice was soft, firm as her gently rounded chin. "Lots aren't." She tugged at his hand, and they drifted slowly across the field toward the darker trees on the other side. "That's dream enough for me."

He glanced at her as they walked. Her hair was a darker blonde than when he had left three years ago. The slightly tanned high school face had lost its smattering of freckles and had taken on something different he couldn't quite determine. Her brow was just as wide and just as clear. Maybe the eyes, he thought. Their blue seemed to have deepened, maybe with the darkness of his brother's death and his mother's grief.

"Sissie write you again?" His voice was even, controlled.

"Three times since you left." The afternoon breeze had finally given up and their voices carried in the silence. "A post card once, something on a piece of notebook paper another time. Mailed one from Albany. Another from New York. I'll show them to you when we get back."

"Pa hasn't changed?"

"His hate—he can't seem to forgive—paralyzes him more than the stroke."

They reached the other side of the pasture and picked their way around clumps of sumac and birch towards the darker and cooler firs. "When Edwin died," she continued, "your Pa just sat and stared. He had been able to move around some till then. Even talk a bit. But he never spoke again. The Sunday after the funeral, we came back from church with your Ma. The whole house was smoked up. He poured kerosene all over the family Bible and took a match to it. Couldn't get it in the fireplace—about burned the house down."

They stopped at a ruined stone wall clinging wearily to the contours of the land. Once it had been the fortress that kept the pines back from the cleared field, but now it sat impotent in the green sun-shafted darkness.

"The one he always carried to church?" His eyes narrowed with the memory. "He set it on the mantel. I never saw him touch it after Sissie left. Remember he never went back to church, either." He bent and picked up a gray fieldstone, its crown covered with a thick cap of lichen and moss. "Sounds like you had your war here—a war that I should've been here to fight." He replaced the stone atop the wall from which, with some winter's frost, it had tumbled. He started to brush his hands off on his uniformed thighs, but stopped short and dusted them off against one another with a clapping motion. The soft "slap, slap, slap," of his calloused hands slipped into the woods and died without echo.

"Too bad God went off someplace else to fight, too. You could've used the help." He laughed bitterly. "Wish I could put this mess to rights as easy as I put that stone back." He glanced at the wall struggling through the pines. "With the mortgage Edwin took out on the farm and wasted, can't afford to go to college now, even on the government." He looked

7

askance at her and refocused his eyes directly ahead of him. "No one else to take care of Ma and Pa. 'Pears to me there'll be a MacIntosh on the hill for a heap o' years."

They picked their way over a low place in the wall, stepping carefully over and between the spilled stones. He grasped her hand and helped her balance. "Ain't at all what I dreamed," he said again.

She stepped in front of him lightly and so suddenly that they had to embrace to keep from falling.

"We'll make our own dreams!" she said, a stubborn, angry flush rising to her cheeks. "You're back, Ira. Nothing else matters to me. We'll do the living that has to be done." She kissed him—firmly, fully—trying to draw through the softness of her body against his, all the anger, disappointment, and frustration of a soldier back from war.

1

As the ancient Dodge truck ground up the first short steep grade of the hill, Ira MacIntosh wondered when it would wheeze its last and die.

"Sounds as old as we're gettin'," said Bea, echoing his thoughts. Her blue eyes drank in the greens of the brush and trees bordering the winding Vermont road.

"Ayuh." Ira's nasal agreement sounded clearly over the groanings and clatterings of the truck.

"Must've come up this hill a thousand times, you and me," Bea added.

Ira glanced sideways at her, his ragged eyebrows drawing together slightly. How Bea could snatch thoughts out of his mind as deftly as she flipped biscuits from a hot baking sheet always puzzled him. "Ayup." Ira nodded his agreement. Counting the child-years, he thought, it must be more than a thousand times.

They had grown up together wandering the fields of both farms, catching frogs in the pond back of the apple orchard, cutting up the shallow slope of the old pasture and trying to swing the birches at the edge of the Rookery.

They called it the Rookery because every spring at snow-melt the winter's frost seemed to exhaust itself by heaving to the surface a crop of roughly rounded field stones.

"It looks like one of those islands where the sea-birds lay their eggs all over the place!" Bea's sixth-grade voice was shrill on the crisp March air. Ira reached down to touch one of the stones. "Dinosaur eggs," he shouted, entering the game. "And the sun's warming them up. They're gonna hatch and getcha and put snow down your neck." He reached down beside one of the white-nested stones to scoop up a handful of snow. Laughing and screaming, they raced across the field. Scampering over the wall bordering the road, Bea glanced back over her shoulder and noticed that he had lost the snow. The threat gone, she waited for him. Together, their hands thrust deeply into their pockets, and throats burning from the icy air, they trudged up the hill to the MacIntosh farmhouse. From that day they called the field the Rookery.

"More than a thousand times. . . ." On one of those humid days in July, the summer before his senior year in high school, he chose to return to the farm the long way from Croughton's Corners in order to pass the Mayer place. Now that he had his license, he wanted Bea to see him driving on the county road—legally.

She was out in the field below her mother's farmhouse. She and her mother had struggled to do the work since her father had died seven years ago. Her mother drove the old John Deere that somehow kept running, with Bea perched behind on the high-seated hay-rake.

Her hair was parted in the middle and gathered behind with a small ribbon. She wore a white blouse with short sleeves. Her figure was no longer childishly awkward as last summer, but flowing and graceful as she controlled the crescent tines gathering and dumping the hay in long, straight windrows. As usual, she wore a pair of men's bib overalls, but now they fit— well, differently.

"More than a thousand times. . . ." He was out of school a

year. It was the summer before Pearl Harbor. Sissie had left. Pa'd had his first stroke. Edwin would sneak off to the Corners when there was work to be done, and Ira was pressed increasingly into taking on the farm. Edwin, older and larger, and deaf in one ear, managed the money and made a show of organizing the work, but when it came time to put plow to dirt, it was Ira who stared into dawn edging the east.

Only Bea and her mother mitigated Ira's granite realities when, from time to time, they invited him to dinner.

"They got a film at the community house tonight," Ma Mayer had chattered after a supper of stewed chicken, potatoes and gravy. Ira had supplied the chicken. "Why don't you and Bea go down t'see it." She had a way of phrasing questions into affectionate commands.

"After we help you with the dishes." Bea reached for an apron.

"And leave me nothin' to do after you're gone?" she chuckled. "Land sakes, no. Get goin' now, or you'll be late."

They had pulled out to the road and headed up the hill to get to the Corners the short way before she spoke.

"No better at home, Ira?"

"Same." He swung around the curve of the hill, the one where the Rookery wall humped old and tired beyond the culvert. He slowed and stopped and shut off the engine.

They sat together in the cab listening to the crickets' silver chirrup saturating the night around them. The moon, just past full, splashed blue so that they could see with unusual clarity the field, and even a hint of the trees beyond.

"You mind if we don't go to the Corners?" He stared across the field through the open window.

"No. It's all right." They sat for some minutes enjoying the crickets' callings.

"Ira, remember the day we named this place?" She smiled softly at the memory.

11

They got out of the truck, each to a side, and closed the doors. He helped her over the culvert and the ruined wall just beyond.

"Ayuh." They followed an old set of wagon tracks along the wall and then swung slightly down a slope and through a stand of pine.

"You chased me with a handful of snow."

"Never meant to catch you."

"I wanted you to."

They stopped at the abandoned cellar. Ira gazed into the excavation, black-shadowed where the moonlight failed to penetrate its corners. "'Nother one of Edwin's big plans." His jaw muscles contracted, making his angular face even harder in the moonlight. "Gonna build my house on the old pasture, Edwin says." He reached down and picked up a small round stone, turning it over and over in his fingers as he spoke. "That was a year ago. Started diggin' out the cellar and found it was too much work, I guess." His voice was low and bitter. "I wanted to go to college, Bea. I wanted more than farming on the hill the rest of my life. Got as much chance now of gettin' off the mountain as this hole has of bein' a house."

"I'm glad it'll never be a house." Leaning against him, she clasped his waist with her arm. Ira awkwardly found the curve of her back with his hand. "The house was Edwin's dream, Ira. This is our field. His dreams don't belong here."

They turned and continued along the tracks. As the meadow grass became more sparse, they glimpsed occasional egg-shaped stones incubating in the moonlight. "Strange we call it the Rookery," he snorted. "What can hatch from granite?"

"All kinds of things," Bea replied. "The day we named it, that was the day I loved you."

"More than a thousand times. . . ." Bea had said.

Ira shifted to second gear and swung the faded gray truck around a curve past Merrick's old summer camp, lurched through a small dip, and urged the laboring vehicle up a gentler part of the hill.

"Everythin' 'round here's fallin' apart."

"Ayup." Ira drove on, his deep-set brown eyes peering from under the crushed bill of the red cap he wore from sunup to sundown. Out of deference to Bea, he usually removed it at the table.

"Shame the way it run down after the Springers left."

"Ayup." Ira's angular Adam's apple bobbed loosely in his throat.

"New owners still let it run down even after you fixed it up for 'em five years ago."

He said nothing. Ahead and to the left, the brush gave way to an old but well-cared-for farmhouse. Bea had kept it for a few months after her mother died. When she married Ira, she put it up for sale. "Don't need two farms in the same family," she had insisted. She used the money against the mortgage on the MacIntosh land from Edwin's debts.

The truck struggled beyond the old Mayer place past several patchwork fields, going to brush now that hay wasn't needed. Low stone walls and a few ancient trees bordered them. Inside the curve, before the road straightened for a last long grade up MacIntosh Mountain, lay the Rookery. For reasons he never cared to share, Ira still kept the field partly in hay, having stayed the advance of the pines at the line they had firmly established for themselves while he had gone to war. He would have taken out those pines too, where they had intruded over the wall, but Bea wanted them to remain—"to remind us that there were worse years," she had said. A mixed patch of woods lay above the Rookery, along the straighter part of the hill. Finally Ira's white farmhouse and weathered barn asserted itself just below the crest. It was separated from the trees by a large vegetable garden on the downhill side. On the side away from the road, a sharply-sloped pasture reached long and narrow up to an apple orchard. Only the first few trees were visible, the rest being sheltered on the backslope. There was another field along the road beyond the barn. The trees crowded against the upper edge, and finally swallowed the road, or seemed to. The road continued beyond Ira's place to find its way across the top of the mountain to Croughton's Corners. They always referred to it as "the short way."

Bea pushed back a strand of hair, tinged more brown than blonde. "Day was heavy and gray like this the day you left for war." She smiled and looked sideways and down—much like her mother, Ira thought.

"Ayup."

He slowed the truck, clanked the gears into low, turned sharply left into the steep dirt driveway and pulled the truck up onto a level patch beside the barn.

"Well I—Ira, we got company."

He had already spotted the youngster huddled in front of the door. Only a slight deepening of the frown lines, chiseled in his face from a lifetime of farming a reluctant ground, betrayed his curiosity.

Ira wiggled the shift lever making certain the truck was in gear and set the brake. By the time he had stepped around to chock the wheels, Bea was almost to the door, her black patent-leather purse swinging from her chubby arm.

"For goodness' sakes, Ira, come see who it is!"

"Ain't goin' anyplace very quick, far as I can see." He quickened his pace, however, and reached the porch shortly after Bea.

"Why, it's Tammi—Tammi Springer."

"Ayup. Figgered. Spotted that checked huntin' shirt I give her." He looked more closely at the girl. "Must be three years ago last summer."

The girl lay asleep on her side, knees drawn up, hands

14

clasped under her chin, her head pillowed on a small blue day pack. She had fashioned her long auburn hair into two heavy braids, fastened at the ends with thick twisted rubber bands. She wore faded tennis shoes, jeans, and a yellow T-shirt. The hunting shirt acted as a makeshift blanket.

"Soul'd think that noisy old truck would've woke her up," Bea said. "Poor thing must be plumb worn out." She leaned down and placed her soft short-fingered hand on the girl's shoulder. "Tammi?" She shook her gently. "Tammi? It's Aunt Bea. Wake up."

The girl whimpered in her sleep a few times but resumed her heavy, regular breathing.

"Sakes alive, Ira, she's exhausted! Pick her up. We'll put her on the couch." Bea fumbled in her purse for her keys while Ira knelt on one knee and gathered Tammi into his arms.

"Sakes alive," she muttered, "it's not right we can't leave a key out anymore. She could've come right in and made herself t'home." Turning the key in the lock, she pushed the door open. "Put her on the couch in the parlor. I'll get a blanket." She shut the door and looked at the rusted nail where the key used to hang. "Not right. Not right at all," she mumbled.

Ira carried the sleeping girl into the parlor and placed her gently on the old blue brocade sofa while Bea hurried to get a blanket. She spread it over the girl, tucking it gently up under her pale chin. "Grew to be a pretty little thing," she said quietly. Her face, grown more round with her years, softened, and the slight creases between her eyes almost disappeared.

They moved out to the kitchen where Bea filled the chipped blue enamelled kettle. "Have some tea for us in a bit." Reaching into the cupboard, she took out two thick crockery mugs and set them on the porcelain table. "Probably should call her folks."

"Think not." Ira's calloused finger traced lightly around the lip of the mug.

"Land sakes, why not?"

"All she has is that." Ira nodded his head to the blue day pack he had brought in from the porch and dropped next to the refrigerator. "If a body were to ask me, I'd say she run away."

"All the more reason to call Jael and Jerome."

"Best wait till she wakes."

"Might be tomorrow morning 'fore that happens," Bea's voice carried her irritation.

"Not likely they'll worry worse tomorrow than today," Ira replied.

"All I can tell is that if I were Jael and Jerome, I'd be worried." She went to the stove, removed the kettle from the heat, and poured hot water into the old blue teapot. "Must be sick with care. 'Specially a minister's child."

"If we call 'em 'fore she's ready," Ira explained, "nothin' to stop her from runnin' again." He paused. "We never could find Sissie, spite of the fact we get a card every year or two."

Bea dumped the water from the warmed teapot, added a teaspoon full of A & P loose blend, and refilled it with boiling water from the kettle.

Ira continued. "Doubt Jerome and Jael'd be able to find her if she was to leave here. Doubt she'd be as safe."

"What'll we do?"

Ira sat silent for a moment. "Well," he sighed and looked up at her. "Guess we better drink this tea 'fore it gets stone cold."

Exasperated, Bea huffed at him. But she set the cream and sugar on the table and sat down, waiting for the tea to finish brewing.

"Then you got supper to fix, and I got a garden to hoe." Ira poured cream into his empty cup and added two spoons of sugar, a custom acquired from his Scottish grandfather. He nodded toward the parlor where Tammi lay huddled under the blanket. "And she's got sleepin' to do."

16

Gulping his tea down almost as fast as Bea had poured it, Ira plucked his cap from the table and stood.

"Ira, shouldn't we just. . . ."

"No." His seamed, angular face and nasal voice sometimes reminded Bea of the granite fieldstones in the Rookery.

"Supper'll be ready in an hour." Her red-cheeked face, usually cheerful, tightened around the mouth.

"Time enough."

The wood-framed screen door slapped tiredly against its stop as Ira went out to the tool shed.

"Hoein' tomatoes," he muttered. "Least that's something a man can understand." He reached inside the shed and took his hoe. "Not like gettin' caught in other people's troubles."

2

By the time the tinny dinner bell rang, Ira had cleared the weeds from three rows of tomatoes. He had bought that bell for Bea on their one trip out of the mountains years ago, a bus tour down the east coast to Washington, D.C. Returning through the fertile Amish farmlands, he had admired the neatly-kept farms and the quiet, productive people who owned them. He purchased that bell as a reminder of the energetic, self-reliant people of the Pennsylvania countryside. Upon arriving home, he had examined the bell more closely. Stamped deep inside the throat he read "Made in Passaic, New Jersey." He almost threw it out in irritation, but his practical side argued that a bell is no less a bell for having been made in Passaic. When Bea found out about it, however, she chuckled, "Well, for a man who keeps on sayin', 'Things ain't always what they appear,' you sure got brought up short that time."

His nerves grated every time he heard that bell. Ever since their trip, Bea had reminded him with the tinny ring of that hypocritical little bell, "Things ain't always what they appear."

"Ira," Bea's shrill call from the house seemed half-swallowed in the gray-green Vermont evening.

Ira came out of his reverie and headed for the house. Leaning the hoe against the porch, he shuffled his feet on an old scrap of carpet, entered, and stepped to the kitchen sink.

"She awake yet?" After the sticky stillness of the evening air, the cool water felt good on his face.

"No." Bea ladled greens and potatoes from speckled pots onto a pair of blue willow dinner plates, their glaze crazed in spots from many years' use.

"You'd think the smell of this supper would wake her up." Ira pulled a towel from the rack fastened by the side of Bea's combination wood and gas stove and rubbed his face and neck vigorously.

Placing a fried pork chop on a bed of sauerkraut, Bea added, "Wouldn't be a bit s'prised. But keep your voice down." As she set the plates on the table, she continued in a softer, sadder voice, "Three years since they been back."

"Ayup."

They sat at the table and bowed their heads. "Lord," Bea prayed aloud, "Thank You for bringin' Tammi." She paused. "We don't know what the problem is, but if we can help, we're here." She looked up and then quickly down again. "And thank You for this food You've given us today. Amen."

Ira grunted his usual, "Amen," to Bea's blessing. Ira himself wasn't sure that the Lord wanted the air cluttered with people telling Him things both He and they already knew. But he had decided that if it made Bea feel better to say it, it wouldn't hurt either God or him to listen.

"She'll be hungry."

"Ayup."

"I put a plate in the oven against her awakenin'."

"She'll like that."

For a few moments, the only sounds were occasional soft clinks of silverware upon dishes and the tink and hiss of hot water in the kettle.

"They never did seem to be able to leave—for good, that is," Bea said, buttering a thick slice of home-made bread.

Ira chewed his food slowly, sipping now and again from a large glass of water.

"That little grave over there in Croughton's Corners seemed to pull 'em back," she continued.

"Ayup." Ira chewed and sipped again from his glass. "Hard to leave a place when part of you is buried there."

"I guess, after the funeral, that's when they set their minds to leave."

"Ayup." Ira took another mouthful of greens. "Him, anyhow."

"Ain't had a preacher who'd stay since."

"Leastwise, not one who'd do more than talk fancy," Ira commented. "Guess that's why I took a likin' to him—that and the fact that little Tammi reminded me so much of Sissie." He chewed his food thoughtfully while Bea chattered.

"Breaks my heart to see that little church down by the lake fallin' apart and the paint peelin' off. We was married there."

"Ayup." Ira chuckled.

"What's so funny about that?" Bea's eyes glinted.

"Nothin'," Ira grinned. "Nothin' at all." His gold tooth gleamed briefly. "Just rememberin' the preacher who married us."

"That was a good long time 'fore the Springers come."

"Yep, 'twas. 'Member the first time we hunted together. Him bein' chased round and round that clump o' maples up near

19

Henry's place by thet deer he thought he killed. Just winged him, though. Must've been the fastest resurrection he ever hope to see when thet buck got up on all fours and started poundin' after him."

"Ira MacIntosh, you stop bein' irreverent right here in my kitchen," Bea scolded, trying to look stern.

Ira sliced half an onion over his potatoes, added a pat of butter, and mashed them with a measured deliberation. "Guess Jerome was the best one, though."

"Don't know but that I agree," Bea nodded. "Leastwise, 'til he got so busy."

"'Twern't busyness," Ira returned. He stared at his water glass as if it were a crystal ball. "Jerome—I really liked him. But he had ambition eatin' away inside like a termite in pine sidin'." He frowned slightly. "Surprised the mountains held him even three years."

"For a man who went to services precious few times when Jerome Springer was here, you sure seem to have him figured out." Bea smiled, but her voice was serious.

"Easier to see what's in a man when he's in his overhauls diggin' a pit for an outhouse than in his Sunday suit."

"Ira," Bea huffed, trying to be indignant, but not quite succeeding.

"It's true," Ira insisted. "Jerome was a good man. Wern't feared of gettin' dirty helpin' folks up here." He drank the last of his water. "Sure hope he found out what he was lookin' for."

"Sure wish they didn't have to leave," Bea said, pouring Ira a mug of tea. "But I guess the baby dyin', and Tammi gettin' burned—couldn't stand to stay."

"That wern't the reason," Ira insisted quietly. "Wern't the reason at all."

"Glad we stayed friends, anyhow," Bea muttered. "Even though Tammi's the only one who writes, mostly." She cleared the plates from the table. "Weedin' after supper?"

"Another couple of rows."

"I'll wake her after I do up the dishes."

"Time enough."

Ira returned to the garden and Bea stood at the sink before the square-paned window, "doing up the dishes" as she had done for the past forty years, "Sure wish they'd stayed," she sighed. "Bet that little girl wouldn't've run." She rinsed the tea leaves out of the pot. "That Jerome Springer was the only preacher Ira put any stock in. He'd probably be goin' to church right now, if they'd stayed."

3

Fragments from past years fueled her mutterings as she kept her hands busy.

"'Fore they come—fourteen years ago this month, it was—that little church was just like the village," Bea thought sadly, "run down and tired."

She added some hot water to the dishes in the sink.

"People sure started coming to church when Jerome took over, though," she smiled. "Come from all around. Even Ira went a few times."

She remembered Ira had said, "I figger if a man'll come help me rake my hay on a Sunday afternoon when it's fixin' to rain, and then send his wife down to keep 'em singin' while we get cleaned up, well, won't do no harm to step inside his church now and again."

"Started to change, he did, right after that the man from the mission came." Her lips turned downward at the corners.

"'Jerome's a fine preacher,' he said. 'Like to use him for special meetins',' he said. 'We'll be sure you have someone for service when he's gone,' he said. Like a bunch of fool old hens we ate it all up."

She wrung out the dishcloth and scrubbed the kitchen table vigorously. "That's what turned his head—got him lookin' for a bigger church." She rinsed the cloth and hung it up to dry. "Made him forget what he was here for in the first place." She dried her hands on the towel attached to her apron and glanced toward the parlor. "Now his little girl's a runaway. Should've stayed here."

Plucking a dry towel from the rack, she snatched a plate from the drainboard and wiped it vigorously.

"Radio program was all right, though," Bea talked to herself in her agitation, her voice a sibilant whisper. "Ira even listened mornings in the barn when we still had cows."

She gazed out the window and slightly to the left. She could just see Ira working the hoe rhythmically as he moved down the rows. "That's when Ira stopped goin' to church at all." Pressing her lips into a thin, straight line, she remembered Ira's clipped tone. "Jerome's not here all that much. Guess the preacher and me have more important fields to plow."

"Should've known that morning Jael come over," Bea thought.

It was a November morning, still gray with sunup and carrying the edge of winter in its wind. Jael and Tammi stood in her doorway bundled and shivering.

"Sakes alive! What you two doing out at this hour of the morning? Come in 'fore you freeze!"

"Thanks, Bea." Jael and Tammi slipped inside quickly. "Think it may snow today?"

"Wouldn't be surprised. Get your wraps off and have some chocolate."

Jael helped Tammi unwind from her scarf and fumbled with her large-buttoned coat. "Jerome had to go extra early today—they want him to make a couple of extra program tapes for Thanksgiving."

"Radio program really keeps him hoppin'," Bea remarked, pouring boiling water into three mugs and adding the powdered chocolate.

"Seems everything keeps him busy, nowadays, Bea—except me." Jael sank into a chair at the kitchen table and rubbed her hands together to get the chill from her fingers. She smiled, but Bea saw the strain. "Heater doesn't work in the car. He said he'd get that fixed today, too." She found a rough fingernail and picked at it with small, nervous movements.

Bea reached for Ira's old quart thermos and its tin cap. "Tammi?"

"Yes, Aunt Bea?"

"Uncle Ira's out in the barn milking. Would you please take this thermos out to him?"

"Can I sit up on the cows?" Tammi's green eyes brightened as she laughed. She shook her head quickly from side to side, enjoying the swish of her auburn hair gathered tightly on either side and thrusting outward and down, like tails of twin ponies.

Bea filled the thermos with tea, glancing first at Jael and then at the excited child. "Wouldn't be surprised if he might let you. You ask him."

"All right." The child slipped down from her chair. "May I take my cocoa?"

"Certainly."

Tammi, carrying her half-empty cup carefully, slipped

through the side door Bea held open for her and disappeared toward the barn.

Sitting across from Jael, Bea laced her cup in her fingers and fastened her eyes upon Jael. They'd had other conversations, and she hated to see the hardness form around the corners of the young wife's lips.

"Trouble, child?"

Jael gazed sadly at her, her face framed by her soft auburn hair, cut short and combed for utility rather than for style. "It's . . . it's not working for us, Bea."

Bea waited for her to continue, but Jael stared into her cup.

"Gets awful lonely in that little house when he's gone, I 'spect," Bea remarked.

Jael shook her head, and then the words came in a rush. "That's not the problem, Bea. I love it here. But Jerome—I don't know what's happened. When we first came, it was everything he wanted—to show people who God is; to show them that God loves them; just to be a pastor and preach God's Word and love His people." Jael choked. She sipped her chocolate to hide her hurt.

"And now?"

"It seems like something inside keeps pushing him." She placed the mug on the table and ran her finger nervously around the thick lip. "When he is home, he'll hardly talk about anything other than 'The Work,' as he calls it." Jael lowered her eyes and stared into the chocolate sludge at the bottom of the mug. "Lots of times he'll work halfway through the night. Says he's going to prove to his father that he can succeed." She sat silent a moment. "Bea, he's so set on success, that's all he thinks about. He even seems too preoccupied to . . . to come to bed with me." Full, heavy tears grew, brimmed over, and slipped slowly down her cheeks. "Tammi and I—we believe in him, Bea! Isn't that enough? Why does he have to prove things to other people?" Her voice ended in a squeak.

Bea got up and moved the teakettle over to the hot side of the new Sears wood and propane gas stove Ira had bought for her the month before. She kept her back turned. "People don't like to be seen cryin'," she thought.

"Bea," she sniffled, "he . . . he's just not the same anymore. He always wants to get more. He never seems to get tired. He has such high expectations for himself, for me, for Tammi—I can't meet them. I just can't keep up. I'm so afraid I'm going to fail him and ruin everything."

Bea turned away from the stove, walked over to Jael and sat beside her. She gathered the younger woman into her short chubby arms.

"Child, buildin' his work is to a man what birthin' is to a woman," she comforted. "Your man ain't any different."

"But why does it have to be his whole world?"

"Just scared of failin', I expect. Just scared of failin'."

"But Bea, it's being left out that hurts. That's what's so lonely. Even when he's home, I feel alone."

Bea pushed herself away from Jael and grasped the younger woman by the shoulders. "Alone?" Her fierce gaze softened. "Ain't nobody not alone. You ain't the first. Doubt you'll be the last." She turned her gaze to the doorway through which Tammi had gone. "Leastwise you have a young 'un." She dropped her hands from Jael's shoulders.

Jael looked at the older woman, her self-pity lessened. "You and Ira, you never had—?"

"Died when he was two. Caught pneumonia," Bea explained simply. "Buried him over in the old cemetery in Croughton's Corners, we did." She gazed at the door leading to the barn.

"How do you manage, Bea?" Jael asked with a puzzled frown. "It must be hard for you."

"Oh, we had plans to leave the farm," Bea said. "Right after the war—Ira got out of the army. He was going to go to college to be a shop teacher in the high school." Her voice edged with a trace of bitterness. "Then Ira's older brother— the army wouldn't take him—had some 'gettin' ahead' of his own to do—only it was with Ira's money."

Jael listened silently.

"Took all the money Ira sent home—he was supposed to put it in the bank—Ira's money to go to school after the war— took it all and borrowed more on the farm besides." Bea's lips tightened. "Lost it all, too. Then we almost lost the farm when Ira's brother got himself killed—tractor turned over on him— he'd put the farm up against the debts." She sipped her hot chocolate. "Took Ira an' me twelve years 'fore we paid it all off." Bea paused. Her lips turned up at the corners for a moment as if the remembered pain had made her wince. "Then Ira's Pa, sick from a stroke since before the war, died—the cancer. Along with that we had Ira's Ma nigh onto ten years. She didn't want to leave the farm—guess she always hoped, somehow, Sissie'd come back. Died right in that upstairs bedroom, she did. We keep it as a guest room, now."

"So you just . . . stayed."

"No point in leavin'."

Jael looked at the older woman, her own troubles less awesome. "How do you do it, Bea?"

"You go 'bout your business, child." She gazed sadly into the bottom of her cup. "You go 'bout your business and do the livin' that has to be done."

Jael shook her head slowly. "Ira must have been very discouraged."

Bea looked at Jael, her eyes large and warm. "That's what a wife's for, child. When a man feels there's nothin' left, she makes him feel he's worth it, that he "ain't a waste." She looked in the direction of the barn again. "Terrible thing, to see a man lose his dream." She turned back to Jael, appraising her.

"You got a good soft young body, child." She chuckled. "Woman's softness gives a man strength." She chuckled again, this time more lightly. "Guess that's why the good Lord made us softest when our men are weakest."

Jael had taken Bea's hand. "Bea," she said, "I—I guess Jerome needs—my softness."

The following June, Jael had become pregnant with her second child.

"Well," Bea sighed, placing the last dish in the cupboard and hanging up the towel, "I ain't as soft as I was." She gazed out the window where Ira had finished hoeing the tomatoes in the failing light. "But he's strong now—and old, like me."

4

"Do the livin' that has to be done," she had told Jael. Bea placed her hands on the front lip of the sink and leaned forward again to glimpse Ira in the deepening gray of the evening. "What with the war and all," she thought, "last thing on Ira's mind to leave again and traipse all over the place." She smiled sadly at the recollection.

That evening, too, had been pregnant with rain. Chilly and damp, they had huddled close one to another outside the gas station at Croughton's Corners.

"I'll write you every day, Ira."

The grind of a heavy vehicle carried from where the high-way curved in the gloom. She stiffened, and then relaxed a little as a truck lurched by, its lights gleaming feebly along the two-laned road. It disappeared in the opposite direction, the tail lights winking a dusty red against the gray.

"I'll write back." Only the pressure of his arm betrayed his pain as he clasped her closer to his side. The brass buttons on his uniform jacket hurt. That pain she understood. Ira's leaving her for the unknown, the blackness beyond the circle of yellow light spilling from the rusty-hooded pole set between the gas-pumps—that was the dark mystery.

She turned her face up toward his. "Ira, I wish we were married."

"No point to it, Bea." The light glaring down from the "ESSO" sign drew strong black shadows beneath his visored cap, hiding all but the tip of his long nose and the bottom of his angular chin. "No tellin' what might happen." He pulled her closer, and the light glinted yellow against the sharpshoot-er's medal on his breast. "Won't start nothin' you may have to finish alone."

They had had the conversation before.

"I wouldn't mind, Ira."

"I would," he said simply. "My family puts upon you enough. Be worse if we married. Wouldn't be fair."

They heard the bus before they saw its headlights glow in the moist air, and she slipped both her arms beneath his and clung to him. She felt anger. Anger at that nameless some-thing tearing him away from her. Anger at the bus and its driver. Anger at his family. Anger at the darkness.

She reached up and touched his cheek. The headlights swept around the curve, and the roar of the bus diminished to a grind as it slowed and crunched to a stop in front of the station.

"Come back, Ira." She meant to speak in her normal voice,

but the burning in her throat forced a whisper. She tried to smile. "I want to make your baby."

The bus door flapped open. The driver, quietly ignoring them, unscrewed the lock on the luggage door and propped it open. He heaved Ira's bulging pack inside. The rain started again, a fine misty drizzle.

"I'll come back, Bea." They kissed, awkward in the presence of the driver and the gallery of curious passengers framed in the yellow windows.

The driver slammed the cover to the baggage compartment, screwed it shut with a small crank, and brushed by them to climb back into the bus. He waited for Ira to board, and the door flapped shut. She could see him, bent almost double, reaching his hand toward her—but the attempted wave seemed to Bea a gesture of anguished supplication.

She walked unsteadily back to the old truck and slid into the worn seat. It started sluggishly, and she lurched away from the station. She took the short way home, over the mountain. Where the road curved at the Rookery, she stopped and turned off the engine and headlights. The rain drummed on the roof in a steady, monotonous drizzle.

Only tears came at first, the tears she couldn't let Ira see. Then came the sobs—long, tearing, lonely sobs carrying all the anger and hopelessness she had hid from both Ira and herself over the last months. At last she sat breathing heavily, her mind numb, her energy drained.

Vaguely she became aware that the rain had lessened. She clambered from the truck and walked slowly to the edge of the field, picking her way carefully among the stones concealed in the darkness. The rain had worn the clouds thin as a worn dishtowel. The moon struggled out, easing the blackness, but then the fabric thickened again and blotted out the glow. The rain returned, heavy insistent drops that soaked the new Sears suit she had bought for Ira's furlough; still she stood there, ignoring the discomfort. Another day, one bright winter-spring day, she had fled across this same field before him, and with each breathless gasp from her running, her heart had sung, "I love him. I love him. I love him."

She came back to the blackness, but now she smiled gently. The dark would not swallow him, or her. When he returned, she would never again allow anything to part them.

She returned to the truck. She would have to return it to Edwin by seven the next morning.

Irritated with herself for taking so long with the dishes, Bea grabbed the broom to sweep the kitchen floor. "It's no wonder they left," she muttered. "All this old woman could tell her was 'be strong.'" She mocked her own tone. "And then her losin' that second baby." Her throat burned. "Ira made that tiny casket right out there in the barn. They buried him right next to our Samuel."

She heard Ira on the back porch stamping the mud from his feet.

"Get your shoes off 'fore you come into my kitchen," she called. Ira's shuffling and heavy breathing replaced the stamping as he struggled out of his high-topped work shoes.

"Slippers are right inside the door," she added as Ira entered in his stocking feet.

"Thanks. Fixin' to rain."

Bea gazed out the window. "Yes, 'tis." Then she added sadly, "He'd have a young one by now, most's old as Tammi."

Puzzled, Ira frowned slightly. Then he walked over and slipped his arm around Bea's waist. Together they watched the evening harden into black.

There was a soft step behind them. "Aunt Bea?" Tammi's voice was clogged with sleep. "Uncle Ira?"

Turning, Bea gathered the girl against her. "Yes, child, yes." She stroked the girl's hair. "My goodness, how you slept."

Enveloped in Bea's soft embrace, the girl wept silently, her tears spilling heavily down her cheeks.

Ira stepped to the stove, moved the kettle over and lit the gas. Dropping open the oven door, he found a potholder and removed the supper plate Bea had saved for her.

Bea disentangled herself from Tammi.

"Sakes, child, come sit! You must be starved," she fussed. Tammi glanced around uncertainly.

"Go ahead, we've had ours. Sakes, you did sleep some."

"I walked from the bus stop at Croughtenville."

"Good six mile," Ira grunted. "Come across the mountain?"

"I . . . I guess so." Her voice was still thick from sleep. "There was a mill or lumberyard or something about half-way here."

"That'd be Sloan's," Bea said, pouring a large tumbler of milk and placing it in front of the girl.

"I . . . I stopped there to ask for some water and directions."

"S'prised he didn't have one of his men drive you over," Bea said, her voice short. "Ira's certainly done plenty o' favors for him."

"They offered," Tammi added quickly. "But I was scared of them, even though one of them—the one who just got a new blue truck—he was going to drive me, and even gave me his lunch." She paused. "But I was still scared." Tears edged her eyes again.

"Must've been young Thomas Brady spoke to you," Ira said. "Only one at Sloan's owns a new truck. Not likely he'd hurt you."

"Go 'head and eat, child." Bea looked up at Ira and inclined her head toward the cellar door. "None down that mill dare lay a hand on you. Not like city folk, we ain't."

Ira stepped to the cellar door and lifted the latch. "Well, you have your supper, young 'un; an' catch up on your gossip. Me . . . I got work to do." He padded down the steep stairs, his slippers making comfortable sounds on the worn risers.

Pausing at the bottom, Ira took a moment to enjoy the smells of wood-shavings, glue, and paint permeating his snug stone-walled retreat. He stepped across to his workbench where one of the dining-room chairs was trussed in rope clamps until the glued repair had hardened and set.

"Hardened and set," he thought. "Ayup. Jerome would have out o' here." He dug in his pocket for his jackknife and began scraping the glue from the newly-repaired joints. "That was Jerome 'fore he left," he repeated. "Hardened and set."

Unable to reach a rung for scraping, he pulled a stick from the center of a twisted rope and released the pressure on the chair. "Always show the hurt, but it'll be strong again."

"Funny," he thought. "That's jest what I told Jerome that night he brought the chest."

He and Bea had barely finished supper the night Jerome's old Carryall had pulled up into the driveway.

"Mercy sakes, it's the preacher," Bea had exclaimed. "And me a mess and the kitchen still cluttered from supper."

"T'ain't likely he come to check up on your housekeepin'," Ira observed. He gazed through the side window at Jerome stepping around to the rear of the vehicle and opening the back. Ira thrust his feet into his worn brown slippers and padded to the kitchen door. Opening it, he called out into the dusk, "Just in time for tea, Jerome, if you're not too busy," he smiled.

"Thanks." The young preacher had missed the gentle criticism. "Sounds good." He stepped through the door Ira held open for him. Jerome carried a wooden chest. Its black boards, cupped from dampness, had pulled away from the ends.

"Looks like it's had the worst of it," Ira drawled.

Jerome placed the chest down next to the cellar door. "Could say that. It's Jael's—was full of her linens and keepsakes. Things she was saving for Tammi." He paused, accepting a mug of Bea's never-ending supply of tea. "Was going to be her hope chest." He sipped his tea. "Got damp when the pipe broke in cellar the day . . . Jael had the accident. . . ." He stopped to clear his throat from a sudden huskiness. He sipped his tea again. "Well, anyhow, most of the stuff was mildewed and stained."

"Woman puts a lot o' stock in things like that," Bea interjected. "Must've hated to have them things hurt. Know I would have."

Jerome gazed sadly at the chest. "Ira, do you think it could be repaired?"

"Maybe I could do somethin' with it," Ira replied. "We'll take a gander."

"How's Jael?" Bea interjected in the short, awkward silence. "Haven't seen much of her since . . . it happened."

"Coming along." Jerome took another sip of tea, still staring vacantly at the chest.

"And Tammi?"

"Oh, lot better. She'll have a scar good number of years, though—going to be hard on her when she gets to be a teenager."

Bea turned her attention to clearing the table. "Whyn't you menfolk get downstairs so's I can pick up from supper." It was not a question.

A few moments later, the chest sat on the cellar workbench. Ira was surprised at both its age and its workmanship. "Man that made this," he said, running his fingers along a carefully fitted joint, "he put a lot o' love into it."

"Jael's great-grandfather I guess," Jerome said quietly. "Been in her family a long time." He stared at the chest a moment and then continued, almost as if to himself. "Didn't seem to bother her at first. I almost forgot about it. Then—I guess it had something to do with the baby dying—I returned from a few days of meetings in the Stephentown area, a big church there for the size of the community. Lot of people attend—" He stopped for a moment as if he had lost track of what he had started to say and stared at the chest. "I came home yesterday afternoon, Ira, and she was just sitting in front of that chest." He shook his head, puzzled. "Sitting and folding all those ruined linens . . . folding and crying."

He shook his head again. "The Mission Board gives me extra for traveling around. People give us love gifts here and there, too. I told her we could buy some new." He shook his head again. "'Whatever you want,' she said. 'It makes no difference—not anymore.' She just looked at me and folded and unfolded her linens again and again. 'Do what you have to,' she said." The young preacher frowned. "I asked her what she meant by that, but she wouldn't talk any more."

As Jerome spoke, Ira examined the chest more carefully. He scraped at a rotted seam with a narrow chisel.

"Bottom split out from the side pretty bad," he muttered. He placed the wooden-handled tool on the bench, and, opening the lid of the chest, ran his fingertips down the inside where the sides and bottom came together. "Womenfolk have different ideas from men." He picked up his jackknife and dug the point into the wood at various places along the inside corners. "Guess they can see things we can't."

"I guess. But I'm going to have to get her out of the mountains. She and Tammi will be better off in a town for awhile—maybe a city."

Ira cocked an eyebrow and continued sounding the wood with the point of his knife. "Tell you that, did she?"

34

"No. Hasn't said much of anything. Matter of fact, she refused to talk about it." He paused again, watching Ira's experienced hands take the chisel and remove some rotted wood.

"Wood's good and sound after you take away what's hurt," he said, glancing sideways at Jerome. "Long's we don't get hasty—or backwards—with the repair, be strong as ever." He put the chisel up on the rack behind the bench.

Jerome looked at him curiously. "I hate to see her unhappy. But ever since we came, she seems to have had a harder and harder time."

Ira placed his hands on each side of a cupped board along the front of the chest. "Warped pretty bad," he muttered. "Could be if we wet it up again, and dry the inside before the outside, we might be able to help some." He looked at Jerome. "Problem's on the inside. Probably not hurt much at all if a body had put a light bulb into it right away. As it was, the outside dried faster and curled up like a maple leaf in the first good frost." He closed the lid of the chest. Ira leaned against the bench, sipping from the cup of tea he had brought downstairs with him. "Sometimes what seems the plainest ain't the worst of the problem." He gazed at the chest. "So you think she'd be better off out o' the mountains?"

"Looks more that way to me with each day, Ira."

"Well," Ira gulped the rest of his tea. "Man's got to do what he's got to do."

Three months later, Bea had returned home from church with news that the Springers were leaving.

"Figgered so," he had responded.

"Night he brought the chest?"

"Ayup."

"Way you fixed it up—first she smiled in a long time."

"Always show the hurt, though."

"Mind made up back then, had he?"

"Ayup. Hardened and set," Ira had replied.

Hardened and set, just like the chair leg he had repaired. Ira often wondered if the preacher had found what he sought in his big city church. "Wonder if he got the mountains out of his wife, too," he smiled sadly. "Looks, though, like they're growed into his daughter clear to bedrock."

He finished scraping the last of the hardened cement from the rungs of the chair. Folding his jackknife, he slipped it into his pocket and then lifted the chair from the bench to the cement floor. He grinned, satisfied. It didn't wobble.

Bea's voice pulled him out of his reverie.

"Ira?"

"Ayep?"

"Young Brady boy just drove in the front yard."

"Be right up."

Tammi's dishes were still on the table when Ira came up into the kitchen, her milk glass only half empty. He heard her quiet retreat up the stairs to the front bedroom.

"My, she lit out o' here when he drove in," Bea remarked, staring up the stairs, her voice low.

Ira walked to the door and opened it before eighteen-year-old Thomas Brady had a chance to knock. "C'mon in, Thomas."

"Thanks, Mr. MacIntosh." The boy stepped in, awkward, his face reddening under his cap.

"How's things at the mill?"

"Right 'nuff." He accepted the cup of tea Bea placed into his oversized hands. "Thank you."

"Git off late, did you?"

"Ah-huh. Overtime makin' up trusses for summer camps." He sipped nervously from his tea cup, his eyes going from the dishes on the table and then to the doorway leading into the parlor. "See she got here all right." He studied the tea in his cup.

"Ayup." Ira remained expressionless as he poured another

cup of tea for himself and motioned Thomas to a seat at the table.

"She wouldn't take a ride. Done it easy on lunch hour."

"Told us," Ira smiled. "She's a mite skittish."

"Up here three summers ago?" The question was casual.

"Remember her, eh?" Ira cocked a shaggy eyebrow slightly.

"Ayea." Thomas mumbled the affirmation, his face turning even redder. "Just drove up to see she got here all right." He stood and shuffled his feet. "Guess I'd better get goin'. Ma'll wonder where I am."

"Nonsense," Bea said firmly, setting a sandwich before him. "That was a real nice thing you did for her, givin' your lunch away like that, Thomas."

"Only a lettuce and tomato sandwich," he mumbled, trying to grin around a mouth full of bread and meat loaf.

"Nonsense," Bea insisted. "When a grown man gives away lunch after workin' all mornin', that's somethin'."

Thomas' face reddened again as he bit into the second half of his sandwich. He chewed for a moment in silence, and then made another attempt at conversation. "Guess she come up for the summer again."

"Wouldn't be surprised if she's here for awhile," Ira replied. "How's your hammer hand?" he asked, changing the subject abruptly.

"'Bout ready to fall off," Thomas grinned, and stood. "But I expect I'll get used to it."

Ira stood, stretched and followed him to the door. "Little rough at first," he agreed," but Mr. Sloan says you're a good worker."

Thomas grinned his pleasure at the compliment.

"Here," Bea interrupted, "You take this home for you and your Ma." She shoved a covered plate containing the rest of the meat loaf into his hands. "Got more than we'll ever use."

Thomas nodded his thanks and retreated toward his truck.

Ira and Bea watched at the screen door as the bright discs of his headlights drew backwards down the steep driveway, swung sideways to point down the hill, and then disappeared.

They stood silently for a moment, enjoying the night air. They didn't need the weather report to know it would rain.

"Let's go outside," Bea said quietly.

Ira held the door open for her, and they stepped through onto the porch.

"Tammi's goin' to have a baby."

"Figgered something like that."

Bea made a face at him. "You're the smart one."

"Jerome and Jael ain't ones to hurt," Ira explained. "Had to be the other way round to make her run."

" 'Too ashamed to stay home,' she said," Bea added.

"She ready to call?"

"Just got to the edge o' that when the Brady boy drove up," Bea replied.

"Just like Sissie," Ira said abruptly.

"Not really," Bea objected softly.

"She run away. Same reason," Ira insisted.

"Tammi has us to run to." Bea's voice carried an edge of determination. "She's not goin' to be another Sissie, Ira." Her voice was more gentle. "We won't let that happen."

The creases deepened at the outside corners of Ira's eyes. "Sissie never found anyone."

"Leastwise, not up to five years ago," Bea added. "Been a good long time since we heard."

"Never would send an address." Ira muttered. "She must know we want her back."

"Your Pa always taught, 'Lie in the bed you make,' Ira. There's no room for comin' back—or forgiveness—in that."

"Ayeah." He glanced down at her. The yellow glare of the porch light softened her features and reminded him of a gold-

38

en-haired girl on a hay-rake many years ago. "Glad your Ma brought you up different."

"Too bad," Bea sighed.

"What's that?" Ira picked up the edge of a new thought in the tone of her voice.

"Brady boy's taken a shine to her," she said softly. "He'll be disappointed when he finds out."

When they entered the kitchen, Tammi was seated at the table, arms straight, open-palmed hands thrust between her knees.

5

When the truck pulled into Ira's driveway, Tammi had escaped from the table and slipped quietly up the carpeted stairs to the spare bedroom.

The room was familiar and comfortable. Three years ago, when she had spent the summer at the farm, she had slept on the lumpy mattress. The window opposite the foot of the bed overlooked an aged, sturdy apple tree. The early-morning sun would stencil patterns from the tree's upper branches across the faded crazy quilt under which she snuggled. Her room at home was similar, even to the apple tree overlooking the front yard.

Her room at home. Her own apple tree. Was it only yesterday she had watched the sun rise on her own apple tree, the one Uncle Ira had dug for her when they left the mountains just before she turned seven? Tammi's mind skipped back to the day when her father had torn them from the mountains.

"Mommy, I don't want to leave," she whimpered, clinging first to Bea and then to Ira. "Why does Daddy have to leave?" she cried. "Why do we have to leave?"

"God needs Daddy in Shelterport," her mother had tried to reason with her.

"But why?"

"Daddy can help a lot of people there," her mother had returned.

"But who's going to help Aunt Bea and Uncle Ira, and the Hobbs's, and that family on the other road that nobody likes?" She turned her tear-stained face up to her mother's.

"God will find someone else to come here, just like He found us to come."

"Why can't God find someone else to go to the city and leave us here?" Tammi cried defiantly. She tore herself loose from her mother. "I hate God! He hurts me! He always hurts me!" She ran toward the apple orchard.

She heard her mother's call, but once out of sight, Tammi circled back around to Ira's gray-planked barn and climbed the ladder to the back corner of the loft. She had made a small hideaway in the mounded hay where she had spent many rainy afternoons. Only she and Ira knew about it, and it was Ira who found her there a little while later. "How about I dig an apple tree special for you to take with you," he offered. His brown eyes glowed warmly. "That way, you can always have something of the mountains to look at."

"Will it be my tree?"

"All yours."

"But it won't want to leave—here."

"Don't think it would mind as long as it has you to take care of it."

She sat silently, pressing herself into the corner of the barn walls, made fragrant by the hay of all the summers of Ira's life. Reluctantly, she stood and followed him silently down the ladder.

The packed car, U-Haul trailer attached, remained unmoved outside the old couple's farmhouse, while Ira and Tammi climbed into his battered gray truck and disappeared down the old farm road toward the orchard. They returned an hour later, Tammi riding on Ira's lap in the cab, steering; and an apple tree, exactly as tall as she was, set in an old five-gallon tin of mountain earth, in the back.

Although her cheeks showed signs of recent tears, she sternly supervised just where her father should set the tree among the rest of their possessions in the trailer. Satisfied, at last, she clung tightly to Ira, enjoying the last of his iron gentleness. Then she turned to Bea, who, holding her tightly against her ample bosom, kissed Tammi's cheeks and then the burned place, the scar still glossy and white. Silently, they left. From an area specially cleared for her among the luggage in the back of the Carryall, Tammi watched Aunt Bea's handkerchief make slow arcs, until, against the dark green of the mountain, it became a white speck. The curve near Merrick's swallowed it.

Often she felt like crying during that drive to her new home in Shelterport; but the young tree nodded its cheerful green head to her as it followed on the trailer, and she dreamed of how beautiful it would be outside her bedroom window where her father said he would plant it.

But board meetings, Bible study, sermon preparation, visitation, and getting acquainted with each family in the congregation, absorbed all her father's time. Struggling to grow in the confines of that five-gallon container, her tree languished, its branches dying, its leaves curling.

On a Saturday morning almost a month after they had left the mountains, Tammi dragged a rusty shovel from the garage to the front yard to dig a hole for the tree. The late September earth, dry from a summer with little rain, was iron to her. Her mother found her almost an hour later, crying in frustrated seven-year-old gasps, her cheeks muddy from tears, her hands blistered from having done little more than scratch the earth. Saying little, her mother got the hose and soaked the ground. Then she took Tammi into the house, cooked a batch of pancakes, and served them with maple syrup.

Together, they went outside again to enlarge the hole. They soaked and dug four times more before the roots of the tree fit without crowding. They finished shortly before supper, and together admired the brave, thin, tree, still alive in spite of neglect. They went into the house and washed their blistered hands with cool water.

"Mommy?"

"Yes, Tammi."

"Will God ever let us go back to the mountains?"

"Maybe someday," her mother had replied as she spread ointment over a particularly large blister on Tammi's hand. "But you'll learn to like it better here," she continued brightly. "There are lots of boys and girls to make friends with."

"Not at school. Not here," Tammi pouted.

"Certainly there are."

"They chase me. They call me 'Scarface.'"

Her mother's face hardened, but her voice was very gentle. "Do they chase you often?"

"They used to chase me every morning," Tammi continued, "but I go to school a different way now."

"Did they hurt you?" Her mother's eyes had narrowed and two spots of red came into her cheeks.

"Yes," she said matter-of-factly, "but a man was working on his boat in the boatyard. He came out and scared them away."

"The boatyard?"

"Yes. He's Mr. Rawlings. He took me into the office and washed my face." She gazed solemnly into her mother's eyes. "Now I go by the boatyard, and they daren't chase me."

"Well," her mother smiled, but it was strained, "I guess we'd better tell your father about this so he can thank—Mr. Rawlings."

"Mommy?"

"Yes, Tammi."

"Is God mad because I said I hated Him?"

Her mother had gathered her into her arms. "Of course not."

"I told Him I was sorry, but He keeps on hurting me."

Her mother held her out at arm's length. "Why don't we talk to God now, and ask Him to help you?"

Tammi watched through the window as her father drove into the driveway between the church and the parsonage and parked the car. He walked across the lawn and stopped abruptly to stare at the pathetic tree stuck into the front lawn. He walked slowly to the house, his face sad.

He ate little supper. At last, he looked at Tammi. "You must have worked very hard putting that tree in today."

"Mommy helped me." Then the dam broke. "The ground was so hard—but we watered it and dug and watered it and dug—and we even got blisters on our hands—look." She held out both hands for his admiration.

Her voice trailed off as she saw her mother glare across the table at her father. Frightened that she had said something wrong, Tammi pulled her hands back and sat toying with her food and trying to hide tears she couldn't explain. Her father met her mother's glare briefly. He also glanced away.

"Some children taunted her on the way to school." Her mother's lips were compressed in a straight line. "A man chased them away."

"Hm. Yes. Frank Rawlings. Came by the church to see me right afterward." He took a new interest in his food. "Good thing I decided to work at the church every morning for awhile." He buttered a slice of bread and tore it in half. "I got busy and forgot to tell you."

"Forgot to tell me!"

"One of those things all kids get into," her father said defensively.

"All kids have not been burned," her mother snapped. "All children aren't called cruel names because of something they can't help." She raised her voice and it had a bitter edge.

"Well there's no point in getting angry about it!" As always, her father's voice was carefully calm. "I took care of it. Tammi's none the worse. I had other things to do."

"When it comes to us, you always have 'other things to do.'" Her mother's eyes turned hard green.

"I had to go downtown to get the permit for the new church sign."

"I'm sure you'd have gone to jail if you hadn't done it on your day off."

"As it was, it's good I was there. The man did come and tell me about it."

"But he could've been—" she glanced over at Tammi, "somebody bad."

"Well he wasn't," Jerome snapped. "He's a guidance counselor from New York—just moved here. He's at loose ends right now." Her father's lips formed a straight line, as they always did when he was angry. "He just lost his wife less than a year ago and decided to move here, take a vacation to get his head collected." He gulped his coffee. "So that's the story on your 'bad' man!" He set his cup down with a sharp "clink," wiped his mouth with his napkin, and left the table.

Hurt and confused by the emotions surging around her, Tammi had sat quietly and stared at first one and then the other parent. Somehow, she knew it was her fault. If she hadn't told God she hated Him, there wouldn't be the scar on her face, the children would not have chased her, and her parents wouldn't be quarreling.

She looked up at her mother. "May I leave the table, please?" The question came out rhythmically, like a liturgy finishing every meal; it had a familiar and secure ring.

"Yes, Tammi, you may." Her mother's voice had lost its edge, but Tammi noticed that her knuckles were white as she grasped her crumpled napkin.

Tammi slipped from her chair and ran to the living room window to gaze at her tree in the gathering dusk.

Growing up with the tree, Tammi shared its struggle to adapt to Shelterport. Over the years, Frank Rawlings had become friend to both. Because the tree failed for so long to thrive, he gave Tammi, as a joke present for her twelfth birthday, a fifty-pound bag of tree food. Tammi had soaked the ground and added the fertilizer. The tree responded, thrusting out new shoots, unfolding rich green leaves, and even presenting a few tentative buds to the spring sunshine. From that time forward, on Christmases and birthdays, Frank Rawlings had presented her with a bag of tree-food—gift-wrapped—for the apple tree.

The year she turned sixteen, she and Ted started dating; as if the tree knew, it covered itself with white blossoms. The trunk, scarred and misshapen from earlier traumas, was no longer its most obvious feature; during blossom time Tammi slipped out of bed mornings and gazed through the window watching the spring sun rise upon it.

But spring passed. The blossoms fell. Insects and disease attacked. Only a few misshapen, scarred apples grew, clinging tenaciously to the black branches. Filled with worms at harvest, the fruit was almost inedible.

A late October windstorm split the largest branch away from the trunk. She had examined the damage with her father the afternoon following the windstorm.

"Daddy, will my tree die?"

"I think we can save it," he smiled. "Here, let's prop up the branch." With rope and lumber they bound the tree back together and gave the branch temporary support. "I don't know much about tree surgery," he remarked, "but let's get some tree tar on Saturday morning and see what we can do."

"Saturday?" Tammi's eyes brightened.

"Ayep." Her father mimicked Ira's swallowed expression. "Morning time."

"Date!" she said. Laughing, they walked together into the house.

Tammi had gotten up earlier than usual that Saturday morning and dressed in an old T-shirt and jeans. She heard her father moving around upstairs as she fried his eggs, over easy, just the way he liked them. She placed them on a plate as she heard him descending the stairs.

When he entered the kitchen, he was wearing his gray suit, blue tie, and striped shirt. She stared at him, carefully hiding her disappointment.

"Tammi—I know we were supposed to work on your tree this morning."

"It's all right," she said mechanically, placing his eggs in front of him.

46

"The director of the rescue mission phoned last night," he continued. "They called an emergency board meeting."

"It's all right," Tammi mumbled. "It's not that important." Under her breath she added, "And neither am I."

He glanced at his watch and gulped his coffee. "I'm glad you understand." He scraped his chair back. "Gotta get. Why don't you eat my eggs? I'm running late. Don't know if I'll be home for lunch; we have an outreach planning meeting this afternoon." He started out the door, turned around and looked back toward her. "Mother's not feeling well this morning. She'll be down later." He was gone.

Tammi stared at the eggs for a few moments, then quietly picked up the plate and scraped the eggs into the garbage. She cleaned up from breakfast and slipped out the back door. The hardware store was a twenty-minute walk. In less than an hour she returned home with a can of tree tar.

She worked all morning pruning away the damage with her father's saw. Using the tree tar, rope, hammer, nails, and odd pieces of lumber, she covered the wound and supported the limb.

The tree lived, but her inexperience showed, and injuries the storm had caused would always be visible. Barely, the tree survived the winter.

The morning she ran away, she gazed at it. "It's still the tree that Uncle Ira gave me," she murmured. "I love it even if it is ugly and scarred, like me." She turned away from the window and lurched over to the side stand near her bed. She fumbled for a moment with a crumpled paper sack, slipped a lemon drop into her mouth, and struggled desperately against the nausea pushing up into her throat. Unable to control it, she ran quickly into the bathroom across the hall, turning the water on full force to roar into the tub, and flushed the toilet to cover the sound of her retching.

6

Tammi bathed quickly and slipped back into her robe. She scurried across the hall to her room, and dressed in her school clothing. Yanking an old three-ring binder out of her bottom drawer, she snapped it open and slipped some papers over the rings. She closed the binder again. It would be discarded. Pulling a paperback from the shelf next to her desk, she threw it face-down on top of the binder. She checked her appearance in the full-length mirror fastened to the back of her door. Her hair wasn't quite right, but she couldn't fix it now. "More important things than hair," she thought.

Stepping into the upstairs hallway, she looked back to make certain she had taken everything she would need. "My purse!" she thought irritably. "Be in a fine fix if I left that behind." She stepped to her night stand to pick it up. Next to it lay the King James study Bible her parents had given her for her sixteenth birthday. She grasped it for a moment and then placed it back on the stand. She had tried to read it these last several weeks, but God didn't seem anxious to speak to her. "God speaks only to people He can love," she murmured. "Nobody could love me anymore." She paused at the head of the stairs, numbed her mind, and went down to the kitchen.

She placed her binder on the kitchen counter and sat at the table.

"Morning, Tammi." Her mother's voice was businesslike as

she performed the breakfast chores. "Asking our own bless-
ings this morning." She took the juice from the refrigerator.
"Oatmeal's on the table."

The last thing Tammi wanted was oatmeal; her stomach
shuddered in agreement. Lifting her spoon, however, she
forced herself to take some. If she made an attempt, she
might be able to get it half down. By the third spoonful, her
stomach decided it had had enough.

"Guess I'm not very hungry this morning, Mom."

"At least drink your juice, then." Her mother filled her glass.
"Can't go all day on an empty stomach."

Tammi gazed dully at the remains of her oatmeal coagulat-
ing into a tepid paste. She knew she should eat it. Her money
wouldn't last long.

"Tammi?" Her mother's sharp voice forced her back to her
charade. "Are you ill?"

"No." She answered too hastily. "No. I just feel a little 'blah,'
that's all."

"Way you're poking at your food—looks like you have the
weight of the world on your shoulders."

The toaster thrust up two pieces of bread with a metallic
sigh.

"Have your toast buttered for you in a minute. Want jam
too? Seems to me you'd get tired of sweet strawberry jam
every morning."

Tammi blinked and pushed back a strand of auburn hair
which had spilled forward over her slumped shoulders.

"Your father's got an important meeting with the area repre-
sentative this morning. It's all settled. They voted him District
Superintendent for the State." A toast plate clattered on the
tiled counter as she worked. Tammi thought she detected a
tired resignation in her voice.

"My goodness, Tammi, sit up straight," her mother continued. "And I think you'd better spend a few minutes with

your hair before you leave—you've been getting awfully careless with your appearance lately."

"Leave me alone. Leave me alone! LEAVE ME ALONE!"

Tammi gripped her juice glass convulsively. A clammy perspiration covered her brow. Had she actually screamed that? Flicking intense glances toward her mother, she waited for the shocked reaction, but her mother continued puttering around the sink and stove. Breathing deeply, Tammi forced herself to relax her hand.

She glanced again to take a detailed mental photograph of her mother: auburn hair streaked slightly with wisps of gray; the wide, clear brow; gray eyes that warmed green with laughter. Tammi couldn't remember the last time they were green. More often they glinted a hard gray in dutiful concern for doing right things at proper times. Tammi stole another quick look. Her mother's long, finely shaped nose had grown a little thinner and sharper over the years. Her lips, once full and soft—Tammi had noticed that in a faded color photograph— were now compressed companions to a preoccupied frown etched indelibly between those gray eyes.

Munching her toast and sipping deliberately from a thick-rimmed mug of steaming hot chocolate, Tammi deadened her emotions by continuing the mental snapshots. Another glance fixed the image of the garish pink and orange flowered housecoat. She knew her mother hated it. When Tammi had asked why she refused to throw it out, her mother had replied, "Use it up. Wear it out. Make it do, or do without." Then, smiling grimly, she had continued, "Tammi, I'm trying to wear this horrid thing out."

Tammi remembered when Mrs. Sharkey, the church chairman's wife, thudded up to them one Sunday evening. Her heavy black pumps beat on the parqueted oak floor like a cannibal's drummed dinner invitation to a doomed mission-

50

ary. She thrust the housecoat, stuffed into a large brown paper grocery sack, into Jael's hands.

"I just can't wear it anymore," her brassy voice cut its metallic way through the hubbub of the departing congregation. "I've lost *sooo* much weight this last few months, and, dear, it's simply *tooo* large." Her too-regular false teeth gleamed in her puffy white face as she contorted it into a hungry smile.

Her mother's eyes became iron. For a moment, the frown lines etched themselves more deeply. But with a massive effort her mother regained the self-controlled mask carefully cultivated through the years as a pastor's wife.

Almost from the day she had received the housecoat, her mother had worn it regularly.

Tammi glanced at the clock. Only two minutes had passed.

This morning seemed like one of the searing, painful, slow-motion dreams that came with terrifying regularity following the night of her scalding. The dream never varied. Always, someone wanted to hurt her. Always she found herself floating with a viscous slowness which now, fully awake, she experienced. It was the same terror, the same evil, the same inability to flee.

One night, when the fire was about to engulf her and the darkness drown her, she had said simply, "I can always wake up just by opening my eyes." Concentrating on that hope, she had forced her eyes open and had indeed awakened. Terrified and sweating, she stared at the blue-gray square of night sky in the black frame of her bedroom window. The cross-shaped silhouette formed by the old-fashioned wooden moldings between the panes had comforted her.

But she could not force her eyes open in this dream, and there was no comfort. Its creeping, suspended terror remained.

She tried to make time move faster by counting the number

of times she chewed her toast. Her heart beat dully in her ears. She glanced at the yellow daisy-shaped clock hanging over the kitchen stove. Only five minutes since she came down? Slowly she slipped her right hand from the table and wiped her perspiring palm against her thigh.

"Tammi? On your skirt?"

"Jael, have I got any clean socks?"

Tammi released her breath slowly, grateful for the distraction her father provided.

"Look in the bottom drawer."

"Oh, got 'em."

A door slammed upstairs. Tammi's father thudded down the stairs in stockinged feet. He carried his shoes in one hand, his tie in the other. He entered the kitchen wearing a gray suit Tammi hadn't seen before. Tammi gazed at him intently. His light brown hair, parted at the side, fell neatly halfway over his ears. His hair used to be straw-colored, she remembered, and cut very short. His active blue eyes gazed alertly from behind heavy-rimmed glasses. He smiled readily, but there was a tightness about it.

He noticed her stare.

"New suit. If I'm going to be asked to be the new D.S., I'd better dress like one." He grinned self-consciously.

"Seems to me," her mother remarked quietly, "a very wise man once said to beware of any enterprise demanding new clothes."

"Bet Tammi knows who said that," her father chuckled, looking up at her expectantly.

Startled, Tammi filled her mouth with toast to avoid answering, and took a large mouthful of juice. She didn't have to exaggerate her difficulty in swallowing.

"Thoreau," he answered a little smugly. "But he stayed in the country all his life." He glanced at his watch. "Besides, all he was interested in was pleasing himself."

Tammi saw her mother's shoulders stiffen under that hated housecoat. "I suppose he would feel right at home on our Church Board, then, wouldn't he, Dear?" She wasn't smiling.

Her father buttoned his soft light blue shirt at the neck and flipped the striped tie, another recent acquisition, into a Windsor knot. He picked up and buttered a slice of toast with slow, deliberate strokes.

"Well, Mother," he grinned, "bet you never thought that you'd be the wife of the next District Superintendent."

"Whatever you want, Dear." Her voice was weary.

He placed the knife down very gently, but the muffled "clink" filled the kitchen. He smiled wanly. "Guess your mother didn't want the boy to take her out of the country . . . or some saying like that," he tried to joke. But the twitch of the jaw muscles and the slight flush in his cheeks signalled that Tammi's mother had struck a nerve.

In the silence, Tammi heard the blood rush in her ears. She glanced up at the clock again, its disinterested electric whirring the loudest sound in the kitchen. It was two full minutes before she dared leave. It seemed two centuries.

"I'm sorry, Dear," Jael said, slowly brushing a wisp of hair from her brow. "I . . . I shouldn't have said that." She turned to the stove. "Would you like an egg?"

Tammi sensed the hurt in her father's voice. "No thank you." He spoke very quietly. "Toast and coffee will be fine."

And now she had to hurt both of them.

"Tam?"

"Yes, Dad?" For the last few minutes, Tammi had swallowed nausea and screams of frustration welling up against the tightly clamped muscles in her throat. She could only whisper.

"I'm sorry, but I won't be able to come to hear you play in the band concert Friday night. The men of the church are meeting to work out a special series of family nights for the summer." He glanced through a letter he had brought with him to the table.

"I should be able to come, Tam," her mother added. "Unless Louella can't solve some family problem. Then I'll have to sit in for her on the planning for the Mother-Daughter retreat."

Tammi's palms and brow felt clammy. Nervously she again dried her hands on her dress. Glancing around the kitchen one last time, she summoned all her concentration to force a casual tone.

"It's all right. Doesn't make any difference, anyhow." She picked up her binder and paperback from the counter.

"Be home late tonight, Tammi?"

"Better not wait supper, Mom." Forcing the words out, she played a robot. She started out the door.

"Tammi?"

She stopped and looked at her father.

"Is that the novel you're studying in English class?"

She could only nod. Her throat seemed about to explode.

"What is it?"

Silently she turned the book face up and tipped the binder so he could see the title.

"I'd think the English teachers would find a more modern book to teach nowadays," he remarked, a teasing twinkle in his usually preoccupied blue eyes. "Have a good day." He lowered his gaze to his letter before he had finished speaking.

Tammi paced down the walk and turned to the right toward school. Just before she left the yard, she stopped suddenly by the low, sagging branch of her beloved apple tree and broke off a leafy sprig. Continuing down the street, she turned again and, out of sight of the house, sank down upon a low wall enclosing a small green around a memorial to the men from Shelterport who died in the World Wars.

She sobbed an almost silent searing cry which turned suddenly into a hysterical giggle. She tried to stifle it with a handkerchief snatched from her purse; but the strange mixture of laughter and weeping overwhelmed her as she recalled how close she had come to giving everything away. She hadn't noticed the title of the book until her father asked about it. It was *The Scarlet Letter.*

Tammi remembered forcing herself back under control and walking to the bus stop, boarding a Beltline 26 bus, and taking the rear corner seat. In order to avoid recognition, she had slouched down and hid her face, pretending to study the papers in her binder. Each stop as the bus crawled downtown was terror. With all the people she knew from church and school, she was certain someone would surely recognize her. That was the one part of her plan she had overlooked. Her stomach constricted into a burning knot. Her hands and forehead became cold and sweaty again. But she arrived at the bus terminal unrecognized.

Tammi recalled less specifically retrieving her day pack from a coin-locker where she had checked it the day before. Confused images—the tiled restroom where she changed her clothes, the coin-operated stall in which she locked herself until the rasping PA announced the bus for Burlington, the stench of stale tobacco, rancid sweat, cheap perfume, and diesel fumes; entering the coach, the endless swaying, changing buses for Croughton's Corners, and the muted roar of the engines—tumbled in her mind like jagged fragments of a shattered mirror. She remembered more clearly getting off at Croughton's Corners, the endless walk to Ira and Bea's, her hunger and thirst, the rough-looking men at the mill, and the red-faced boy who gave her his lunch. She remembered most clearly her fright when he offered to drive her over the mountain to Ira and Bea's. Another long walk. Ira and Bea gone. Awakening, downstairs, on the sofa.

From her retreat in the upstairs bedroom, Tammi heard the kitchen door open and then close. An engine started in the driveway, and the grind of a vehicle gradually diminished into a whisper and finally was absorbed in the evening blackness.

She waited for a few minutes, unwilling to leave the quilted softness of the old-fashioned bed. She listened for the pattern of Ira and Bea's conversation, but they had stepped outside, and she could hear nothing.

Finally, she slipped out from under the covers and sat on the edge of the bed. "She must have told him why I ran away by now," she thought. "I hope he won't hate me." Her eyes felt hot and dry. She stepped to the door and went downstairs.

7

Bea bustled about the stove, pouring herself the last of the supper tea and placing the pot on the sideboard to be washed with the remaining dishes.

Ira pulled an old white-painted kitchen chair out from between the kitchen door and the refrigerator and tilted back against the wall, ankles crossed, legs thrust forward. He yawned loudly, stretched, and glanced up at Tammi, his brown eyes sad.

"Well, guess I'll have me some ice cream. How 'bout you?"

Tammi nodded her head. "Please."

Except for rain-sounds sifting in through the screen door, the kitchen was silent.

"Seems to me you're partial to strawberry," he drawled. Tipping the chair forward, Ira stood and opened the freezer door at the top of the refrigerator. He pulled out two brightly-printed cartons and stepped to the counter beside the sink. "Want some, Bea?"

"No. I'll just finish my tea."

"Best way to end a long, hard day," Ira commented, spooning pink mounds into two plastic cereal bowls.

"Been usin' that excuse for the last twenty years, he has," Bea sputtered. "Every summer, every night, ice cream before bed. Don't understand he doesn't tire of it." She winked at the girl, remembering a much younger Tammi, three summers ago, delighting in sharing Ira's ice cream ritual at day's end.

"Well, figgered out what to do yet?" Ira asked the question casually, cutting his soup spoon into the ice cream.

Tammi stared down into her bowl. She had eaten little. She shook her head. "No. No. Not yet."

"We got that bedroom up there." Ira swallowed and paused while the cold hurt his throat. "Stay's long as you want."

Tammi looked up at him and then at Bea. "I feel so ashamed, Uncle Ira. Aunt Bea, I feel so—bad."

Bea looked at the girl and placed teacup, hands, and elbows on the cool white of the table. "We know, child." Her voice was gentle. "We know."

"Uncle Ira, what'll I do?" Tears started spilling again.

"Well . . ." Ira held the back of his neck with his left hand and leaned back in his chair. "Ain't much good at givin' advice." He gazed at her, his eyes unblinking. "But I ain't never been able to run far enough away from somethin' I'm scared of but that it wasn't there at the other end."

She stared at the mound in her bowl. "You want me to go back home, then."

"Nope."

She looked up, surprised. Bea stared at Ira, incredulous, her blue eyes unblinking.

Ira took another mouthful of ice cream and replaced the spoon in the bowl. He leaned back and continued. "'Member three years ago you went down to pick some raspberries up near the sugarin' house? Got yourself right smack into the middle of them thorny berries and stepped into a bee's nest?"

Tammi glanced at her hands. "Yes. You told me to be careful for the bees."

"Twixt the bees and the berry bush, you got stuck good and painful. No way we knew to help you, though, till you come back to the house."

"Sakes alive, do I remember that," Bea chuckled. "Your face puffed up like a chipmunk and scratches all over your little arms and legs."

"Bein' on the edge o' grown like you are is like steppin' into that bee's nest in the berry patch. Some spots, after you get into 'em—you're goin' to get stuck good and plenty whatever you do." Ira filled his mouth with a large spoonful of ice cream and sat silent for a moment, enjoying the chilled sweetness. "Best thing to do, you did then. Hot foot it home out of harm's way." He swirled his soup spoon around in the bottom of his ice cream bowl to get the last mouthful. "Goin' to hurt as much goin' back as goin' away. Body's got to decide."

"Mom and Dad—they don't know yet."

"Leastwise, they didn't when you left," Bea contributed. "They must be worried sick, child. Why don't you call them and let them know you're all right?"

Tammi looked down at her ice cream melting in the bowl. "I'm so scared. I can't. Not yet." She looked from one to the other. "I just don't know what to do."

"Only got three choices, seems t'me," Ira said.

Tammi looked up, waiting for him to continue, but he said nothing more.

"You mean," she faltered, "going back home."

"Ayup. That's one of 'em." He cocked a shaggy eyebrow at her. Tammi gazed at Ira with large green eyes. "I . . . I could stay here?"

"Possible." His eyebrow lowered as he considered the possibility. "S'pect your folks'd be here right quick though to fetch you home agin."

Tammi remained silent a long time. "I guess I could go someplace by myself . . . where no one knows me."

Ira stared into the bottom of his ice cream dish, spooning the last of the thick pink syrup. Bea watched him, her lips pressed together a little more than usual.

"Reckon you could git a job—waitress or somethin' till your time come," he said slowly.

Tammi sat silent, dabbing at her ice cream. "My folks'll hate me."

"No such thing, child," Bea interjected. "Sure, they'll be upset some. Real upset." She reached across the table and grasped Tammi's trembling hands inside her own soft comfortable palms. "And they'll be terrible hurt. But they'll come through. They love you."

"But my Dad . . . and, the church . . . they're going to make him District Superintendent. They'll talk behind his back . . . my Mom won't be able to look at anyone at church again . . . they'll hate me. They'll all hate me! They'll never want to see me again!" She dropped her spoon and clutched the napkin to her face as tears overflowed again.

"Well," Ira replied calmly, "leastwise wouldn't hurt to find out for sure. Be no worse off then, than now."

The tears stopped coursing down her cheeks, and Tammi arranged her napkin on her lap with nervous, twitching movements and fiddled with the edges of her ice cream bowl.

"Prob'ly better," Ira continued. "Now you ain't sure." He raised his eyebrows. "Not much to lose as I see it."

"I'm scared," she whispered. Bea reached across the table and took Tammi's hands again. "Child, your folks are as scared as you are. There's nothin' about bein' growed that takes away bein' scared." Bea squeezed her hands before releasing them to finish the tea, now cold in her cup.

Red-eyed, Tammi stared through the window into the night.

"Not much else to do, is there?" Tammi sighed. "Nothing that will help."

"Leastwise, not for long," Ira agreed. He placed his spoon inside his empty dish and ran his calloused hand through his fine gray hair, as if the absence of a cap made him uncomfortable.

"Do I have to call them tonight?" Her voice quivered.

"Wouldn't hurt," Ira responded quietly.

Tammi glanced helplessly at the door frame leading to the parlor—and the telephone. She gathered her feet under her and leaned forward as if to stand, but then sank back again. "I . . . I can't. Not tonight." She started to weep again. "I know I have to go back. I just can't call tonight."

There was another long period of silence. Tammi toyed with the ice cream in her bowl. She sighed again and hiccupped slightly from her weeping. "Uncle Ira, can you take me to the Corners tomorrow? I guess I have to go back."

"Reckon so." He stood and walked to the kitchen door. "Have to get a new chain for the saw, might's well do it then."

"You're goin' to call, aren't you, child?" Bea urged.

"I'm . . . I can't. Not tonight."

"Well, certainly first thing tomorrow, then," Bea continued.

"I . . . I'll try," Tammi promised. Then she looked at Ira, "Uncle Ira—maybe—could you—I mean—after I get on the bus . . . ?"

Ira turned his warm brown eyes upon Tammi again. They had a faraway look in them as if he were remembering another time, another girl. "If you can't," he said gently, "we'll call—let 'em know you're comin' home."

Bea got up from the table. "That old oak wardrobe up there's got some old flannel nightgowns in it—an' there's plenty o' hot water for a bath." She started placing the kitchen to rights for the night. "Ira's old bathrobe's up there too. Sakes, it's gettin' late."

Ira stood and took his hat from the top of the refrigerator. "Guess I'll lock th' barn."

Tammi, standing also, stepped over and hugged him, clinging like a frightened bear cub. "Thank you, Uncle Ira. Thank you," she whispered.

Awkwardly, Ira smoothed her hair with his work-roughened hand. "You'll be all right, young 'un," he said. "It'll be all right."

Tammi looked up into his face, but he seemed to be gazing into a past she could not enter. She kissed him on the cheek and went up the stairs to her room.

Bea wiped out the sink and stood with him for a moment. "Guess I'll get to bed too," she sighed. "Got a big day tomorrow with that young 'un." She shuffled off quietly to their bedroom. "Turn out the lights."

"Ayup."

Ira stepped out on the side porch to listen to the fine rain that had started shortly after the Brady boy left. He could just see the black outline of the aging gray-boarded barn behind the old Dodge. Sissie had run away on a night like this. He stepped out of his slippers, thrust his feet into an old pair of rubber boots beside the back door and trudged up the drive to padlock the barn and tool shed.

8

Sissie had been gone for three days before Ira thought to look in the drawer of the tool chest.

He had made it for his carpenter's tools, a large box with a generous compartment across the top and three shallow dovetailed and finely-fitted drawers one beside the other across the bottom. It had won the prize for "Best Crafted" in the manual-arts fair the month before.

He remembered the evening he had lugged the chest home along with his award and set them in the corner of the living room.

Edwin had glanced at the chest and plaque and reminded him that Ma didn't like tools in the house. His father had grunted, "No point in makin' so fancy a chest—good hard work'll tear it up, anyhow." His mother reflected the hurt in his own eyes. She had run her hand over the velvety varnished lid and said, "It's lovely, Ira. Just like your Grandpa's work."

Only Sissie had come later out to the barn workshop and asked to see every cranny and corner. Sissie had sat on the sawhorse and let him show her the special things he had worked into the chest; and her eyes glowed, pleased with his craft, as she listened to him ramble on. Finally he finished, and placed the tray into the top of the box and slid the drawers shut. After he showed her how spring-loaded pins locked the drawers shut with the closing of the cover, Sissie had asked, "Ira—can I use one of those drawers?"

"Edwin get into your stuff again?"

"Not just Edwin. They don't seem to see I'm 'most a woman grown, Ira. There are some things I like to keep special." Her eyes flashed their resentment.

"How'd you like me to make a lock-box for you?"

She smiled strangely, "I'd like that, Ira." She glanced at the toolbox. "But till you get it done, can I use that drawer in the middle?"

Ira lifted the lid to release the catch on the drawer and slid it out. "All right. I put a hasp on the box to lock it." He reached into the top tray, removed a padlock with two keys, and handed her one. "You know I won't bother it."

"I know, Ira." She clutched the key in her hand. "I'll give you your key back when I'm through with the drawer." She kissed him, too suddenly for him to back away in embarrassment, and ran out of the shop.

Two weeks later, she left. For the first three days of their search, they turned up little more than that someone thought she might have been at the bus at Croughton's Corners. The police had found no further trace.

Needing to think, he decided to work in his shop after supper. Working with wood always calmed him, and he planned to start fitting her lock-box together. Somehow, making something for Sissie helped him to believe she'd come back.

Not bothering to put on a jacket against the night drizzle, he stepped quickly across the lawn and up the rutted path to the barn. He slid the door back on its slanted iron track just far enough to enter and let it squeak closed after him. He reached up, pulled the string on the drop cord he had rigged and opened the hasp on his toolbox. Lifting the lid, Ira reached for a chisel in the top tray. He stopped, poising his hand over the box like a preacher giving a benediction. The other key—the one he gave Sissie—lay in the tray next to the chisels.

". . . *when I'm through with the drawer,*" she had said.

His hand trembling, Ira opened the center drawer. The note was there, folded once. He opened it and smoothed it on the bench—his hands shook too much to hold it.

> *Ira: I'm sorry. I got to go away while I got the chance. Don't worry about me. Tell Ma not to worry. Pa and Edwin don't care. I hate to leave you most of all. I love you.*
> *Sissie*

Ira stood, dazed, reading the note again and again. Finally, he folded it, slipped it into his pocket, and made his way back to the house.

That day was the beginning of the "black years," as Bea

later referred to them. They looked, but Sissie had disappeared. "Probably went to the city," the sheriff had said. "If a person don't want to be found, all they have to do is stay law-abiding." He had shuffled some papers. "Easier to find a three-legged tick on a hound dog."

His father had torn from the family Bible the page bearing her name, and he spoke her name only once again—just before he died in the upstairs bedroom. "Sissie," he had whispered. "Tell Sissie I never meant to hurt her."

The day she saw the note, his mother changed. Her eyes went lifeless. Though she lived another twenty years, she became passive and silent. At the last, she spent most of the days sitting in her room with all the shades drawn. Some said they should have put her in the county hospital, but Ira and Bea cared for her until one day, she simply stopped breathing, and died.

And it was raining tonight—the night Tammi came—the same way it rained the night he found the note. He had been seventeen when Sissie ran away. And from the first, he suspected that Edwin and his father were hiding something.

"Sure found out quick enough what they wouldn't tell me," Ira muttered as he struggled with the hasp on the barn door.

The week following Sissie's disappearance, Ira drove to Austin's gas station in Croughton's Corners for a case of oil. Jake Austin's son was counting out the green and white quart cans for him when they heard the car drive up to the pumps.

"Be right back, Ira. Gotta pump gas."

"Sure. I can get the rest of these."

Ira watched through the dirty windows facing the pumps as

Jake Junior pumped gasoline for Carl Hartley, a dropout last year from the Central School.

"Sure thing she run away," Carl sneered, his voice carrying through the open door of the station as he bragged to the four younger men riding with him. "She put on airs, like all those MacIntoshes. Well, she didn't put on any airs for me. She's no better than the town pump."

Jake Junior glanced toward the station, a worried look on his face. He replaced the hose and took Carl's money.

Coming in to put the cash in the old brass register, Jake Junior saw Ira standing in the storeroom doorway. He glanced out front, and then back at Ira. "Nothin' but a lot o' talk," he said awkwardly.

"He's the one made her run away," Ira said, his voice soft, dangerous. "That's what no one would tell me." His eyes narrowed as he stared down the road where Carl had driven. "He ain't seen the last of the MacIntoshes." He dropped some money on the counter, picked up the case of oil and silently carried it around back to his father's truck. He would have forgotten his change, had Jim not run around and thrust it through the open window at him.

Shortly after sunrise the following Saturday, Ira crept to the living room and slipped his father's deer rifle from the corner of the closet. He found the box of shells in their usual place, the center drawer of the old oak sideboard, and took six of them. Closing the door silently behind him, he stole from the house and cut across the mountain behind Mayer's cow pasture, which bordered on a pine woods. Cutting through the pines, he reached the back edge of the Hartley's farm. He dropped on his hands and knees when the woods thinned and crept silently forward on the thick pine-needled carpet until he was hidden behind the decaying black trunk of an ancient tree. The barn and the house, its back porch splashed golden with the new-risen sun, were both clear shots. He lay on his stomach. The log had fallen across a younger tree, and one end had remained slightly raised.

Ira slipped the shells into the magazine and thrust the rifle barrel through the space formed by the log and the smaller tree upon which it rested. He waited. It wouldn't be long. The cows were lowing to be milked.

Young Carl came out, black-haired, smiling, strutting his manhood like a buck in rut. He stretched in the morning coolness. The dark patch of hair on his tanned chest made a perfect aiming point. Ira cocked the rifle and aligned the gold bead of the front sight in the middle of the rear notch, drawing the gray iron "v" down the center of Carl's form a hundred yards distant. It rested a moment on the arrogant face and dropped to the dark patch on his chest. The second joint of Ira's finger whitened against the trigger as he raised the sights just above and to the left of the aiming point. He drew a deep breath and held it.

"Won't do no good to kill him, Ira."

He froze. Every sound carried to him as if each had created its own world—the rushing of blood in his ears, the whine of mosquitoes in the damp grass, the lowing of cows in the Hartley's barn, the rhythmic clanking of the pump on the back porch as young Carl drew a basin of water for washing.

Gently he relieved the pressure from his trigger finger and silently released his breath. Sliding the rifle back slowly from the top of the log, he set the hammer on the half-cocked position and rolled quietly on his side to face the voice.

Blonde-haired Bea Mayer lay beside him, her voice an earnest whisper. "You'll still be hatin' him even after he's dead." She rolled onto her stomach and peered through the space from which Ira had withdrawn the rifle, "Then who you gonna shoot?" She turned her head sideways and cradled her face on her crossed arms. "Saw you cut 'long the edge of our land up toward the mountain while I was gettin' the cows out to pasture," she whispered. "Heard 'em talkin' 'bout Carl and Sissie at school, too." She gazed at him, her eyes warm and blue. "Saw you carryin' the rifle—an' tenth o' June ain't deer season." Sixteen-year-old Bea had placed her slender fingers over his. "Ira, killin' Carl ain't gonna bring back Sissie."

That was the only time Ira had ever cried in front of Bea.

Carl Hartley had gone on to fight in the war. He had lost a leg and more and had returned to the mountains. Bitter and solitary, he had made himself a hermit on the farm he inherited from his father. Each year the farm became more and more run-down. Carl provided for himself with the government disability check each month and what he could grow in his small garden.

Since the day with the rifle, almost forty years ago, Ira had never spoken to Carl. "You stopped me from killin' the man, and I'm thankful," he had told Bea. "But he's dead so far as I'm concerned." He saw her expression. "Know it's wrong to hate the man—so be it. I can't help the way I feel."

Sissie had never returned, and except for an occasional card bearing no return address, he had heard nothing of her whereabouts.

Trudging back down the path from the barn, Ira shook his head and stepped out of the rubber boots at the kitchen door. Wiggling his feet back into his slippers, he went inside, locking the door behind him. He padded across the kitchen linoleum, through the parlor, and into the bedroom.

Already asleep, Bea lay on her side, one soft, white arm flung across his half of the bed. He was always surprised at how much smoother and younger her face looked in the subdued light of the nightstand lamp. Undressing, he lay beside her. He slipped his hand beneath her outstretched fingers and thought about how this same gentle hand had kept him from murder.

9

Tammi watched Ira's and Bea's figures slip sideways from the frame of the green-tinted bus window, their plain faces reminding her of a Grant Wood painting.

Rising early that morning, they had breakfasted on pancakes and maple syrup and then crowded into the cab of the old gray pick-up for the hour-long trip.

"Might's well take you right on down to Burlington," Ira had said. "More likely to have what I need there."

"And you'll be on the same bus till you get home," Bea added.

Grateful there were few other passengers on the coach, Tammi retreated into the foam and vinyl upholstery. The bus roared and hissed out into traffic, and shortly afterward, the steady thrum of the muffled diesels lulled her into a half-trance.

As the bus loped along, in rhythm with the tarred seams of the concrete highway, she wondered at how drastically her life had changed.

"Hey—does it ever get above freezing here?"

Those were Ted's first words to her last September.

"June tenth through twentieth," she had replied, trying to turn away the burned side of her face and be clever at the same time. "Snow melts too much to use the sleds."

She lowered her face toward her books and shot glances to see if the other girls in the study hall noticed that he had spoken to her. "Thank you, Mr. Simpson," she breathed, "for your fetish for alphabetical seating." Tammi glanced at Sandi Beech who had turned herself a little sideways and fiddled with her hair so that the movement would catch his eye; but Ted Tolleson glanced her way only briefly, ignored the quick invitational wrinkle of Sandi's nose that other boys seemed to find irresistible, and continued chatting with Tammi.

By the time the day ended, Tammi had discovered that Ted was in three of her six classes. When she saw him in speech class, his face broke into a wide, warm smile; and Tammi's ears burned red under the envious gaze of the other girls in the room. "The alphabet caper," he had joked, pulling his schedule card from his books. "What other classes do we share?"

Tammi glanced at the peach-colored card. "Chemistry." She glanced at it again, and noticed that Ted had transferred in from Oceanside, California.

In chemistry class, Tammi was the only student without an assigned lab partner, and Mr. Burroughs placed Ted with her.

"Well," Ted chuckled, "you going to keep me from blowing this place up?"

Tammi stood a little sideways, and tossed her long auburn hair a little, hoping it would fall over the side of her face. She sensed Sandi's stare, two tables back. "If you do, warn me first so I can run."

When school ended that day, Sandi had swayed up to Tammi's locker. "Hi Tammi." Her smile was cold, her eyes narrowed a little.

"Oh, hello, Sandi." She bowed her head and peered into her locker, making a lengthy task of pulling out a book.

"It's all a put-on, you know," Sandi said coolly.

"A put-on? What do you mean?"

"His paying all this attention to you." She no longer smiled. "I've seen guys do it before—make believe they're interested in a 'Plain Jane' to make all the other girls start chasing them."

"I don't know what you're talking about, Sandi," Tammi snapped. "I sit in front of him in three classes because of an alphabet." She grew bolder with irritation. "I doubt that he'd answer your advertisements from across the classroom, in any case."

Tammi stopped abruptly, unable to believe she had said that.

"Well—Miss Goodie-Goodie has another side," Sandi sneered. "When you get hurt, don't tell me I didn't warn you." She hitched her bag higher on her shoulder and turned away. "Hey! Guys! Wait for me!" She ran down the hall after a group of three girls on the cheer squad.

Ted's impact rippled throughout the school; but while he was friendly to the other girls who seemed always in his vicinity, Tammi noticed that he seldom paid more attention to one than the other. That he spoke to her at all puzzled her.

"You sure are creating a stir among the girls around here," Tammi remarked casually as they cleaned up from an experiment.

"Dunno," Ted shrugged. "Lot of 'em go with the guys on the football squad." He checked to make certain the gas was off to the Bunsen burner. "Transferring made me ineligible to play this semester, but I want to go out for spring sports." He rinsed a beaker and continued, "First commandment for a transfer student who wants to get into sports: 'Thou shalt not mess with another guy's girl'—especially if he's bigger than you are." They laughed, and Tammi felt a new warmth quite unlike anything she had ever felt before.

Two weeks later, Ted turned to her after the bell dismissing speech class.

"Hey, Tam?"

"Yes?"

"How 'bout going to the game with me next week?"

Tammi felt her face redden and her palms sweat. She glanced down and fumbled with her speech notes. "I . . . I don't know." She scooped her books up and held them tightly against her chest. "Can I tell you tomorrow?"

Ted looked at her, a puzzled frown on his face. "Sure."

"A date with Ted Tolleson," she whispered to herself over and over again as she walked home. "A date with Ted Tolleson!" She couldn't help laughing. "Sandi Beech would *kill* for a date with Ted Tolleson, and he asked me!" She giggled to herself as she turned down the walk to the parsonage.

Her mother looked up as Tammi entered through the kitchen door. "Well—what are you so happy about today?"

"Oh," Tammi smirked, "a boy asked me to go to the ballgame next week."

Cocking an inquisitive eyebrow in her direction, her mother smiled and turned the meat in the pan to sear the other side. "Anybody we know?"

"Just the most popular boy in school, that's all!" Tammi couldn't stop grinning.

"And who's the most popular boy this week?" her mother asked playfully. She removed the creamed corn from the heat.

"The boy who transferred in right after school started, Ted Tolleson."

"Oh?" Her mother sliced an onion over the meat and slipped the lid covering the potatoes to one side so they would not boil over. "Where does he go to church?"

Tammi stopped giggling and turned her lips down at the corners. "I don't know, Mother, he just asked me to the game. I—I didn't get his pedigree!"

"Tammi, you don't have to get sharp," her mother soothed, "but it is good to know those things."

Tammi snatched her books from the counter. "No guy in school looks at me because of this burn that makes me look like a leper—and when the most popular guy in Shelterport asks me—." She sighed and started for the stairs.

71

"Tammi?"

"Yes?" Her voice was surly as she turned and faced her mother.

"I didn't say you couldn't go." She smiled. "Why don't we talk about it at supper, when your father comes home."

"Whatever." She turned and continued to her room.

A half hour later, Tammi heard her mother answer the telephone, speak for a few moments and then hang up. Shortly after that her mother called her for supper. When Tammi came down to the dining room, there were only two places set.

"That was your father." Her mother's lips were set.

"Oh?"

"He won't be home until late. The building committee has hit a snag." She sat and hitched her chair closer to the table. Her quick, nervous movements betrayed her anger. "Would you return thanks, Tammi? To be perfectly honest, I'm not in a praying mood."

Tammi prayed and they ate. She waited until they were on the dessert before saying anything.

"Ted told me he'd ask me tomorrow if it's all right with you and Dad." She tilted her head so her hair covered more of her face.

Her mother finished the last of her dessert and then looked up. She smiled sympathetically. "It wouldn't be polite to keep him waiting, would it?" She looked deeply into Tammi's eyes. "Dad's not home for us to talk to, so I'll make the decision." She cocked her head a little to one side, as she always did when she was thinking, and frowned slightly, making the inside ends of her thin eyebrows slant upward. When she did that, it seemed to Tammi that her mother appeared more sad than thoughtful. "A ball game is public enough but—" she calmed Tammi with a hand on the shoulder. "You'd better find out about his 'pedigree' as you call it before you come asking again, understand?"

"Yes, Mom. Yes!" Tammi wiggled around in her chair with excitement.

"Oh—go shoot some baskets or something before you explode," her mother laughed.

The next day before speech class, Ted leaned forward over his desk. "Well, can you go?"

"Yes. I'd like to."

"Good," Ted smiled. "Pick you up at seven?"

"Okay."

"We'll go to Barney's afterwards for something to eat, all right?"

"Yes. That'll be fun."

Barney's, she thought, as she walked back home from school that afternoon. *Barney's.* Only those who were popular congregated at Barney's on Friday nights. Never before had anyone even suggested Tammi meet them there. And now she would go there as Ted's date!

Tammi drifted rather than walked home. Only partially aware of her mother's greeting, she floated through the door and up to her room. She sat on her bed, its apple-blossom counterpane preserving springtime. Maybe her tree, with its stark branches outlined by the late fall sunlight, would take the hint for next spring.

Vaguely, she heard her mother making supper sounds downstairs.

Ted Tolleson. Barney's. He had even seen the scar on her face and neck, and it hadn't mattered! She had tried to cover it by wearing her hair long and full around the sides of her face, but she knew, sooner or later, he would ask. People always did. Finally it came during a lab period.

"How'd you do that?" The question was casual, sincere. It didn't mask pity and disgust she had sensed in others making the same query.

Before she knew fully what she was doing, she had told him

simply and naturally the whole story as they worked. It hadn't made any difference. He hadn't turned away. He hadn't stopped talking to her. And now, he had even asked her for a date. To Barney's. By unspoken codes, no "weirdos" went there—at least not while the regulars were there.

"Tammi." Her mother's call floated up from the kitchen. "Tammi—supper."

She'd order a hoagie—a Number Five—just this once—all those calories—but everybody ordered hoagies—a Number Five: cheese, provolone, ham, tomatoes, onions, shredded lettuce, just enough green chilies to give it a little bite, and a restrained shake of salad oil to keep the French bread from being too dry. She'd bought them for herself on occasion, but always when the place was mostly deserted, and never on the weekend.

"*TAMMI!*" The accented second syllable finally brought her back.

"Coming."

"It's supper time."

"Yes. I'm coming."

She tried to transform the heavy odors of searing liver and pungent butter-fried onions into the deli fragrance of a Barney's Number Five, but her imagination rebelled at the attempt

Friday night, when Ted called for her at her house, Tammi's mother answered the door. She heard a mumble of conversation downstairs as she combed her hair one last time to fall correctly alongside her face, and then went down.

"Hello, Ted." She smiled self-consciously. "I see you and Mom have already met."

"Yeah." Ted's smile seemed a little tense. "She invited me to church on Sunday."

Tammi felt her ears burn as she shot a glance at her mother.

"You two have a good time, now," her mother had said. "Remember, eleven-thirty."

They walked out together in the gray evening light. He opened the door of his truck for her, walked around the front, and slipped in the other side. As he started the engine, he turned and slid his gaze over her. Tammi reddened. She had never really felt a boy's look before, not like that. She felt confused.

With Ted at the game, Tammi felt more self-conscious than if she had been voted Homecoming Queen. Girls who never had spoken with her before approached with a friendly, "Hi Tammi, Ted. Great game, huh? See you at Barney's." Even Sandi Beech came over between cheers, a wide smile on her face. "Good to see you tonight, Tam! Ted!" Tammi stiffened as she saw Sandi's eyes narrow slightly. "Your hairdo is beautiful, wearing it forward and long, the way you do, Tammi!" She smiled again, and said in a low voice that Ted couldn't hear, "Careful, Goodie-Goodie—he's out of your league."

At Barney's they sat in a booth back in the corner and ate their hoagies.

"Sandi told me your father is a minister."

"Yes." She filled her mouth with a large bite of her sandwich so she wouldn't have to talk for a moment.

"That's neat." He continued, "Mind if I come to church Sunday?"

Tammi sat, her mouth filled with hoagie, unable to chew or swallow. She couldn't believe it. *Ted is actually asking for a second date? A church date?* All she could do was wag her head dumbly from side to side until she managed to swallow her food. "Mind?" She coughed and took a sip of her soft drink. "No . . . no, not at all."

Ted paid the bill and they went to the parking lot. Several students gathered around the vehicles in the unusually mild evening, chattering and joking with one another in the parking lot. Tammi and Ted joined them for a few minutes. Finally, she forced herself to look at her watch. "We'd better be going, Ted. It's getting late," she said.

"Sure," he smiled. "Everybody's leaving now, anyhow." Leaning forward to open the door, he brushed against her. At the time, she thought it was an accident.

10

When Ted appeared at the church door the following Sunday, he wore a brown sport coat and beige slacks. His dark brown shoes gleamed like a pair of wet coke bottles. He had trimmed his hair and combed it carefully. He wore a tie, not the clip-on kind that made young men look like little boys again, but a carefully-knotted striped tie that harmonized with his brown-tinged shirt. His tan, left over from a California sun, had not yet faded to a New England paleness, and it accented his blue eyes. The smile was relaxed, but respectful.

Tammi felt a little smug. Her father hated overly-long hair and sloppy attire, especially at church. There wasn't a thing he could complain about with Ted. He would have to like him. But she held her breath anyhow when she introduced them before Sunday school.

"Dad, this is Ted Tolleson. Ted, this is my father." She searched her father's face for reactions.

"Well, hello, Ted." He reached out to grasp Ted's hand and grinned.

Tammi relaxed.

"Been hearing a lot about you." He released Ted's hand, and stood easily, his arms folded loosely across his chest. "I guess this is some change from the beaches of California."

"Yes, sir," Ted replied.

"Sure picked the cold time of year to come here," her father chuckled. "Hope you brought your long underwear with you."

Tammi felt the red flood into her face. "Why does he have to do that?" she thought. "No matter what Ted says now, he'll sound like a 'smart kid.'"

Before Ted could answer, however, Carl Henry interrupted with some deacon business, and her father launched into another conversation. Tammi stood with Ted for a moment and then touched his arm. "The high-school class meets downstairs." She doubted her father knew they had left.

Ted seemed to enjoy that first morning as well as she did— except for a moment when he had leafed aimlessly through the pages of both the Old and New Testaments looking for First Corinthians. Finally, he grinned helplessly and glanced over at her. Irritated with herself for embarrassing him, she moved over closer and smoothed the pages of her Bible so he could share it.

During the morning service, she sang loudly enough to cover his stumbling through unfamiliar hymns. At the door he shook hands with her mother and her father and declined an invitation for dinner.

"My uncle and I go out to dinner on Sundays," he grinned.

"Your uncle?" her father's curiosity was aroused.

"Yes," Ted explained. "My aunt died five years ago. He has a large house and lives alone." He paused for a moment, and then added, "During the week I work for him at his marine hardware store in Colonie Town." He smiled a little self-consciously. "Sunday is the only day he takes off, so he sort of looks forward to it." His face became serious. "Guess he gets lonely."

Tammi noticed Ted's quick glance toward her and the quick blink when he caught her eye. There was a hint of something that she couldn't understand, but she said, good-bye to him and watched him walk to his truck parked across the street. "How many other boys would think of a lonely uncle?" she thought. She had trouble keeping from smirking. "His pedigree might not be what some of the others are, but he's as good as anyone else—better!" the thoughts tumbled fiercely through her mind.

"Seems like a very nice boy," her father said at dinner that day. "Very polite, respectful, but confident at the same time," he added. "Very few of those around these days."

"He told me he went to a large church in Oceanside before he came here," her mother added.

Tammi stopped chewing for a moment and frowned. There was something nibbling at the edge of her mind. She finally gave up trying to think it out of its corner and went back to trying to line up three green peas on the tines of her fork. But the question still bothered her.

"You know more about him than I do," Tammi grinned.

"He told me while we waited for you to make your entrance Friday night." She smiled. "Just getting his 'pedigree.'" She winked at Tammi and rose to get the rolls from the oven.

Tammi finished her soup in silence. Ted had said nothing to her about going to church in California. She wondered how much they used the Bible or sang, but she shrugged it off. Different churches worship differently.

After that first Sunday, Ted attended church regularly. He appeared at youth meetings and evening services. Most of the time she found him sitting next to her, but since he came so often, she didn't really consider his being at church a "date."

At school, they congregated in the cafeteria at the same table as all the popular students. Delighted in no longer finding herself a "leper," Tammi buzzed near the center of the hive that frequented Barney's after school. She sat with them in the bleachers during football games. Later in the fall, she joined the skating parties at the ROLL-A-SKATE rink between Shelterport and Colonie Town. During the winter, when the ice hardened on the pine-fringed lake two miles west of Shelterport, the others took it for granted that she would join them in ice-skating parties. Sometimes, when the party finished, a couple stayed at the lake after the others left. She paid little attention to them, or to the scraps of gossip at school. That was their business. It was enough that she no longer had to sit solitary at the lunch table or make excuses to get home as rapidly as possible.

Only Sandi Beech seemed determined to ruin it for her.

"Junior-Senior Winter Dance coming up, Miss Goodie-Goodie," Sandi had taunted in the girls' lavatory one morning. "I hear tell you 'don't'—that is, you don't dance." She gave the double meaning time to take effect. Her eyes grew round with mock innocence. "Aren't you going to share him with anyone else just a—little bit?" She ran a comb through her hair once more and left.

But Ted didn't seem to mind. The night of the Christmas dance at school, he took her to a Christmas concert at the Junior College instead, and drove her to Barney's afterward.

The after-dance crowd hadn't yet packed the place with laughter, corsages, suits and semi-formal gowns; all but two of the booths were empty.

"Name your poison," Ted grinned.

Tammi looked at the menu posted over the counter with black stick-on letters. "Ummm . . . I think I'd like a hamburger."

"Want everything on it?"

"No onion."

"That's good—the tables aren't long and my truck isn't wide."

Ted placed the order for two hamburgers, milkshakes and fries, and they sat in a rustic circular booth just inside the door.

"I sure enjoyed this evening, Tammi." Ted's eyes sparkled; there were droplets of water where snow had melted on his hair.

"So did I. You really didn't mind missing the dance?"

"No. Girls who'd go to a dance with me are a dime a dozen." He paused while the waitress brought a new bottle of catsup to the table with their place setting. "Now, a girl who would turn me down—because she doesn't dance—now that's a challenge." They laughed again, but a quick, hard glint had appeared for a moment in his eyes.

Tammi moved the subject to safer ground. "Did you miss not being in California for Christmas?"

"No," he said quietly. "Never made much of it. Suppose if my folks had gone to church and all like your folks, it would have meant more." He changed the subject abruptly. "I'll keep busy in my uncle's store during the vacation. Maybe we can get together for some skating." He grinned, his teeth white and even. He glanced toward the order counter and then back to Tammi. "Thanks for going with me tonight. I was a little down, with Christmas coming on and all."

Tammi frowned slightly. There was something uncomfortable about what he was saying; something her mother had said, but she couldn't ferret it out.

Misreading her expression, Ted added hastily, "But tonight was kinda neat. Really different."

"Didn't you do things with your folks at Christmas?"

"My folks did almost nothing as a family—y'know?" He shrugged his shoulders. "Mom is only interested in her politics, and her job. She's a buyer for imports of some kind or another. Dad lived in his law office during the week and in his sailboat on weekends. They don't care for much besides that." He shrugged. "They do their own thing, you know?"

"Doesn't your mother like to sail?"

"She hates it." Ted shook his head. "Dad used to take me along a lot. Then he found other crews—prettier than I was." He studied his fingernails for a moment, and the hard look came into his face again. "I hated that."

Tammi remained silent, her eyes encouraging him to continue.

"My mother finally divorced him. Guess it's better all around."

"I don't think it is better for you, Ted." She reached out and placed her hands gently over his. "I couldn't even begin to think of what it would be like. It must be—well, like being abandoned."

"That's why I'm out here, I guess," Ted sighed. "Mom doesn't want me back there alone while she travels all over; Dad is too busy keeping people out of jail,—and I don't think my uncle is too thrilled about my living with him back here, either."

Tammi pulled her hands back and unfolded her napkin as the waitress placed their hamburgers and shakes on the table. She frowned slightly. Something was out of adjustment. She still couldn't spot it.

"Don't you see your father at all?"

"Naw." Ted took a sip of his milkshake. "He writes a note with a check once every couple of months, but that's all I ever hear from him."

Ted looked down at his food, and then back up at Tammi again. "Dad did teach me one thing, though."

"What's that?"

Ted looked stern, sat up straight, and in a baritone parody of a courtroom lawyer, said, "Son, if you remember nothing else, remember this. You get only one chance to get what you want. Grab it or forget it. Don't blame anyone else if you miss it."

They laughed together again, but the subtle gnawing uneasiness Tammi had fought all evening refused to go away.

She picked up the catsup bottle and tilted it over her hamburger. No catsup came out. She gave it a gentle tap. Still, it refused to flow.

"Here, I'll come to your rescue," Ted grinned.

With mock helplessness, she handed the bottle to him. He inverted the bottle, tapped the bottom with the heel of his hand, and waited expectantly—for nothing. He tapped again. Still nothing. He grunted, gave the bottle another preparatory tap and followed it with a resounding "thwack!" with the heel of his hand. Something inside the bottle gulped, and a river of red belched from its reservoir. Cascading thickly, it inundated Tammi's hamburger, spread quickly over the rim of her plate, and dripped off the edge of the table into large red splotches on her pleated beige skirt.

Open-mouthed, Ted stared at the bottle, too paralyzed to right it. Tammi gasped and finally squealed, "Stop!"

Panic-stricken, Ted recovered, set the bottle upright, stood quickly, snatched a napkin, and tried to keep the red ooze from spreading further.

Several couples, early arrivals from the dance, stared in their direction, and Ted's face burned red under their gaze. Tammi knew hers must at least match it. She snatched a handful of paper napkins from the holder and dabbed at the mess on her skirt. The waitress saw them and laughed. "Hey, Ralph," she called in to the cook, "get the snow shovel! We got a little catsup problem out here."

Tammi felt her face glow as red as the catsup on her skirt. She glanced up and glimpsed Sandi Beech seated in a booth with two other couples. Sandi's look was not sympathetic.

Tammi turned her eyes back to Ted. He had seen Sandi, too. His embarrassment edged toward anger.

Tammi looked around helplessly, and then took her father's

advice for impossible situations: "Laugh," he had said. "Laugh long and loud. It beats crying and puts everyone at ease."

Tammi raised her eyes until she locked gazes with Sandi while she worked a peal of laughter around the lump in her throat. She looked at Ted and laughed again. *I will not let her win!* she vowed. *She will not see me humiliated.* She faked a good-natured gasp, "I guess someone had better hose me off." She stood and accepted a wet towel from the waitress.

Finally, she heard what she had worked for—a faint snicker, then a giggle, and finally laughter—the free open laughter of others laughing with her, not at her. Two of the other girls went into the ladies room with her to help with her skirt, and when she returned a few minutes later, Ted had joined the others in a large booth on the other side of the aisle. Sandi was seated on his left. He had saved a place for her to his right, and a newly-cooked hamburger was waiting for her. "Compliments of the house," the waitress smiled. "I'm sorry about your skirt."

"Casualties of war," Tammi smiled back.

She sat close to him as he drove her home. For the first time in her life she had been able to control a situation rather than be a victim of it. With a sense of new confidence, she pushed her long hair back from the side of her face and leaned her head against Ted's shoulder.

Ted shook his head. "Tammi, I'm really sorry." He shook his head, took one hand from the steering wheel and placed an arm around her.

Tammi laughed, quietly. "It's all right. The stain'll come out."

"It's not just that. It's—well it was so embarrassing for you."

"For me?" Tammi laughed. "The look on your face as the catsup came and came—blurp, blurp, blurp—I couldn't believe it!" They laughed together again, and then rode silently for a few moments.

Noticing that he still seemed unconvinced, Tammi added,

"It was a little embarrassing—for both of us. But my father says embarrassment builds character."

Ted rolled to a stop in front of her house. "Well—I sure helped you build a monument!"

They laughed again, and he kissed her. By now, she had learned not to let her nose get in the way.

She couldn't tell exactly when the fun disappeared. She sensed, one day, that the lunch table no longer overflowed with the "tossed salad" fragments of conversation she had grown used to over the weeks. She did remember the strange look Ted gave her when they glanced around toward the end of one lunch hour and discovered that they were alone at the table.

To be with Ted. To talk to him. To feel him warm, strong, and close. To know she needn't worry about her burned face, or being a "sideshow attraction," to know that he loved her—these made her world blossom.

When she allowed Ted to caress her, a warning light blinked feebly deep inside her conscience. But Ted was so lonely, his parents so far away, and he had been hurt so deeply. She remembered how her mother's softness had comforted her those long months after the burn. Maybe her own softness could comfort Ted. Surely there was no harm in that. The warning light winked one last time and died.

They had stayed to make certain the fire was out and the trash was in the rusted iron barrel at the edge of the lake.

Ted had slammed the tailgate shut and they stood together in the silence.

Toward the east, Shelterport's glow crept above the piney

crest of the mountain and was absorbed into the crisp silver-blue of the moonlight.

The winter sky rang with a carillon of stars, silver against purple. Tammi imagined the three large stars of Orion's belt as deep-throated iron bells, solitary and authoritative; and the dust-like particles of the milky way as the silver-voiced soprano octaves. She remembered a story, long ago, that described moonlight as silver music spilled over the landscape, so those without ears to hear could enjoy its beauty.

"Wow." Ted's exclamation hung on the night air. "We don't get nights like these where I come from."

"It's even prettier away from the city," Tammi murmured, thinking of Ira and Bea and the apple-orchard hill. "No glow to dim the stars."

Ted reached into the truck bed and picked up a thermos jug. "Let's sit and have a cup of chocolate before we go."

"That'd be nice." She peered into the camper shell on the truck. "Cups got shoved back. I'll get them." She stepped up on the bumper and over the tailgate. "Oof! Not much room back here." She reached back for the bag containing the cups. "But it's not nearly as cold as out there."

"If that's the case, I'm drinking mine in there," Ted replied. She felt the truck lurch slightly with his weight as he climbed in.

They sat beside each other, sipping their chocolate and watching the night on the ice-covered lake. The pines along the shore formed a darker purple collar between sky and ice. The only sounds were their quiet breathing and faint squeaks from the truck, as they made themselves more comfortable close to each other while they talked.

As before, he spoke of his parents and their failing him. As usual, she pressed tightly against his side, trying to comfort him with her closeness.

At first, his caresses were comfortable and hesitant. Then

they became exploratory. She moved to halt his hands, but as she did so, she felt a barrier come between them. She didn't want to lose him. It would be all right. As his gentle caresses became hypnotic and insistent, she had no will to listen to the screaming from deep inside her mind, and no energy left to push his hands away. Mind, body, conscience, seemed strangely dissociated from the only reality that mattered: Ted.

Then the music of the stars and night and the spilled moonlight screamed. Her mind and her conscience and her hypnotized senses rushed back in a reality of cold, of darkness, of parallel steel ridges beneath a thin carpet.

Tammi lay stunned, devastated, her emotions paralyzed in the vortex of a black silence.

She pushed Ted away. Her hands shaking, she had attempted to refasten her clothing—and fumbled, and fumbled, and fumbled.

A fountain burst like a cistern and thrust up tears from deep inside. They flowed, burning from her eyes, at first a trickle, and then a full course, increasing with the muffled, almost silent gasps of her weeping. She had turned the silver night-music black. It would never be silver again.

"Here's a tissue, dear," the voice said. "It's far too nice a day to go on crying like that."

Confused and frightened, Tammi looked around, disoriented by the sway of the bus and the rush of the air conditioner. Her heart pounded heavily in her throat and she gasped for breath.

"My goodness, dear, do you want me to ask the driver to stop? You're not going to faint, are you?"

Painfully, Tammi turned her head toward the voice. It belonged to a tiny lady dressed in a splashy print blouse and gray slacks. Her stern-looking, high-cheekboned face formed a striking contrast to her kind, gravelly voice.

The lady's raised eyebrows required an answer—to what? Tammi dug painfully for the question as she tried to bring herself back to the present. "No. No I'm all right. I just felt . . . I'm all right." She took the tissue. "Thank you. Thank you very much."

"You must be tired out, dear," the gravelly voice continued. "You were just past the edge of a doze when I got on a half-hour ago." She gave Tammi another tissue. "I would not have awakened you except you seemed to be having a nightmare. You thrashed about, and then, when you started to cry—well, I thought I'd better awaken you."

"Thank you." Tammi wadded the tissues in her hand.

"Do you want to talk about it? Strangers are safe, you know." The lady smiled gently.

"No. Thank you. I'm all right."

Gravel-Voice tried to make more conversation, but Tammi answered only in monosyllables. Finally the lady capitulated, and they rode silently until she got off the bus in Keene.

Tammi stared out the window at the departing passengers. Gravel-Voice walked toward a doorway marked "Gate 3." Before she disappeared inside, she turned to glance toward the window through which Tammi was watching. Startled, Tammi quickly dropped her eyes, but the image of the woman's plain friendly face with its sad sympathetic smile etched itself on her mind. Not wishing another seatmate, Tammi started to place her checked hunting jacket beside her. There, lying in the center of the seat-cushion, was a folded sheet of lined paper, apparently torn from a small spiral-bound notebook. Picking it up, Tammi read on the outside, "To my Troubled Friend." As the bus rumbled away from the station, she opened the note and read it.

Dear,

As I rode with you, I prayed for you. You have obviously a great sadness and a great trouble.

God loves people who have great sadness and great trouble. I am praying that He and you will find a place of meeting in the midst of this and that He will strengthen you as you go through whatever it is you must face.

God bless you.

S.M.

11

The bus thrummed eastward, and the seacoast smell seeped into the air-conditioning system. The ground flattened and the trees thinned. The endless monotony of tidal marshes, small estuaries, and flat gray overcast slipped past the green-tinted window. The mud, exposed at low tide, stretched a sticky gray-brown toward the sea.

Her spirit sodden as the marshes, Tammi recalled Ted's puzzled response to her tension and her refusal on their next date.

"I thought you loved me."

"Ted—I do love you, but we—I"

"But people who love each other show it."

"No! Not like this." She pulled her arms in, clenched her

fists up under her chin, and pushed against him struggling to break his embrace.

"What'sa matter?" His blue eyes had lost their softness, but his voice became persuasive. "Even if you do get pregnant, we can always get married—if we have to."

"It's not just getting pregnant."

"Well, what then?" He frowned in his frustration.

"It's wrong."

"Wrong!" He snorted. "You didn't think much about 'wrong' last week." He started to reach around her.

"No, Ted, NO!" She pushed against him. Her stomach suddenly knotted and heaved against the bottom of her throat. Gagging, she thrust Ted away and fumbled for the doorlatch. She yanked upwards on it and slipped to her hands and knees on the frozen ground. She coughed and retched, convulsion following convulsion, until finally she leaned, panting, against the inside of the opened door. She pulled herself to her feet and slipped, exhausted, back into the truck.

Hands clenched tightly on the steering wheel, Ted sat unmoving. He stared at her coldly, incredulously. "I'll take you home." His voice was flat.

"Ted, I'm . . . I'm sorry." Tammi still gasped from exertion. "I couldn't help it."

"Forget it." He pressed his lips together angrily and said nothing more until he jolted to a stop in front of her house. Tammi waited for a moment for him to step out, as he usually did, to open the door for her. He remained seated behind the wheel, his eyes glaring straight ahead. She reached over to touch his hand. It tensed under her fingers. "Ted. Please. Don't be angry. I do love you. Don't be angry. I just feel so dirty and guilty—and scared—I always get sick when I get scared. I just couldn't help it."

"Forget it," he snapped.

"I'll see you tomorrow?" Her voice was anxious.

"Yeah. Sure." He still remained seated, his lips pressed into a thin angry line.

Tammi lifted the latch and slid out. Almost before she let go of the door handle, Ted had jammed the truck into gear and, wheels spinning in the hard-packed snow, skidded out into the street. Tammi stood in the darkness watching the red tail lights disappear around the corner.

Confused and hurt, she ran into the house, up the stairs and into her bedroom. "Just a loser," she thought bitterly as she lay across her bed. "Just a loser if you don't give in." She wept silently. "God. Why can't someone love me?"

The next morning, Tammi took particular pains to dress nicely. When she saw Ted coming down the hall, she forced a cheery, "Hi."

He glanced sidelong at her. "Uh, hi—" he said, and continued talking with one of the boys on the basketball team.

When the bell rang ending class, Sandi Beech sidled up to Tammi's desk and smiled victoriously. "Well, Miss Goodie-Goodie, looks like you have been brushed off—told you," she cooed, swishing her skirt from side to side as she swayed away.

The cold treatment lasted all that week. One after another, Tammi's new friends drifted away. The week following, Mr. Burroughs asked her to remain after chemistry class.

"Tammi, your grades have been going down quite a bit on the last three tests."

She felt her face turn hot and tilted her head down so her hair fell over the scarred place. It always showed more when her face reddened. She said nothing.

"I've noticed that both yours and Ted's labs have been. . . ," he smiled and fixed his eyes on her face with an intensity that even his tinted glasses couldn't diminish, "well, far below their usual quality." He grinned slightly to take the edge from the criticism. He waited for a moment and then continued. "Do you have any suggestions to remedy the situation, Tammi?"

She shook her head, not trusting her voice.

"Well, I think we'll try switching lab partners for a while."

Tammi turned to face him, her eyes wide and pleading, tears following one after another down her reddened cheeks.

Mr. Burroughs glanced away and fumbled for a tissue from a box on his desk. "Now, there's no need for that." His voice was gentle. "You are a good student, Tammi. I want to be able to give you a grade that matches that high quality you have inside."

Still silent, Tammi took the tissue and dabbed at her eyes. "I already spoke to Ted," Mr. Burroughs added. "As a matter of fact, when I asked him how he thought he could improve, he said he was probably holding you back because you had to slow down so much for him."

The next day, Tammi found Al Muhr as her new lab partner. She cringed under Al's lecherous gaze. He gave the impression that he was always stretching to glimpse something he shouldn't see.

Tammi slipped back into an isolation far lonelier than she had known before meeting Ted. Then, she had only the scar to hide. Now, guilt had become much more tangible than the scar ever was, and it had to be locked up so securely that no one would ever suspect.

"PORTSMOUTH—PORTSMOUTH, NEW HAMPSHIRE—MEAL STOP, THIRTY-FIVE MINUTES."

The rhythm of the bus changed, jolting her from the past nightmare to the present one. She sensed that there would be no awakening, no running. She glanced again at the note "Gravel-Voice" had written her, creased and damp in her hand. She thrust it into her pocket as the bus sighed to a stop in front of the loading gate.

Tammi stood and pulled her day pack down from the overhead rack and dropped it onto the seat she had claimed. She opened the top, removed her purse, and followed the last of the passengers off the bus. Pushing her way through a smudged glass door, she entered a grim-looking cafeteria. Although not really hungry, she took a clammy plastic tray, slid it down the runners paralleling the streaked counter, and pulled a doughy-looking serving of apple pie from an eye-level shelf. She slipped by the hot foods as rapidly as possible. The greasy smell of reheated sausage and the sight of rubbery scrambled eggs made her feel twitchy. She gulped, forcing her stomach into submission, and shuffled to the hot chocolate dispenser. Choosing a thick mug, still hot from the dishwasher, she filled it, paid the cashier at the end of the line, and chose a seat in the corner of the cafeteria. She sat apart from the rest of the passengers, but where she would still be able to see the driver when he boarded the bus.

Three weeks ago. The smell of frying sausage on a rainy Saturday morning permeated the house when she awakened, and her stomach heaved uncontrollably. Fortunately, her parents were downstairs in the kitchen, and her rush to the bathroom had remained undetected.

Then the terror nibbling at the base of her emotions leaped fully into consciousness. It had started its insidious gnawing the same night the stars stopped singing. It had swelled when her body broke its monthly rhythm. She tried to convince herself that she was just upset, that she would be all right next month. She wasn't.

Now, morning nausea. She peered through the crack of the cautiously opened bathroom door and stumbled back to her room. Slipping into bed, she pulled the warm darkness of the quilted apple-blossom counterpane over her head. She breathed in deep gasps. She tried holding her breath for a moment and then releasing it in long, controlled exhalations. For a long time she lay in the dark of the quilted covering. At last she pushed out from under it, sat on the edge of her bed and stared dully at the upper branches of the apple tree tracing their thin gnarled pattern against the early spring sky.

"Tammi? You up?"

Terror again.

"Tammi?"

She had to answer. "Yes . . . Yes, Mom." She rolled slowly out of bed and fumbled with her bathrobe.

"Your father and I have to go downtown. There's some scrambled eggs and sausage in the oven for you."

Tammi leaned against her doorframe, trembling, silent, exhaling another held breath.

"Tammi?"

"Yes. Yes, Mom. I hear you. Thanks."

Hearing the front door slam shut, Tammi stepped behind the curtains at her window and watched through the bare-branched apple tree as her father backed their old Plymouth down the driveway. The tires left long muddy slashes in the snow, now grimy with April's uncertainty between winter and spring.

She turned and stepped to her bureau.

PREGNANT!

Trance-like, she moved through the routine of dressing and struggled to pray.

"God—why me? Why did You make me pregnant?"

As a child, when she first learned to pray, pictures would come to her mind. "God's pictures" her mother called them. "That's God talking with you in your mind when you pray, Tammi," her mother had said—her mother's lips then were full and soft, and when she smiled, her face would glow, and Tammi would somehow feel her mother's glow envelop her.

She tried to make her mind form just one of "God's pictures," but found only a bleak grayness to match the day.

"My parents don't deserve the disgrace, God. Why do You have to punish them?"

She swallowed, trying to moisten her throat and mouth.

"I deserve the punishment, God, just me. My folks didn't do anything."

The same emptiness continued.

"Why an innocent little baby, God? Why do you have to punish an innocent little baby?"

As she rolled heavy white socks onto her feet, her heartbeat thumped its two-syllable accusation, "PREG-nant . . . PREG-nant," it mocked, "PREG-nant . . . PREG-nant." It pulsed through every inch of her body.

"I'm such a hypocrite," she breathed. "They'll all think my folks are hypocrites too." She slipped on a worn pair of tennis shoes and tied the frayed laces.

"Oh, God. I'm so scared." She walked stiffly down the stairs to the kitchen. The empty house oppressed her. The chill, drizzled dampness of the early spring morning fed her fear as she stepped out into the side yard.

She trudged slowly across the yard to the old wooden door at the rear of the church. Opening it, she stepped down the steep dark stairway to the basement. The familiar scent of old varnish, furniture wax, musty hymnbooks, and pine-scented disinfectant created a pungent incense in the cold gloom of the fellowship hall. Tammi slipped through a door to the right of the small raised platform at the front. It led to the classroom where, as an eight-year-old, she once had knelt to tell a gentle Jesus she loved Him and wanted to live for Him. She had hoped, at the time, if God were pleased enough with her for doing that, He might replace the shiny, white, wrinkled scar on her face with healthy skin, so she could be like other little girls. He hadn't.

She sank into a small chair and gazed slowly around. The pictures on the walls testified of David and Goliath and Adam and Eve. In an aged and curling print, a confident Daniel gazed bravely up from the lion's den. Over the teacher's table hung a picture of a seated Christ surrounded by young children. He held a little auburn-haired girl in his lap, her smile pure, innocent, trusting.

Tammi stared emptily at the picture. Finally she bowed her head into her hands, her palms pressing her eyes as if to keep them inside her skull. "Oh, God. I wish I were dead."

The words slipped out deliberately, coldly. She tried, in fragmented, half-formed pleas and images to reach out to that Jesus she had clung to as a little child. But unlike the little girl in the picture, she couldn't find the security of His lap or the confidence of the child's innocence.

"I'm so sorry, God." The words were lead in her mind.

God didn't seem to be accepting apologies.

She looked up at the picture again. "I wish I could go back. Little kids are so lucky."

She sat in the silence straining for some comfort, some pictures from God. There was only a terrible loneliness.

"God. I need You."

Nothing.

Crossing her arms in a kind of self-embrace, she rocked slowly from side to side, whimpering from the terror now completely engulfing her. "Oh, God, how can You do this to me? I told You I was sorry." The bitterness grew larger and stronger inside. "Why aren't You a God of love? Why must You always hate me?" She was almost frantic now, doubled over, sobbing, holding her sides as if to prevent her body from bursting. "What'll I do . . . what'll I do . . . what'll I do?" She sat panting, hopeless.

Then, Tammi sat straight, her eyes widening, her face pale. Into her mind had slipped a picture and a strange, sibilant whisper. *"There is still time,"* it hissed. *"You don't have to have the child."* She shuddered in the basement's chill air. Crossing her arms, she again slid her hands up to grasp her hunched shoulders. She inhaled short desperate gasps of air, releasing them with whimpering animal-like moans.

Someone had answered.

It wasn't God.

"COACH FOR BIDDEFORD, PORTLAND, BATH, AND POINTS NORTH, NOW BOARDING AT GATE THREE ... LAST CALL FOR PASSENGERS FOR BIDDEFORD, PORT-LAND, BATH, AND POINTS NORTH, NOW BOARDING AT GATE THREE."

Startled, Tammi pushed the partially eaten slice of pie aside and gulped the remaining chocolate from the thick-sided mug. She scrambled from her place and hurried past the stool where the bus driver had sat. *Stupid,* she scolded. *"All you need to do is miss the bus. Never get the courage up to go back then."*

The driver, standing by his seat at the front of the coach, grinned when she clambered aboard. "Had one more ticket than I had heads—saw your pack back there and had 'em call again."

Tammi flushed red. "Thank you." She went to her seat and watched the city slip past as the driver threaded his way through the narrow downtown streets.

Once on the turnpike, the familiar rumble of the engine and the cool sighing of the air conditioner again insulated Tammi from her surroundings. She lapsed back into tracing the stream of experiences that had drawn her toward Shelterport again. Somehow, she had made it through that Saturday.

"Whether he wants to or not," she told herself, "he's going to talk to me—alone—on Monday."

The Sunday between had lengthened into the Millennium. She kept out of her parents' way by doing more than her share of the household chores. Setting the table and doing the dishes kept her and her mother too busy to talk about anything other than meat and potatoes, serving forks and worn linen. After dinner, scrubbing pots and pans and putting away the dinnerware provided solitude and avoided conversation with her parents and Sunday afternoon visitors. She had just time to go to her room for a short nap before the evening service.

During the service, Tammi sat alone in the rear corner of the church, hoping no one would speak to her.

Avoiding the after-service chatterers and the other young people from the church, she slipped across the drive and up to her room. Although she could hardly hold her eyes open, she slept only in fragments. Dreams of a gray fog searing the side of her face as she groped her way through it troubled her sleep, and she awakened in a sweat, heart pounding, and gasping for breath as her mind screamed for God to talk to her. But God remained silent, and she slipped off again into the gray world.

Monday morning.

By now she had discovered that rushing immediately to the bathroom, letting the water roar at full flow into the tub and flushing the toilet served to mask her retching sounds. She dressed quickly, grabbed only orange juice and a sweet roll for breakfast, and left for school early.

She heard Sandi's and Ted's laughter echoing along the hall before they turned the corner to see her waiting outside the classroom. Ignoring Tammi, they sauntered on by to join a group of students waiting at the next room down the hall. When the bell finally rang, they returned to the door where Tammi stood. Sandi gave her an elaborate, "Excuse me!" as they squeezed by. Tammi tried to pluck at Ted's sleeve to get his attention, but he was by her and into the classroom before she overcame her hesitation. She slipped in quietly among the last of the students and took her usual seat in front of Ted.

She glanced up, saw Mr. Carston was busy with attendance, and turned around to face Ted.

"We have to talk," she whispered.

"So? Talk." He fixed his eyes carefully on his speech notes.

"Alone. It's important."

"I don't have a lot of time anymore." He studied the advertisement on the side of his pen. "Sports are starting and I have to get to work, too."

Tammi bit her lower lip. She felt like screaming, "Make time—I'm pregnant—you're the father!" Instead, she took a sheet of scrap paper and wrote, among the confused jottings from other classes "pregnant." She turned back to Ted and, cupping her hands around the word so only he could read it, placed it under his gaze.

Ted's arrogance vanished. "What're you tryin' to pull?" His whisper carried no farther than Tammi, "Just once? and you're . . . ?"

Tammi scribbled heavy black lines over the word until it was obliterated.

Ted glanced around nervously. "See me after school." His face was flushed except for a whitened area over each cheekbone.

As soon as the last bell rang, Tammi hurried out to Ted's truck. A few moments later, Ted strode angrily from the locker-room and opened the driver's side door.

"Get in," he commanded.

Tammi opened her door and slid into the passenger seat.

Ted started the engine, and they sat silently for a moment. "How do you know?"

"I know." Tammi blushed.

"Been to a doctor?"

"No," Tammi admitted, "not yet."

"Better make sure."

"I don't know who to go to," Tammi whispered helplessly, "and I have no money."

"What a mess. What a real mess," Ted hissed. He sat silent for a moment. Then, strangely, he changed. The blue softened in his eyes. "Look, Tammi." He paused, choosing his words carefully. His eyes narrowed a little and then widened as if he had made a decision. "You go to a doctor—just to make sure." He reached into his back pocket and removed his wallet. He placed two twenty-dollar bills between them on the seat. "You have a family doctor, haven't you?"

"Yes, but . . ." Tammi thought for a moment. "I'm afraid. My parents could find out if I went to him." She spoke just above a whisper. It was so good to have Ted close to her again, to feel his concern and protection.

"Well, look—find someone," Ted rasped harshly.

"I'm sorry, Ted." Her fingers trembled as she took the money from the seat. Feeling cheapened, she put it in her purse and wiped the palms of her hands on her skirt. "I didn't mean to spoil things."

Ted stared through the windshield.

"There's a doctor some of the ladies in the church go to. He's way on the other side of town, and my folks don't know him."

"Yeah, good." Ted's jaw muscles tightened, but his voice was controlled, gentle. "Don't worry," he smiled. "We'll do whatever has to be done." He turned to face her, his eyes nervous. "Just don't tell anyone, okay?"

"All right."

He looked at his watch. "I gotta go to work now." He looked over at her. The hardness in his eyes and mouth contradicted the softness in his voice.

As she opened the door to step out, Ted leaned toward her almost as if to kiss her. Instead, he added, "If you are—well, we can figure out a way to get it taken care of." He pulled the door closed and drove from the parking lot, his tires screeching as he turned the corner.

12

In a little over an hour she would be home.

She almost wished that Dr. Claymore had picked up the telephone on his desk and called her parents when she went to see him.

It was Tuesday, a little over a week after she had told Ted. The activity calendar beside the kitchen telephone reassured her that both her parents would be busy with church activities through the afternoon and well into the evening, so there would be no questions to answer when she came in two hours later than usual.

Dr. George Clayton Claymore was very kind and very gentle, and the nurse remained in the room, giving Tammi's hand reassuring squeezes during the worst of the examination. In spite of the kindnesses, Tammi's face burned hot and dry from shame and embarrassment. Her stomach hurt even more than usual from fear. Finally it was over, and Tammi dressed herself.

"The doctor wants to talk to you, Tammi," the nurse said. "But we need to do a little lab test first." The paper covering the thin mattress on the stirrupped examining table rattled as she pulled down and fastened a fresh length. "There's no one else in the waiting room now. Why don't you go out there for a few minutes, and I'll call you when he's free."

Tammi felt caught in the middle of another of her nightmares. Again, she couldn't wake up. Again, everything floated in inexorable slow motion, and there was no escaping the fresh terrors to follow. She walked mechanically out to the waiting room and sat in a chrome and vinyl chair.

She faced a panelled wall covered with pictures of cooing, drooling babies smiling toothlessly into the camera. On sides, stomachs, and backs; dressed in diapers, dresses, and sun-suits; each picture celebrated life and personality. Many prints were signed with the flourish of a joyous parent declaring the name and birthdate of a new human being.

Somewhere from behind the doors leading to the examining rooms, she heard the muffled slap of a metal chart cover. The door opened, and the nurse gave Tammi a white-uni-formed smile.

"Dr. Claymore will talk to you now, Tammi."

She followed the nurse to the doctor's private office and sat down in the chair facing his desk. A few moments later he entered and sat opposite her.

Tammi tried, but there was no way she could meet the sad gray eyes of Dr. George Clayton Claymore, M.D.

"Well, Tammi, you're going to have to tell your parents."

She stared at the leather bindings of the thick books on the shelves behind his desk. "I . . . I can't." Her throat closed tightly over the words. Losing the slow-motion, nightmare calmness with which she had controlled herself for the last hour, she sobbed silently, dabbing at her face with a handkerchief.

Finally she calmed herself and sat, hiccupping with each intake of breath. Dr. Claymore handed her a tissue from a box on his desk.

Tammi slumped back into the overstuffed embrace of the living-room style chair, her hands listless in her lap.

"Your parents are going to have to know sometime, Tammi," he insisted. "There's no way you can avoid that." His voice was incredibly gentle.

She moved her head from side to side, unconsciously punctuating her words. "I can't tell them. They'll be so ashamed of me."

"What happened, Tammi?"

"I . . . we didn't mean to do anything . . . anything wrong," she hiccupped. "He was the only boy I ever met who seemed to care what I thought or liked. . . . and he needed me." Her fingers clenched, wadding the tissue and her handkerchief together. "No one's ever needed me before." She remained silent for a few moments.

Dr. Claymore waited, his gaze kind.

"We saw each other at school and then at church, and then . . . then at youth group." Her eyes were dry now. "His parents got a divorce, and he was so lonely . . . we'd go for rides in his truck, and . . . and we'd go ice-skating." She paused for a moment and then continued. "He'd tell me about sailing with his father off the California coast. His mother always stayed home. She didn't like sailing. Then one day, she told his Dad it's her or his boat." Tammi looked up at Dr. Claymore. "Don't people who get divorces ever think of their kids?"

Dr. Claymore returned her gaze. His eyes were tired and sad. "Sometimes, Tammi, . . . sometimes our eyes get so full of ourselves, we have no room to see anyone else."

"After the divorce, Ted came to live with his uncle," Tammi

continued. "He seemed so lonely . . . he was so comfortable to be around . . . I could be me around him." She finally looked Dr. Claymore in the eyes. "I didn't . . . we didn't mean for it to happen . . . it just did."

The tears came again, and she took another tissue. "I feel so dirty." She turned the wad over in her hands and dabbed at her eyes. "We never again . . . he wanted to . . . but I got so scared I got sick."

Dr. Claymore waited again until she had composed herself. "Tammi, your parents are going to have to know."

"How can I tell them? They'll be so ashamed of me."

"Putting it off won't make it any easier."

"They'll be so angry and hurt."

"For a little while, certainly, but the shock wears off, Tammi." He paused for a moment and then continued. "Parents are pretty durable human beings, Tammi. Often, when they're hurt the worst, and angered the most, they love even more. Especially when you need them the most."

Dr. Claymore glanced down at her chart. "From what you've told me about your background, Tammi, I'd say they'll come through just fine."

Tammi followed his gaze and stared at the neatly-ruled yellow pages. "He said he'd do whatever he had to if anything . . . hap . . . happened."

"Does he know you're pregnant?"

Tammi had reduced her weeping to occasional sniffles and hiccups. "Yes."

"What did he say?"

"To see a doctor."

"What else?"

"To try to get it . . . fixed."

"He wanted you to have an abortion?"

There it was, the word she couldn't bring herself to say, the thought she wouldn't allow herself to think. She nodded her head and focused her eyes stubbornly on the thick books behind him.

"Did he say anything about marriage?"

She shook her head. The tears came again. She took another tissue. "But he loves me. He said he loves me."

"Tammi, look at me for a moment." Dr. Claymore's voice was gentle.

She brought her tears under control and met his calm, warm gaze with her frightened green eyes.

"Tammi, if he really loved you, he would not have jeopardized you like this."

She sat, her fingers plucking one and then another of the wadded tissues in her lap. A fresh supply of tears started down her cheeks.

"Do you still see him?"

"At . . . at school mostly." Her voice was thick from weeping. "He doesn't come to church anymore." She sat silent a moment, gulping and sniffling. "All we seemed to do was argue and fight after . . . but it's because he feels as bad as I do . . . he still loves me," she whispered around the burning in her throat.

"How do you feel about an abortion?"

Tammi lifted her gaze again. Finally, gathering the fragments of her self-respect, she met Dr. Claymore's eyes. "What we did was wrong. But I can't kill a baby." The images on the walls of the waiting room flashed through her mind. "It's not the baby's fault," she whispered. Remembering the hissed suggestion in the church basement, she repeated, "I can't kill the baby."

"Well, Tammi," Dr. Claymore leaned back in his chair. "From the looks of things, marriage doesn't seem an option, does it?"

She shook her head.

104

"And you do have a healthy sense of right and wrong, Tammi. That's why you don't want an abortion."

She sat unmoving.

"What's left?"

She stared at the books again, focusing her eyes deliberately on the finely imprinted gilt letters on their bindings. "I just can't tell my parents. Not yet." She switched her gaze to his face, her eyes wide, terrified. "Dr. Claymore, you won't tell them, will you?"

"If they call, Tammi, I won't lie to them," he said gently. "But, no, Tammi, you're my patient. With that one exception, I won't disclose information without your permission."

She sat a few moments longer. "Is . . . is that all?"

"Well, you'd better see the nurse and make another appointment for next month."

She stood awkwardly. "Thank . . . thank you." She started out the door of his office.

"Tammi?"

She turned to face him. He stood behind his desk. "I meant what I said. You'll come through all right. I'm sure your parents will too, if you give them a chance."

As she expected, the house was empty when she arrived home. She had gone upstairs, undressed, and had stood under the shower until all the hot water was gone. The April air had seemed unusually humid, and no matter how many showers she took, she couldn't feel clean. Dressing in an old pair of jeans and a sweat-shirt, she went down to the kitchen and fixed supper. She was glad her parents weren't home. She would have been unable to sustain the hypocrisy of small-talk.

When she saw Ted's desk empty in speech class the next morning, she was frightened he would be absent. But he entered late, took his unexcused tardy slip from Mr. Carston, and slid into place behind her. Halfway through the first student speech, Tammi felt the pressure of the end of his pen below her left shoulderblade. Reaching back under her left arm with her right hand, she grasped Ted's note without having to turn around. Neatly and precisely, Ted had written only one word: "WELL?"

Beneath the cryptic question, Tammi scrawled, "AFTER CLASS." She checked to see if Mr. Carston was watching and then passed it back.

When the dismissal tone sounded, she swung around in her seat as she heaped her books in a messy pile. "It's true."

Ted fixed his eyes carefully upon a broken fingernail. He picked at it. "Can he fix it?" His voice was hard and tight.

"I—I didn't ask him to."

Ted deliberately stacked one book on top of another and stood. They walked out into the hall together.

"Why?"

Tammi couldn't believe the conversation was happening—right there, in the hallway of a busy high school, between classes. "Can't we talk about this someplace else?" She glanced around, frightened, but the clatter and the noise of the other students protected their privacy.

"I have to work this afternoon."

"It won't take long—just after school is out." She felt her stomach go queasy and her face become hot.

"Well . . ." The hall was almost deserted now. "Make it fast. I can't be late."

Tammi slipped into her algebra class just as the bell rang. Five of the six problems she had done for homework were wrong.

She had trouble working the combination on her locker after the last bell sounded for the day. She couldn't keep her eyes from watering. When she finally got to the parking lot, she saw Ted's red truck turning out into the street. His tires screeched and smoked as he shifted gears and lurched toward the Colonie Town Road.

Tammi stared at the rest of the vehicles flowing through the gate. The tears came freely now. She clawed in her purse for a handkerchief and stepped around the corner of the doors through which the last of the students filtered. They came more casually now, small clusters of friends chatting and relaxing after the main rush.

"Springer?" A boy's laugh rang hollowly down the almost deserted hall and spilled through the opened doorway. "Man, she sure fooled everybody . . . hardly have to ask her. . . ." Laughter again. ". . . can tell you three or four guys who know what she's like. . . . Sandi says she's not what she tries to make everybody think she is. . . ." Laughter again. A group of five boys jostled through the doorway and swaggered toward the parking lot.

Slipping quickly into a locker-lined recess next to the doorway, Tammi jammed her handkerchief against her mouth and pressed herself against the cold gray metal. Terrified that they would turn and see her, she whimpered slightly and worked herself forward to the corner where the wall and lockers joined, shielding her from view. But the boys didn't look back, and she heard their van drive away.

Tammi waited until she could see and hear no other students. She had just enough time to catch the downtown bus and get to the bank before it closed. One hundred sixty-two dollars wasn't much to travel on, but it could get her back to Aunt Bea.

But there was no running. The bus pulled her relentlessly back to Shelterport. She wondered what her parents had said to Ira when he called.

13

"Good to see you again, Jerome." Dr. Soberman extended a large soft hand. "And you too, Mrs. Springer," he added, nodding at Jael, standing with her husband behind the old oak desk Jerome had owned since seminary days.

"I'm sorry this has to be so, ah, early, but I have a meeting immediately after I leave here—with your church board, you know—just a formality." He smiled and shook his head. "And then I must leave for Boston right after lunch."

"Quite all right, Dr. Soberman," Jerome smiled. "I realize that there is a lot of work keeping us pastors on our toes." The three laughed together as Jerome held a chair for Jael.

"Well, it won't be long, Jerome, and you may well be taking a little of that burden from us." Dr. Soberman settled his slightly bulbous form in the chair facing Jerome's desk. "Tell me, how do you two feel about that?"

Jerome glanced down briefly at his left sleeve and whisked away an imaginary speck of lint from his new suit. "Well," he said quietly, "I hope I don't disappoint you." He looked up fully into Dr. Soberman's eyes. "I have to be honest with you. I have wanted to try my hand at this job for a long time." He felt Jael beside him stiffen slightly in displeasure over his admission.

"I'm not surprised, Jerome." Dr. Soberman returned the gaze, his watery gray eyes blinking slowly. "We've been looking carefully at the work you've done here in Shelterport, and, ah, we've been impressed."

"I've tried to do my best."

"So did the four pastors before you, ah, um. Point is, you succeeded. They didn't."

Jerome shifted slightly in his chair to see how Jael had responded to the compliment, but her face remained impassive. "The Lord did the work, Dr. Soberman," Jerome insisted. "I tried to obey."

"Yes, yes, that's well understood." He chuckled. "After all, we both went to the same seminary—we're not taking anything away from the Lord." His gray eyes widened slightly under his arched eyebrows. "But the Lord does use the talents his servants bring, and you have used your talents well." He paused for a moment to clean his glasses. "He also grants spiritual gifts, Jerome, and we feel your gift lies particularly in administration. From what we can see, you've developed it well in both pastorates you've had under us." His chair creaked dangerously as he leaned back and fumbled with something in the breast pocket of his hand-tailored suitcoat.

"Miserable thing's stuck," he muttered. "Here it is." He pried a thick business envelope from his pocket and removed a sheaf of folded papers. "Brought along a copy of your file, Jerome. Your name will be going in a different place in the Denominational Directory. Want to make certain that we've got all our facts straight."

"I'm certain you have, doctor," Jerome replied. He glanced nervously at his fingernails and picked at a rough spot on his right index finger. "It's really not necessary to. . . ."

"It is, it is, ah, Jerome." Dr. Soberman leaned forward and supported his short forearms on Jerome's desk. "Well, ah, you started with us in Croughton's Corners, Vermont. Fine job you did there." He looked up quickly, "You, ah, had some—unfortunate experiences there, didn't you." He lowered his eyebrows and knit them together as he read the entry silently and looked up again. "Lost a child. . . ?" Behind his watery eyes lay sincere sympathy.

"My . . . our only son." Jerome gazed for moment at a spot on his desk blotter. "Happened when I was away to Burlington making a radio program we used to have." He paused again. "Same time our daughter got burned." He glanced at Jael.

She stared, impassively, at plaques and awards documenting Jerome's success. They covered much of the panelled wall facing his desk.

14

"Benni." Jael's lips formed his name silently, and the memories tumbled out from some mental box too long locked. "Our Benni. My Benni."

It was their third winter in the mountains, and by February, Jael had grown large and clumsy with child. She had rolled over toward Jerome in the sagging iron bed and had pressed herself and Benni, kicking gently in her swollen abdomen, against his back. She felt Jerome's breathing change as he awakened.

"Time to get up already?"

"Got another ten minutes."

"Oh."

She could never understand his ability to become completely alert the moment he awakened. "Wind really blew last night."

"Heard it. Radio said it would get to twenty below."

"Stayed warm in here, though."

"Thanks to Ira and that load of wood he brought in."

"He said he noticed you gone a lot—hadn't a chance to do your own cutting."

"I wanted to bring in some more coal in the trailer, but the snow came before I did it."

Jael giggled. "I felt strange—burning coal up here with all this wood standing around."

"Burns longer than wood. Takes no more work to get it. Hotter than wood, too."

"Wood smells nicer. Cleaner."

"That's the mountain country talking." Jerome swung his feet from the bed to the floor and then pulled them back under the covers again. "Whoo. That linoleum is cold." He felt under the edge of the bed for his slippers and positioned them for the next try.

Jael turned away suddenly and fumbled on the rickety table beside the bed for a lemon drop. "Wretched child of yours is making me sick to my stomach again." She popped the hard yellow candy into her mouth. "He's going to have such a sweet tooth by the time he's born that— Oh, look."

"Huh?" Jerome turned toward Jael's side of the bed and looked out the window with her. "Oh, no."

"It's beautiful."

"Not when you have to drive through fifty miles of the stuff, it isn't."

The February night had begun its incremental gradation into morning grays, and the heavy, wet snowflakes settled thickly and silently through it. Clinging to every branch, roof, fencepost, and stump, they had transformed the usually humdrum side yard into an abstract study in humped grays.

"The wind hasn't dropped much."

"I'd better start a little earlier. Liable to have drifts across the roads." Jerome rolled back over to his own side of the bed and finally sat up and thrust his feet into his slippers. "When we leave here—" he shuddered from the chill as he stood, "we are going to have a big, deep carpet on the bedroom floor."

"Only if we can take the neighbors with us," Jael smiled.

"And the springtime, and the summer, and the fall, and the view from the kit. . . . ow!" Jael yelped as Jerome smacked her playfully.

"Can't understand why you like it here so much."

"People don't put on airs," she replied, slipping out of bed and standing clumsily. "They decide to like you or dislike you without looking in your pockets."

"What there are of them," Jerome grinned. "Sure hard to build a church without the people to make it grow. Three years now, and still only thirty-five people as members and fifty in the building on a good Sunday."

"Seems to me, the Lord's more concerned about building Himself into people's lives, than He is in building people into a congregation." Jael felt irritated with herself. Her voice had started to become edged again, and she had started an argument. She followed Jerome out of the bedroom. "I'll get some breakfast."

Through the window above the sink, Jael noticed the grays had lightened considerably. Snow clung to the north sides of the aged, black-trunked pines in the back yard, and their boughs sagged patiently under its weight. She loved this view. Whoever had built this house had placed the kitchen sink and window exactly so for her pleasure, hers and all the wives before her who spent otherwise colorless hours "doing up dishes" or peeling vegetables. The pines stood like a frame on either side of the square-paned window. The path between them, carpeted with matted needles or fallen snow, curved in a graceful "s" to the lake. In winter, white; in summer, green or blue depending upon the time of day, the lake drew her eyes to the far shore where maple, oak, poplar, and white birch trees hunched next to the water like bushy-headed fishermen. In the fall they formed a line of rusts, yellows, and reds contrasting with the purplish pines on the mountain ranges, stretching towards Massachusetts like successive wrinkles in an old man's brow. Through the window, it seemed to her, she could sometimes gaze backwards and see a little auburn-haired girl wandering through her father's woods in Pennsylvania. But now, she could see only slightly past the ancient black trunks of the pines.

She turned away from the sink and placed the coffeepot on the stove. As soon as she was up, she had stirred the banked fire, added several thin sticks of maple, and followed those with heavier hardwood chunks. Now the flat iron lids were heating. Holding her hand over first one and then another she placed the pot on the hottest one.

"Coffee be ready soon. Eggs and bacon?"

"Uh-huh." Jerome's grunt echoed from the bathroom where he was shaving.

"'When we leave here.' That's what he said," Jael thought. She placed six thick strips of bacon neatly in the bottom of a heavy black skillet and broke three eggs over them. He had frightened her when he said that. "Why do people always want to leave places?" she wondered.

She had learned to hate "leaving" as a teenager. "Just like Elmer and his wife."

Jael was sixteen and had been a Christian for only a year. For the three years before that, though, Elmer Perkins and his wife had made the run-down church in their Appalachian community vibrate with laughter and color and real affection. They had pushed back the epidemic bleakness she and her brothers and sisters had always accepted as their only reality. And then it was over. Elmer and black-haired, plain-faced Debbi—the woman who had shown her it was all right to laugh and hug and cry—were gone. The little church, just a mile from their home, had once again wrapped itself in the same bleak blanket of former times.

"God," Jael had prayed with all the faith her sixteen years could muster, "I want to be a missionary. I want to come back and help people in the mountains. Please—find some way."

Please, God, find a way.

Jael closed her Bible carefully so the first sixteen pages containing the table of contents and part of Genesis wouldn't fall out onto the rough planked floor of the loft.

"Jael, you get down here to breakfast or you'll miss the schoolbus."

"Coming." She stepped to the side of the attic, stooping so she wouldn't hit her head on the rafters, and pulled from the narrow space the cardboard box with "DUZ DOES EVERYTHING" printed on the side. She pawed through the contents for a moment and shoved the box back into the corner.

"Adey!" she snapped at an elongated lump on the far side of the mattress. The lump didn't move. Jael reached for the covers and yanked them off the bed. Adele clutched at them but wasn't fast enough.

"Leave me alone! Give me my covers back."

"Did you wear my good blouse?"

"How do I know what's your 'good blouse?'"

"The one I save for Sundays. The one with the ruffles and the long sleeves."

"How was I to know that was royal property?" Adele wasn't too sleepy for sarcasm. She waved an arm to a heap of clothing on the floor in a corner near her side of the bed. "Prob'ly in there someplace. Now leave me alone." She reached for the covers again.

Jael stepped around the end of the mattress, fumbled through the clothing, and came up with the blouse, rumpled and unlaundered.

"You could at least wash it out and put it back when you finish wearing it," she scolded, her voice pitched high with frustration.

114

"You girls quit bickerin' and get down here or I'll come up with a strop to you both." Her father's voice, heavy with sleep and irritation growled up from below.

"Well she doesn't have to be an old grouch just because she's gettin' some kind of award today." Adey wrinkled her nose and lifted her upper lip to give a sing-song quality to her voice.

They heard the springs of the downstairs bed groan as their father turned quickly to get up. Muffled curses accompanied the effort as he struggled with both his belt and the previous night's drink.

"We're comin' down, Pa," Adey grumbled.

Jael reached back into her box and snatched another blouse from the neatly folded garments, a plain white one with a rounded collar, pockets, and short cuffed sleeves. "Might as well be a man's shirt," she murmured, her fingers quick and impatient as she buttoned her clothing. All the others would be wearing pretty stuff—pressed, starched, clean. Even her best looked drab beside them. Now she had to wear something that even the slovenly waitress at the "Lazy Daze Tavern" down at the junction would refuse.

She swallowed her resentment and went down the stairs to the large room beneath. She didn't dare say more to Adey. It would be just like her father to make her stay home from school to keep Timmy and William quiet until the drink wore off.

The heavy curtains, green carpets, and upholstered seats in the auditorium absorbed the sharp-edged noises of the students filing in for the awards assembly and allowed only muted shuffling sounds, occasional snatches of conversation, and authoritative voices of teachers. The students stood while the school orchestra played the "Star Spangled Banner," and then sat buzzing and rustling as they waited for the principal to come to the podium.

Jael sat silent, her sad green eyes drinking in every detail. Up until last January she had given up hope of going to college. Deliberately, she had planned the rest of her life. She'd probably get married—but no drinker or smoker. He'd be a man with a steady job. Their house would be small, but it would be clean and they'd have a bedroom to themselves. And wallpaper. And inside water and toilet. She and her husband would open the church, too. If she couldn't go to college, she was determined not to let despair imprison her.

Then Mr. Simms, the principal, had called her to the office on the Monday following exams. She stood awkward before his desk, conscious of her ill-fitting clothing and worn shoes.

He glanced up from a sheaf of papers on his desk. "Well, Jael, you've gone and done it this time!" His face seemed very stern, but there was a smile around his eyes. Jael stared down at her feet and let her auburn hair fall to conceal as much of her face as it could.

"I want to show you something," he continued, thrusting a slip of paper toward her. It bore her name and three sets of numbers.

She took the paper, but in her fear, the numbers were gibberish.

"Sit down, Jael." There was a smile in his voice that reassured her. She sat in the brown wooden chair facing his desk and glanced up to find a broad smile had replaced the stern look on his face.

"You made the highest score in the Senior Class on the college tests you took last fall."

Jael listened to the rest numbly, hearing only fragments: . . . local businessman . . . scholarship . . . tuition and books . . . college of your choice . . . supply your own room and board . . . awards assembly. . . ."

"Jael Caldwell."

If only Adey hadn't taken her blouse.

But she would go to college. No matter what, she would go.

"Ever run a dishwasher before?"

"Uh, no." She reddened.

"Well, nothing to it," the young man replied cheerfully. "The trays come in there," he pointed to a window where a steel trough-shaped counter met the wall. "You have to scrape the dishes and rinse them with the spray. Slide 'em down to me and I place 'em in the racks. He extended a soapy hand. "By the way, my name is Jer."

She raised her eyebrows and stared awkwardly at his hand, not quite sure whether she wanted to take it. "Jer?"

"Short for Jerome, Jerome Springer. I'm a theology major. What's yours?"

He ignored the refused handshake and unobtrusively returned to scrubbing a seemingly endless supply of pots, pans, lids and skillets. "I—I. . . ."

"Don't worry. You've got plenty of time to choose one. Don't even start it until your third year." His easy smile and friendly blue eyes relieved her uncertainty a little.

"Thought I'd get a start on these before the first dinner dishes start through."

Irritated with herself for bungling the conversation with the first boy that talked to her, Jael stepped forward and picked up a scrubbing pad. "Guess I might as well make myself useful," she stammered.

"Great! Never turn down help with a mountain like this!"

For the next two hours they worked side by side scrubbing

pots, spraying dishes, and feeding the square maw of the dishwasher. She wondered if he ever stopped talking. She smiled as she scraped, scrubbed, and sprayed the parade of dinner dishes marching one behind the other down the trough in front of her. All through high school, few boys ever noticed her enough to say "Hello." Now a tall, sandy-haired, blue-eyed sophomore chattered at her about getting on the debate team during his freshman year, preaching at the mission—and by the way, can she play the piano? They really need one for Christian service assignments; the large department store his father owns, and his own hopes of becoming a missionary-pastor. He was a little pale, she thought, and a little too thin. The tufts of hair sprouting thinly from his upper lip made him appear more childish than mature, but there was a sincerity and an intensity about him she liked.

She hadn't decided upon her major, but she hurried to the office before registration closed for the semester to change a course. She dropped Art and replaced it with Beginning Piano.

In the middle of November, she first heard him preach in the mission. They piled into Paul Redding's old green Pontiac for the ten-mile trip to town. Paul led the singing. Grace Mangino, another freshman girl, played the piano. Jerome preached. Jael was to give her testimony.

She didn't remember what she said in her testimony. She did remember the terror, the pungent smell of skid-row whiskey and sweat, an old man propped in the back corner getting sick in the wooden-slatted theater style seats.

She remembered also riding to and from the mission. Paul and Jerome rolled down all four windows when they reached town. Each taking a part—hers was an uncertain soprano—they sang choruses so loudly that passers-by on the sidewalks turned their heads. At first Jael was self-conscious; for when the old green Pontiac with music spilling out its windows paused at a stoplight, passers-by and passengers in other vehicles stared. But gradually she pushed her reticence aside. Over and over she reprimanded herself, "If I'm going to be a missionary—or a pastor's wife," she added as an afterthought, "I've got to get over being embarrassed about strangers hearing me sing and talk about Christ." But there was still a hesitation which she never, even in later years, quite overcame.

She didn't remember what Jerome preached about that evening, but she did remember the excitement on his face as a man came forward at his invitation to accept Christ. She remembered also the ride home, with Jerome seated next to her—confident, strong. It was easy to sing with him. She decided she didn't really mind the stares when she was with Jerome.

They were postcards at first, two each week throughout June. Then came letters.

> Dear Jael,
> The Gospel Team is Great! Getting lots of practice preaching. This is what I really want to do with my life. We had seven people come forward last night— most so far. This summer is really going fast, though it must be dragging for you, having to work and being one of only three in the whole dorm. Bet you'll be happy when everybody comes back. Must be like King Tut's Tomb there now. Be brave. We'll be back to school in three more weeks. . . .

The letter went on for two more paragraphs, but Jael read the last sentence again and again.

> I don't know how to say this, so I'll just come right out with it. I love you.

She sat on the edge of her bed and stared at the lush August greens outside the window. The whole lonely summer suddenly swelled with life. "I love you," he had written. Never before had anyone spoken or written such words to her, not even her mother. She felt something come from deep inside that made her breath catch.

Three more weeks of working in the store in town. Three more weeks and Jerome would be back. She folded the letter carefully and placed it in her purse.

"Going home for Thanksgiving?" Jerome asked.

"No. I don't have the money."

"Paul is driving me back home. Why not come and have Thanksgiving with us?"

"I—I don't know, Jerome. It's only a few days. It won't be like last summer."

"Nonsense!" He smiled at her. "I'll call my mother and tell her you're coming."

"No, Jerome. I can't."

"Jael." His voice was suddenly serious. "What's the real reason?"

She felt the blood drain from her face, and her hands trembled. "I—I can't."

"But why?"

She felt the tears but was powerless to stop them. "You've . . . well you . . . they're not the same, my family and yours."

"I should hope not," he grinned.

"I mean it, Jerome. You come from a nice house and your father's the owner of a big department store. Your folks have nice things."

"So?" He shrugged his shoulders. "Nice things aren't all that important."

She gazed straight into his eyes, forcing the stark truth into each word. "I haven't told you, Jerome. I'm sorry. I've been unfair to you." Tears flowed freely now.

"Unfair?" He chuckled. "I doubt that."

"It won't work, Jer. Let's just call it off and forget it." She tried to turn away, but he grabbed her shoulders and made her face him.

"Wait a minute, Jael. Nothing is that bad. Walking away without telling me why—that's unfair."

She waited passively for him to release her, but his grip remained firm. Finally she looked up and challenged his gaze with hers. "I've led you on, and it won't work."

"Led me on?"

"Jer—at home—I live in a mountain shack." Now that she had started, she didn't dare stop. "It's a one-room shack with an attic and we don't even have finished walls." She had stopped crying, and the words came out harsh and resentful. "Seven of us sleep up in a loft, and . . . and our toilet is an . . . an outhouse." She blurted out the last word angrily.

He held her silently for a few moments more. Finally he cleared his throat, and she tensed for his reply. It would be very polite, of course, but she held no illusions.

"Well. . . ," he grunted and waited a moment. "This does change things a little."

Her last shred of hope vanished. "I thought it would." Her voice was hard. All she wanted was to run, but his hands on her shoulders prevented it.

"Yep. Sure does," he sighed. Then he smiled. "With that outdoor plumbing, I'm going to have to buy a pair of long underwear when I come up to visit you at Christmastime."

"Christmas?"

"Sure," he laughed. "That's a month after you come home to spend Thanksgiving at the Springers."

Her grandmother gave her the chest three days before the wedding.

"C'mon up t' the attic with me," the old lady had commanded with a secretive, almost mischievous tone.

Jael followed her up the stairs and along a narrow pathway between old furniture, papers, trunks and cardboard boxes. Her grandmother stopped at the back corner of the house. "Pull that junk out of there," she commanded.

Jael got on hands and knees and moved three cardboard boxes and a stack of old clothing away from a bulky burlap-covered box.

"Slide it on out here."

Jael moved it out, sliding first one end and then another over the planked attic floor.

"Take off that burlap. Mind, be careful now."

Jael untied the cord holding the burlap against the chest. She folded back the dust-rotted material from the top of the box and gasped. Quickly she tore away the rest and stood amazed.

"Oh, Grandma."

It was almost three feet long and came to just below her knees. Its hardwood planks had been carefully butted together to make the height, and the sides were fastened one to the other with carefully hand-fashioned dovetails. Elaborate stylized tulips in a Pennsylvania Dutch motif played in primitive symmetry across the front and the lid, their bright reds, yellows and greens set boldly against the flat black base. Hasp, hinges, and handles, like blacksmiths used to make, were of hammered iron. An ancient padlock, the kind which opened by swinging to one side, carried its original key.

Still puffing from the exertion of climbing the stairs, the old lady sat on the ochre-rimmed lid.

"When my grandfather made it for me I was a little younger than you, and almost as pretty," she said, blinking her eyes rapidly as if to peek back through the years. "Just before I married my George." Her voice had a sort of faraway sound. "Made me promise I'd give it to my first granddaughter—sort of a second-hand gift from him.

"Well, 'bout soon's I saw you poke your head out 'to this world, I knew you were the one."

"It's lovely!" Jael exclaimed, unable to take her eyes from it.

"Quilt and good linens inside. Cedar lined, too. Wish it was more," her grandmother mumbled. "Wish it was better."

"Grandma, nothing could be better than this." She gathered the old lady into her arms and hugged her. "Nothing." They stood, one generation clasped to another, each one's tears dampening the other's face.

At the funeral a year later, Jael refused to view her grandmother's body. "I want to remember her like she was the day she gave me the chest," she had explained to her mother.

"I don't blame you," her mother had answered, straightening from her stooped posture over the chipped enamel dishpan. She massaged the small of her back with both hands and glanced at Jael seated at the round oak table.

"Heard you get up this mornin'."

Jael nodded and sipped her coffee, putting the handle on the wrong side of the mug to avoid the chipped spot on its rim.

"Sure you're not goin' back to school?"

"Jerome needs to start seminary this fall, Ma." She gazed into her cup as if the coffee's black reflection could tell the future. "With the baby coming and all, well, we just can't afford two tuitions."

"What about your scholarship?"

"That was for full time. It'll end when I drop out to have the baby. I'd have to go back part-time and pay."

Her mother came to the table and poured herself a cup of coffee. She sat down opposite her daughter and gazed intently into her eyes.

"You happy, Jael?"

"Yes, Ma." She placed her hands upon her mother's. "Happier than I ever thought possible." She returned her mother's gaze and sensed in the usually lifeless eyes, a momentary glow betraying that she herself had once had dreams.

"When the hard times come, Jael, remember now." Her eyes became a little watery and she regained her self-control with a rapid blinking.

"Is that what you do, Ma?" Jael nodded toward the creaky iron bed, one caster replaced by an old Sears-Roebuck catalog. It occupied the corner of the room opposite the kitchen.

"Yes." Her mother's gaze followed Jael's. "Wasn't always like this. None of us meant it to be like this." She sipped her coffee. "Glad you got free of it."

Jael blinked, tried to speak, swallowed and tried again. "Jerome and I are going to do missionary work in the mountains, Ma." She felt her mother's hands stiffen under hers.

"No, Jael, not you. The other kids—they're for the mountains. You always had something finer in you. Don't waste it here. Get away from the mountains."

"Ma, it's—it's where God wants me." She fumbled for words. "For a long time—when I first went to college—I wanted to get as far away as I could. But I learned in college, Ma, and I learned from Jerome, that the place doesn't make the person fine or common, it's what a person chooses when she finally realizes God's love." She hurried on. "If Elmer and Meg hadn't come, I never would have known. They didn't stay long, but they gave me something, Ma. It made me free. I don't know how to explain it, but it's—it's like I owe."

Her mother studied Jael's face through narrowed eyes.

"Well, guess there is a difference in stayin' because you want to, not because you have to."

She nodded toward the stove where, on the round iron lids, two pieces of thick-sliced bread lay face-down, pungent smoke curling from the edges.

"I learned when I carried every one of you—burnt toast and burnt pancakes settled the stomach." She went to the stove and flipped the charred bread to toast on the other side.

"Eggs ready yet?"

"Couple of minutes." Jael placed two slices of white bread on a cast-iron stove lid. "Tammi still asleep?"

"Yes. She had a cold. I'll try to keep her down today."

"Snowing heavy still."

Jael looked through the window facing the road. "You'll have to dig the car out. Plow's not been through yet."

Jerome grunted.

Jael sat with him and they gave thanks together. She jumped up to turn the toast before Jerome finished the "Amen."

"Can't you go to Burlington tomorrow?" She poured coffee into their cups, checked the toast until it was a gold color in the center, buttered it and set it on the table with the coffee.

"Have to catch up on the programs or we'll be off the air." Jerome sat back a little self-consciously.

Jael looked again through the window. "Just a day home—together," she said quietly as she served the eggs and bacon from the heavy skillet.

Jerome raised an eyebrow and finished chewing, a thoughtful expression on his face. "It must get awfully lonely for you and Tammi cooped up here in the house." He glanced through the window. ". . . especially in weather like this." He picked up a slice of crisp bacon with his fingers and bit off a piece.

"I love it here, Jerome," Jael smiled. "I can help people here because I'm one of them and I know how they think." She followed his gaze out the window. "It gets a little lonely some-times," she caught his gaze with hers as she continued, "but I'm only lonely for you. You work so hard and you're gone so much." She bit into her toast and washed it down with a mouthful of black coffee.

"Well, there are some things in the wind," he smiled. "I may well have a lot more time to spend with you." He glanced around, ". . . and you won't have to spend many more winters in this place with its wood-burning stoves and its rusty pipes." He wolfed down the last of his breakfast and held his coffee cup in both hands, sipping from it now and again. "Um. That was a good breakfast."

"I don't mind the winters or the stoves." Something inside made her want to push toward a resolution. "The rusted pipes took us through last winter. You'll have time to fix them in better weather." She caught his eyes again with hers. "And Jerome, we both believed when we came, that small as it is, Croughton's Corners is where God wants us." She took an-other sip of her coffee. "The people are just beginning to trust us. I wouldn't feel right about leaving."

"Well, it's a long ways off, anyhow," he reassured her. Then he grinned. "Reason you don't want to leave is that you can go barefoot from spring to fall without having to worry about what people will say."

Jael glanced down at her plate and picked up a slice of crisp bacon in her fingers. She took a mouthful and chewed for a long time, masking the hurt of Jerome's criticism. "Yes—and I can eat bacon without a fork if I wish," she said defiantly. "The people need us here, Jerome," she said more seriously.

126

She didn't know how to tell him about color, and laughter, and love, and bleakness. "They just—need us."

"Never tell it by the way church attendance has been falling off."

"That's because you're gone so much," she tried to keep her voice gentle and persuasive. "They want to see *you* in the pulpit instead of a Bible school student who's a stranger." Her voice became sharper than she had wished.

Jerome gulped the rest of his coffee. "If they come to church to hear a man, they come for the wrong reason."

"They've only had a pastor for the last three years," Jael said gently. "Someday, they'll know that. Until then, they need you—and me."

Jerome stood. "Well, way things are going, Lord's going to make them grow up faster than they want." He stepped to the coat hooks by the door and started wrapping himself against the cold. "There are people who are willing to make the effort to hear His Word. You haven't been able to be with me a lot, but more and more people have been coming to the special meetings where I've spoken." He grasped a scuffed black overshoe, thrust in his foot, folded his trouser leg flat around his shin, and slid the metal buckles together with obvious irritation. "It's a real encouragement that I don't get here." He stood and looked at her. His face softened as he let Jael glimpse something deep inside. "I've always seemed to be— well—just on the edge of average, Jael." He fumbled with his coat. "I took this pastorate because I thought I wouldn't be able to succeed in a larger city church." Jerome gazed out the window at the falling snow. "I don't know. Maybe it's because my father kept on telling me all my lie that I'd never be able to do anything right." He lifted his cap off the hook and pulled the ear-flaps down. "Well, I decided I'm not going to be a failure. I'm going to go as far as I can go and be more successful than my father himself ever thought of being." He hugged her for a moment, leaning awkwardly forward to keep pressure off her abdomen. "Grab another cup of coffee soon's I get the Carryall started."

Shivering in the blast of cold air swirling in through the door as Jerome went out, Jael turned to the stove and added a new chunk of hardwood to the fire. After refilling her cup, she pushed the coffee pot into a back corner of the stove where it would stay warm without boiling. Carrying her cup carefully, she padded to the living room using the gentle, clumsy gait that women well along in pregnancy adopt. She sat in the overstuffed chair near the front window and placed her cup on the mail-order table beside it. Her hands felt the gently turning bundle in her abdomen.

"What Psalm do you want to hear this morning, little baby?" Only her soft, full-lipped smile betrayed the silent conversation with the infant. "Do you want to hear how well God knows you already?" She rested for a few moments, mentally reaching toward the new human growing inside. "Be patient. Another month and a half, and you'll see Mommy and Daddy and sister Tammi." She chuckled. "And Aunt Bea will probably spoil you terribly. And I suppose you'll hardly wait to be big enough before you ride Uncle Ira's hay rake in the summer."

She glanced through the window for a moment. Jerome had swept the snow from the Carryall and white exhaust from the cold engine advertised that he had just started it. The snow had drifted less deeply than she had feared, and he would be able to drive out without digging. "Well, little baby, you'll have to wait a few minutes. Daddy looks cold out there. He'll want another cup of coffee before he leaves." She grunted as she pulled herself to her feet. Her slippers slapped softly on the linoleum as she waddled back toward the stove.

A half-hour later she watched Jerome force the old green Carryall through soft snow drifted to just below the bottom of the bumpers. "I'll see if Ira'll come up tonight and plow it out," he had thrown back over his shoulder. "No point in his coming before it stops. Only fill in again."

As if the snow wanted to obliterate all evidence of Jerome's presence, wind and flakes combined to fill in the twin furrows of his departure. She sat heavily in the chair and watched as the flakes swirled against the gray sky. They came thickly, like the flakes falling around the fairy-tale house in the center of the glass ball her mother kept in the corner she called the "living room." Fascinated, Jael would invert the globe again and again to gaze at the imitation snow storm. Her mother would sputter at her to stop wasting time and get out to weed the garden or wash the dishes. She smiled at the memory. Now she was in the center of her own glass ball.

The snow completed its work on the tracks and began to fill the rest of the countryside in earnest.

"Well, little baby. We're all alone here with the whole day to ourselves—you and Tammi and I." She reached for her Bible. "I think you'd enjoy hearing about how God knows you even right now." She turned to the Psalms, flipped a page or two to find her place, and began reading in a half-whispered murmur.

> "O Lord, Thou hast searched me, and known me.
> "Thou knowest my downsitting and mine uprising, thou understandest my thought afar off.
> "Thou compassest my path and my lying down, and art acquainted with all my ways. . . .
> "Thou hast beset me behind and before, and laid thine hand upon me. . . .
> "Whither shall I go from thy spirit? or whither shall I flee from thy presence?
> "If I ascend up into heaven, thou art there: if I make my bed in hell, behold, thou art there.

"If I take the wings of morning, and dwell in the uttermost parts of the sea;

"Even there shall thy hand lead me, and thy right hand shall hold me.

"If I say, Surely the darkness shall cover me; even the night shall be light about me.

"Yea, the darkness hideth not from thee; . . . ."

Jael moved her gaze from the fine-printed pages to the snow swirling outside. "God has built a house around you, little baby," she murmured. "No matter where you are, He has a special love for you." She shuddered slightly. Someplace at another level in her mind, she noted the chill creeping in through the walls of her house. She would need to add more wood to the stove. "Even out here—that's what God meant when He said 'the uttermost parts of the sea'—He loves you. Even in the darkness inside where you're hidden and warm, God loves you."

Jael shivered again. "I guess I'd better put more wood on that stove, little baby, or you'll get cold." She placed her Bible on the stand and heaved herself to her feet. As she slipped a new chunk of hardwood into the firebox, she heard Tammi rustling around in the small bedroom to the side of the kitchen.

"You awake, Tammi?"

"Cold in here." The voice was muffled.

"Nice and warm out here. Want some pancakes and cocoa?"

"Uh-huh."

"Would you like to come out and sit next to the stove while I fix them?"

"Uh-huh."

As she took the flour, baking powder, and salt from the

130

cupboard shelf, Jael heard Tammi slide from bed and pad across the floor.

"I brought my blanket."

"That's all right. You just drag that chair up and wrap up nice and snug." Jael felt Tammi's large eyes fastened upon her as she mixed the batter. She poured some maple syrup from a half-gallon tin into a small saucepan and slid it next to the coffeepot at the back of the stove. The chunk of butter she had dropped into the black cast skillet sizzled, and she added it to the batter and mixed it in. The skillet had been a wedding gift from her mother. Well-cured from almost a generation of use, food never stuck to it. It had a solid, substantial feel, not like the pots and pans that had caught her eye shortly after she and Jerome were married.

She shook her head as she recalled her gullibility. Maybe she was too anxious to affirm that she was a woman in her own home, she thought. In any case, she had been eager to make that first major kitchen purchase, a set of hammered aluminum cookware. But with several years of constant use, most of their black wooden handles had loosened. "Heat resistant," the salesman had bragged. "Attractive . . . set off the silvery velvet of the aluminum." Jael used the set less and less as the metal fastenings loosened in the handles. Jerome had promised to repair them; but for almost six years, he had not found the time. Her mother's skillet, heavy and black from forty years' use, remained as solid as the day it was purchased, its handle an integral appendage thrusting solidly from the thick rim.

"I like pancakes," Tammi babbled excitedly. "Is the syrup warm yet?" The statement and the questions tumbled out one after the other.

"I think it lacks a few minutes yet," Jael replied, gazing for a moment at her auburn-haired replica.

"Is Uncle Ira having pancakes this morning?"

"I wouldn't know," Jael laughed. "But I wouldn't be surprised."

"I wish he would come and have pancakes with us." She looked up, her narrow chin making her face look more mature than her six years. "Why doesn't Daddy like to have pancakes with us?"

Jael drew in her breath sharply. She couldn't tell if Tammi's question or the baby's kick generated the pang. "God's got a lot of important things for Daddy to do," she said quietly. Jael kept her hands busy dropping ladles of pancake mix into the skillet. "Lots of times Daddy has to leave before you wake up in the morning."

"Mommy?"

"Yes?" Jael poured the syrup from the saucepan into a small pitcher and set it on the table in front of Tammi.

"Will I ever be important enough so God can send Daddy to me?"

Jael turned to Tammi. Kneeling clumsily, she bundled Tammi and her blanket into her arms. "You're important enough right now." Her voice was husky. "I'm sure God's said something to Daddy about you."

"That's good. Oh! I felt Baby kick."

"He's telling you he likes to be hugged," Jael teased. She disentangled herself from Tammi and returned to her pancakes. She would eat the first ones. Her mother had always said that burnt toast or burnt pancakes settled the stomach.

15

All morning the snow hissed against the windowpanes with sudden gusts of north wind. White and heavy, it drifted across the driveway, heaped up against door and wall on the windward side of the house, and swirled in eddies, forming cold, graceful hollows in the sheltered areas. The bracken edging the farther side of the road, usually visible from the living-room window, was quickly obscured. Behind the brush, the woods smudged darker gray between the flat whiteness on the ground and the thick grayness of the sky. As Jael prepared the bread for baking, she reached up now and again to wipe the frost from the window over the sink and peer out. Only the stern black trunks of the patriarchal pines framing the window showed themselves clearly. The rest of the world disappeared in swirling confusion toward the lake. She shuddered and turned the kneaded bread into the bowl.

The telephone rang at midmorning.

"I'll get it, Mommy," Tammi shrieked. She scurried from beneath her blanket house draped between two chairs beside the stove. "Hello?" She paused. "Hello, Aunt Bea." Another pause. "Mommy, Aunt Bea wants you."

Wiping her hands on a dish towel, Jael made her way to the chair beside the desk and sank down onto it. "Hi, Bea."

"Just callin' to see if you're all right," came the full voice at the other end. "Figured the pastor might have to be out and around."

"Yes. Thank you. He had to go to Burlington."

"In this weather?" Bea snorted. "Roads'll be closed all afternoon." She paused. "Need anything?"

"No, Bea. Thank you." She watched Tammi go back to her tent. "Tammi's playing 'Desert Island,' and I'm baking bread. Jerome's Carryall should make it all right, even with the roads drifted."

"Well, won't harm none to give you a call now and again."

"Thanks, Bea. I'd appreciate that."

Jael sat silently for a long time after she hung up the phone. She felt a twinge of fear from someplace deep inside, the same fear she used to experience when her father returned home late and drunk, shouting her mother's failures. Sometimes from the loft she'd hear the slaps. Her mother never cried out, but Jael could tell how severe the beating had been by the way she moved about the kitchen at breakfast the next morning. Jael forced the memories back into her "locked box," as she called the place where all dark and painful things were stored.

They ate cinnamon rolls and drank hot chocolate for lunch. "Isn't it ever going to stop snowing, Mommy?" Tammi wiped the sticky sugar and chocolate mustache from her lips with a damp cloth. "Ugh. I don't like to be sticky."

"It will—probably tonight."

"Will Daddy come home soon?"

"He'll probably be quite late tonight."

"Can I stay up and wait for him?"

"If you can stay awake."

"What do they eat on desert islands?" Tammi asked suddenly.

Jael gazed through the window at the gray and white landscape, always changing, and yet, like the sea, relentlessly the same. "Probably the same thing they eat in Vermont," she replied, laughing. "A ship sank and some boxes floated ashore," she grinned, entering the fantasy with Tammi. "And they washed up on the other side of the island—over there." Jael pointed to the cupboard next to the stove."

Tammi's eyes widened. "What washed up?"

"SPAGHETTI." Jael laughed again, a free laugh filled with shared delight. "It was an Italian ship, and they were carrying boxes and boxes of spaghetti." Jael watched Tammi slide from her chair and scurry to the cupboard where she pulled a package of spaghetti from the bottom shelf and stood for a moment examining it. "Do they have to eat it raw?"

"No," Jael laughed, holding her abdomen against the pressure. "A box of tomato sauce washed ashore right next to the spaghetti."

Tammi's frown relaxed. "That's good." She placed the spaghetti and the can of tomato sauce on the table. "And fresh bread?"

"And fresh bread," Jael added. "But you're a sick little girl. You need to go and take a nap with your dollies for a while after lunch."

"Can I sleep in my tent?"

Jael appraised the blankets arranged over the chairs and on the floor. "It should be nice and warm there. Get another blanket from your bed and put it on the floor. The heat from the stove will keep you warm."

"It's not a stove, it's the summer sun," Tammi declared, padding to her room after another blanket.

As Tammi settled herself in her tent, Jael punched the dough down in its bowl to rise a second time. She placed it far enough from the firebox to avoid becoming too warm, but close enough to continue rising, then spread a clean cloth over it. She would bake the bread when she cooked the spaghetti late that afternoon. She pulled a black-handled cast aluminum pan from the cupboard and emptied a can of tomato sauce in it.

Hammered aluminum cookware.

Her mother had never had a set of matched "cookware." The salesman had come to the house one day while Jerome was in class at seminary.

"Keep the vitamins in your food. . . ." the salesman said authoritatively. "Last a lifetime . . . never have to buy another pan. She visualized the silver pans hanging neatly in an early American kitchen. "Wooden handles . . . best insulator against heat . . . black handle contrasts with the aluminum color of the pan. . . ." Surely they could afford "a pan a month." She signed the contract. Jerome would be pleased. They would finally be starting to gather something nice of their own. Jael's mother's cookware, like her marriage, represented battered necessity rather than choice.

"You what?" Jerome stormed. "Why . . . why on earth did you do that?" He slapped his books down on the small desk. "We just paid tuition for seminary, and we'll have a hospital bill for a baby in another month, and you bought a set of. . . .of pots?"

Jael's lips trembled. "Well. . . . I'll send—send them back then." She hiccupped, covering her frightened sob, just as she had as a child in front of her father.

"No." Jerome said grimly. "You signed a contract to buy them. You gave our word." He went to the door. "I've got some research to do at the library. Don't wait supper." He slammed the door as he left.

Within the first year, the black handles loosened. Continued use enlarged the holes drilled lengthwise through them, and the black finish wore off the edges of the flat faces to expose the wood beneath. She asked Jerome once or twice to repair them.

"Yes, dear," he would say, absently turning a leaf in a book. "Saturday morning." But Saturday never came.

She grew to hate the pans and felt guilty each time she used them. The payments never seemed to stop.

Tammi's birth had been difficult, and Jerome dropped out of seminary for a year to pay the bills. Finally, they were free. Jerome finished seminary, and they had come to Croughton's Corners.

The pots gleamed from duty rather than love; Jael had to grasp the largest by the opposite rim as well as the handle in order to lift it when it was full, for fear it would come apart in her hands. She had been burned several times when hot liquid had splattered and soaked through her thick pot holder.

A pound of ground meat, a sliced onion, and various pinches of spices completed her preparations for the spaghetti sauce. She browned the meat and onions, combined it with the tomato sauce, and set it to simmer toward the back of the stove. "Might as well draw the water for the spaghetti," she thought. She pulled the large pan with the loose handle out of the cupboard and filled it at the sink. Placing it in front of the sauce pan on the stove, she dried her hands and walked to the comfortable chair in the small living room. The occasional pops and muffled hisses of the burning hardwood in the chunk stove in the corner opposed the "shishh" of wind and snow against the house. Floors and walls creaked from heat on one side and unrelenting cold on the other. Moisture from the baking and housework had steamed the centers of the windowpanes and hardened into intricate icy designs at each corner where the glass met the frames. "Jack Frost's been here again," Tammi would say when she saw it. Jael pushed herself to her feet and waddled to the bedroom. A nap for just a few minutes would feel good.

"Mommy, I'm cold."

How could it be cold? It's May, and we're lying in a field of timothy. The wind's cool on my arm when I raise it above the grass, but down here in my nest, in all its green fragance. . . ."

"Mommy wake up. It's dark, I'm cold."

The timothy turned white, and then dissolved as Jael opened her eyes.

Tammi stood beside her bed, wrapped completely in her blanket. With only her eyes and the tip of her nose showing, she looked like a gnomish Bedouin in the gloom of some faraway twilight.

Jael came fully awake. She could see the moisture from their breath. Evening filtered in dark through the bedroom window; and the wind and snow still hissed as if some evil white serpent, angered at their safety, coiled and struck repeatedly at the panes. "It is cold in here." She sat up shivering as she placed her feet on the chilled linoleum. "I'll stir up the fires. Crawl up into Mommy's bed, Tammi." Jael drew back the covers. "Mommy made a nice warm spot for you."

Irritated with her own carelessness, Jael hurried to the kitchen stove. Both the sauce and the water were only slightly warm. She slid them aside and lifted the round black lid. There were still live embers. Pulling some kindling from the corner of the woodbox behind the stove, she placed the thinnest pieces against the embers and watched as they caught. She added several thicker pieces and then hurried to the living room to repeat the ritual. That fire was in better condition, however, and stirring with a poker, opening the draft, and adding a small chunk started it again.

"Bea hasn't called since this morning," she thought. "It's only five. They're probably not eating yet." She lifted the telephone. Its round black plastic felt cold against her ear. There was no tone. She jiggled the cradle, but no reassuring electronic stutter clicked back at her.

Jael replaced the receiver. "Storm must have taken the lines down," she whispered to herself.

She heard the kindling crackling merrily in both stoves. Quickly she went from one stove to the other, adding larger, longer burning chunks of wood. She could feel the heat now, and the translucent icy filigrees which had crept completely over the windows while they slept had again yielded to a cold wet circle in the center of each pane.

"I'm hungry."

Jael glanced toward the bedroom door.

Tammi stood in the opening. She still clutched the blanket tightly around her, but she had slipped her head free and now stood, a pale dwarfish Indian staring solemnly from the door-way of a longhouse.

"Ugh. Cold One is now Hungry One," Jael said forcing a laugh.

"Will Daddy be home soon?"

"He may be late. It's still snowing very hard."

"Daddy doesn't like to play Desert Island. He always has to leave."

"That's because he has to see other people on other desert islands."

"Can I help you make supper?"

"You can fill the kettle for me."

"All right." Tammi disappeared into her room and returned a moment later minus her blanket. She scampered to the stove, the feet of her pajamas making soft padding noises, and lifted the brightly polished kettle from the cold side over the oven. She lugged it to the sink, lifted it with both hands and placed it under the faucet.

Jael checked the bread dough while Tammi occupied her-self with the kettle. "Looks like we'll have to eat store-bought bread tonight, Tammi."

"Look, Mommy, even the water is too cold to run out the faucet."

"In the cold the dough couldn't rise."

"Mommy, the water won't come."

Jael turned. "Try again, Tammi. Uncle Ira told us that the spring across the road doesn't freeze." She stepped to the sink and watched Tammi reach up to try the faucet again. It remained silent and dry.

Jael sighed. "Leave it off in case it decides to flow again."

"I guess we won't have spaghetti."

"I guess we will." Jael forced a cheerful tone in her voice. "The cold might have spoiled our home-made bread, but I filled the spaghetti pan before we went for our naps." Looking for something to keep Tammi further occupied, she added, "Why don't you go to the cellar and get a jar of the applesauce Aunt Bea put up for us?"

Tammi padded to the cellar door and flipped the light switch almost out of her reach. She lifted the iron latch, opened the door, and stood there.

Jael stirred the meat sauce, enjoying the spicy aroma filling the kitchen. She felt a coldness from the cellar and turned toward Tammi. "Don't leave the door open, Tammi, go ahead down and get the applesauce."

"I can't."

"Now, there's nothing down there that will hurt you," Jael snapped, allowing her tension to surface. "Remember Mommy taking you down and showing you?"

"I can't. Look."

Jael knocked the excess sauce from the spoon and placed it in an old, cracked saucer she kept on the stove. "Certainly you can. I'll stand in the stairway and watch." She wished they had never had the Halloween party at church. Tammi had been frightened of dark places ever since. Sighing, she stepped behind Tammi, and gasped.

The one yellow light bulb reflected up at her from the surface of a spreading, black puddle of water. Still shallow, it betrayed the unevenness of the floor where occasional dry areas refused, here and there, to reflect the same slick blackness. From someplace back in a corner, she heard the slow, invisible splashing of water.

Jael pulled Tammi gently back from the door. "That old pipe Daddy said might break, just did."

Tammi's lower lip trembled slightly. "Is Daddy coming home soon?"

"He'll be home before you know it," Jael said brightly, attempting to calm Tammi. Inside, she swallowed a lump of resentment against Jerome's having left them. Tammi had been right, she thought. When would they be as important in God's eyes as the others, so that Jerome could be there when they needed him? Quickly, she clamped a lid on her own feelings. "Why don't we make the spaghetti now? We'll save some for Daddy for when he gets home."

"All right." Tammi had lost her animation and stood uncertainly in the center of the kitchen.

Desperately, Jael gave her a task to do. "Why don't you set the table for us?"

"All right," she said quietly, and padded back and forth between the cupboards and the kitchen table, carrying one object at a time, like an ant at a picnic. By the time she had completed her task, some of her cheerfulness had returned. "It's just like a real desert island now, Mommy, isn't it?" Her voice was still troubled.

"I'm afraid it is, Tammi," Jael chuckled. Tammi never failed to lift her own depression. "But we can always melt some snow, if we have to."

The spaghetti water hissed and gurgled into a boil. Jael added the spaghetti, and it stilled from the sudden drop in temperature. She slid the pot forward and lifted the rear stove lid to check the fire. It needed another chunk of wood. Jael turned to the woodbox behind the stove.

"That water's going over, Mommy—I'll get it." Tammi ran to the stove, and grasped the pot by the handle.

"NO! IT'S TOO HOT!" Jael shouted, turning to reach for the potholder.

The next few moments remained burned indelibly into Jael's memory. Tammi in her faded pink pajamas with the sewn-in feet. The boiling spaghetti. The handle separating from the large pot as Tammi tugged at it. The evil yellowish water and strings of matted paste cascading over Tammi's head and body as it slid from the broken-handled pot and gathered in a serpentine nest at her feet. Her own rush to help. The terrible full pain from her abdomen as she slipped on the evil mess on the floor. And Tammi's screams.

Picking herself up from the floor, she ripped open Tammi's pajamas and pulled them off. Tammi's screams—prolonged, deep, and agonized. No longer the reaction to initial shock and hurt, they were the terrible hopeless howls of a child who knows the pain will not soon end. Leaving the pajamas in a soggy heap on the floor, Jael scooped Tammi up in her arms, rushed to the door, struggled with the latch for a moment, and then opened it. She slipped on the ice on the steps and fell again. Pain seared up her back as she landed hard, sitting, trying to protect Tammi. Fighting nausea, she struggled to her feet and thrust Tammi into the soft snow drifting against the house. Tammi continued screaming. The sound echoed hollowly against the disinterested black-trunked pines. The snow fell, indifferent to the child's screams and the mother's despairing, "Tammi, oh my Tammi. Oh Tammi."

Jael gathered Tammi against herself again. The child's screams had grown weaker, and Jael feared sending her into shock. Her own knees felt rubbery, and the four steps seemed an impossible climb. The doorway to the warm living room stood open, inviting her in from the storm. But it was so far away. Everything seemed to float. A warm fountain gushed from someplace inside. She wanted again to lie in that green nest of timothy and be drenched in May sunlight. The warm, green-smelling timothy and the golden May sunlight.

She shook her head, forcing herself back to the reality of the numbing cold, the gray-black gloom, and the climb up the icy steps. Her legs wouldn't work. Turning backwards she sat on the bottom step with Tammi in her lap. Placing her hands behind on the next step up, she pushed. Her body felt leaden. She pushed again, straightening her back and moving her hips painfully from side to side. She managed to work her body over the edge of the next step. Turning, she glanced at the open door, the cheery light spilling through it, a mocking, golden carpet of warm May sunlight splashing towards her. Again she placed her hands behind her upon the next riser. Tammi, ominously calm, lay in her lap.

She had just reached the top step and was dragging herself toward the open door and the warmth and the sunlight when Ira chugged into the yard plowing the way for Jerome in the Carryall.

Jael remembered little of the rest of that winter. There was a stark fragment of a gray, snowy day. White ground. A dark hole, rectangular, deep. An untidy heap of brown-black earth. A small, white painted box. Jerome reading, "I am the resurrection and the life. . . ." How could he? Yet he stood there, his face red with cold, a whitened circle on each cheek. His thin, blonde hair caught heavy, wet snowflakes, and his bulky gray overcoat whitened across the shoulders as he stood at the graveside. He seemed as insensitive as the impassive granite monuments dotting the graveyard around him.

She remembered bitterly the Psalm she read to the baby on that evil day:

"If I ascend up into heaven, thou art there: if I make my
bed in hell, behold, thou art there.
". . . If I say, Surely the darkness shall cover me; even
the night shall be light about me.
". . . Yea, the darkness hideth not from thee; . . . ."

Benni was with God. Of that she was confident. But the darkness had hidden God from her.

Vaguely, she heard Jerome praying. She sagged against the Carryall and tried to cry, but couldn't. Instead she felt like screaming, "You should have been there! If you had been home, this would not have happened!"

Bea slipped a stout arm around her waist. "Come," she said tenderly, "Let's sit inside."

Jael allowed herself to be led to the door and helped gently into the front seat.

"Terrible cold out there. Get some heat." Bea started the engine and checked the heater control to see that it was set at "full."

Terrible cold. Dark earth. God's monstrous joke! He had let her grow to love Benni and then He snatched the child from her body. He allowed the infant to struggle for two weeks in a hospital incubator until her hope had returned, and then He had killed him.

And His servant had helped. How subtly God had drawn Jerome away when she needed him!

Tears surged up from the newly empty place where Benni had lain for the past seven months. Jael sat silently, clutching Bea's hand. Still the tears would not come. She sat, green eyes large with accusation, staring at Jerome.

Side by side with the simple farmers and laborers who had attended the funeral, all members of the little church, Jerome labored to refill the grave, wielding the pointed shovel deliberately, heaping dark, dispassionate earth soundlessly back upon earth. To Jael, Jerome had become as cold and unfeeling as God.

"Yes, a true servant of His," Dr. Soberman beamed. "Wouldn't you say so, Mrs. Springer?"

Struggling to pull herself back into the present, Jael glanced helplessly from Dr. Soberman to Jerome and back again. "I'm, I'm sorry . . . I didn't quite catch that."

"I was just mentioning," he chuckled, "that a wife can tell better than anyone else when her husband is a true servant of God." He cocked an eyebrow, waiting for a reply.

"Jerome . . . Jerome has always placed his God before anyone or anything else," Jael said, gazing coolly and unsmilingly into Dr. Soberman's eyes as she closed and locked her box of painful memories. "Always."

Jael fixed her eyes again on the panelled wall of plaques and awards facing Jerome's desk.

16

For almost ten years Vice-Principal Frank Rawlings had crowded out loneliness with the discipline of a quiet, well-ordered life, and an intense interest in sailing. He preferred loneliness to love. There was less pain. What human warmth he needed, a few friends held at arm's length provided.

But the pain was nibbling again at the corners of his life, and he shrank from it. He slouched back in his chair, stared at the telephone, and frowned. Under most circumstances he had taught himself not to frown—it gave away his feelings. But, alone in his office, it didn't seem to matter.

Except for an ineradicable sadness around the eyes, his expression was as habitually relaxed and pleasant as careful schooling could make it. There was something in the sandy hair, unruly as beach grass, and the angular face, tanned and slightly crinkled from sun and wind, that demanded a no-nonsense respect from both student and colleague.

He propped his elbows on the arms of the oak office chair and supported his square chin with steepled fingers. The chair's curved oak frame hooked his lean, wide-shouldered back just beneath the clavicles and at the juncture of his thighs and buttocks. Thrusting his legs straight before him, he guided his heels to the worn spot on the carpet under his desk

for a third point of support. He was a contradiction in image—
the monk in prayer, and the athlete in repose.

Above his pointed fingers his lips compressed into a thin
straight line, capped at each end like a sideways letter "I".
"How on earth do I tell them?" He closed his eyes to shut out
the view of the telephone. "Same way Nate Rosen told me, I
guess."

The thick gray clouds had bulged heavy with snow through
his first two history classes and through the morning study
hall. At noon they had ruptured, scattering at first a few gray
flakes upon an even grayer city, and then released heavy white
wet silent swirls, filling the air with a Christmas card winter.

Frank smiled and gazed through the tall square-paned windows lining the side of the classroom like a half-dozen parade
soldiers at attention. In an hour the snow would blanket the
gray and turn the city briefly white. Carrie would want to walk
across the park to Guido's for supper before they finished their
Christmas shopping, but they would take a cab. With the baby
seven months along, he'd make her save her energy.

Frank grinned at the empty seats in the classroom. He had
already finished his shopping.

He withdrew a narrow black silk-finished box from the
breast pocket of his tweed sportscoat. Flipping back the
spring-loaded lid, he shifted his gaze from the windows to the
exquisitely fashioned silver and diamond pendant. He had
found it almost by accident months ago. A silver heart, almost
an inch high, encompassed a simple cross. A tiny diamond
chip at the heart of the cross seemed to gather light all out of
proportion to its size and prism it back with first one hue and
then another. The jeweler had agreed to set it aside on depos-
it, and Frank had paid a little on it from each paycheck over

the last seven months. Now he would be able to give it to Carrie.

A bell clamored in the hallway outside his room.

For the three years of their marriage, he had never been able to give her anything like this. But now, he'd be on tenure, only one payment remained on his college loan, and his aunt's legacy would make a home of their own possible. "It's about time Carrie had something special," he thought. That it was beautiful was reason enough to buy it. He didn't have to justify the purchase by its having to be useful.

Frank grinned and snapped the box shut. He wondered if the students filling his classroom knew that he was as anxious as they were for the last two hours to pass.

Ten minutes before last hour ended, Frank had turned from the ancient slate blackboard and glimpsed Nate Rosen peering in. The principal's head and shoulders were framed in the glazed door like one of the portraits hanging in the main office. His sparse grizzled hair, balding brow, wide set eyes, and prominent cheekbones provided a setting for a nose magnificent in proportion to the rest of his face. The skin was drawn and tight over the septum and the nostrils flared widely. But after first notice, the viewer forgot it, engulfed by the warm eyes behind the peculiar half-lensed spectacles.

A hand slid up from the bottom edge of the portrait and beckoned to him.

"I guess Grant will have to wait until after vacation," he smiled. He dropped the stub of chalk he was using into the tray. He worked his way among the chatting students to the back of the room wondering what problem could be important enough to bring the principal to his room. Dr. Rosen sent for teachers. He seldom came for them.

The door opened as Frank neared. The principal grasped his shoulder to guide him away from from the gaze of curious students.

147

"Frank." Dr. Rosen's voice was thick and hoarse. Then Frank saw the policeman accompanying the principal.

"What's happened?" He glanced quickly at the policeman and back again to the principal.

"Your wife has been hurt." Dr. Rosen lifted an eyebrow quickly toward the policeman. "She is in the hospital."

Of what followed, only scattered images remained for Frank. The siren's scream along slippery streets. The smell of rubbing alcohol and green soap. The clatter of stainless steel on formica. The scent of fresh bedclothing. The details of the police report: "Accosted by three assailants, male, late teens. Struck repeatedly with heavy object. Kicked repeatedly. Purse missing. Escaped in early 70's red over black Mercury sedan."

It was almost midnight when he saw her try to open her eyes against the pain of swollen purple lids. Just that morning as they lay in bed, her eyes had been large and black, drinking him in as if their thirst would never be slaked.

"Carrie," he whispered. "Carrie." He felt her fingers twitch against his. "I'm here. It's all right." His face was inches from hers as he whispered. She strained to see him through her pain.

"Frank." She extended her fingers, cold against his palm.

"Yes, Carrie. I'm here." He bent his ear close to her lips to catch her low whisper.

She stopped straining and seemed to drift off to sleep for a moment. Then her breathing changed with her effort to speak. "Don't be frightened, Frank."

He reached up with his free hand and stroked her cheek. "It's all right, Carrie. You'll be all right."

She smiled. "Yes." She rested again, and when she spoke again, her voice was a little girl's—brimmed with wonder, shy. "Kiss me, Frank."

He touched his lips gently against hers, avoiding the swollen and torn area where the doctors had stitched.

"Poor Frank," she whispered. She pulled her fingers free and stroked the back of his hand. "We'll be waiting for you—Baby—and Jesus—and me." She rested again and her breathing grew more shallow and rapid, but she didn't struggle or gasp. Once more she said, "Don't be frightened, Frank."

When Carrie was buried, she wore the cross and heart-shaped pendant hidden beneath the high-collared blouse she liked most. That blouse was all he could afford to give her their first Christmas together.

"Frank, you're one of our strongest teachers. I don't want to lose you." Nate Rosen peered at him over those half-rimmed spectacles.

Frank gazed down at the long white envelope containing his contract and ran his finger along the edge. "I have to, Dr. Rosen. I—well, I just can't come back."

"Sit down, Frank." The principal took the envelope from Frank's hand and placed it to one side on the desk. "The truth, Frank. Why?"

Frank drew a deep breath. "You really want to know." It wasn't a question.

He stared for a moment into Naté Rosen's eyes—pale gray eyes struggling to understand the tangles in his soul. "All right." He folded his hands across his chest and stretched his legs forward as he slouched in the chair. He grasped for words.

"The police never found them." His voice caught as he recalled Carrie's image.

"Yes." Dr. Rosen's voice was soft, encouraging.

"I've thought about that," Frank continued. "A lot." He shifted his weight in the chair. "Here I am teaching American history. For what?" He lifted his eyelids and challenged Nate's gaze. "Look around you, Dr. Rosen. We're caught in a grotesque lunacy. We think we can make a difference—have some significance." He paused and stared at the pen holder on Dr. Rosen's desk. "Since Carrie died, I see more clearly. No one can make any significant difference. Not you, not me, not the school, not the police. No one."

"But you make a difference to some, Frank." Nate's eyes returned the challenge. "If we can make a difference for even one, that is significant."

"Why? And for how long?" Frank replied. "Why survive in an evil place?" He inclined his head toward the window where springtime noises of students leaving school drifted through. "Here, there are two kinds of people—the brutal and the victimized." He glanced back toward the envelope on the desk. "Well, there has to be another choice. Until I find out that there is, I'm through." His voice dropped to a whisper with his agitation.

"Frank, what hope do the victims have if we stop trying?" Nate pleaded. "If we give up, it won't be just here. So go someplace else—someplace far away?" He flared his nostrils in derision. "I'm a Jew, Frank. Learn something from a Jew. A Jew knows there is no place to run. A Jew knows there is no shelter from wickedness. A Jew knows there is no port safe from evil." Dr. Rosen's eyes burned intently into Frank's.

Frank lowered his eyes and then glanced up again. "Even if you're right, Dr. Rosen," he shifted his gaze to the envelope on the desk, "I've paid my dues. I can't teach anymore. I look at those students and wonder which one will be the next to kill another Carrie. Then I feel anger. I cannot face a class again, at least not here. Not yet."

The two sat silently across from one another. Finally Dr. Rosen spoke.

"Where will you go, Frank? What will you do?"

"There was good insurance. I have an inheritance from an aunt. We were saving it for a home out on the Island." He smiled sadly and fixed his eyes upon a framed diploma on the plastered wall behind the principal. "Carrie and I dreamed about owning a sailboat. Nothing fancy or ostentatious. Spend the summer sailing. Quiet. Away from things. Thought I'd do that for a time."

Dr. Rosen studied his face for a few moments. "Dreams are for the living, Frank." He paused for a moment and then continued. "You buried Carrie last winter. Don't try to live her dreams. It won't bring her back."

"What have I got left?" Frank snapped. "You tell me, Dr. Rosen, just what have I got left?"

"You are a teacher, Frank." He placed his hands palms down on the blotter in front of him. "Sooner or later you will have to teach again. If not here, someplace else, and. . . ," he added, "you will be able to care again." Dr. Rosen glanced down at the manila folder on his desk. "You've been working on your credentials as an administrator to add to your teaching certificate. Contact me when you are ready. I will give you a good recommendation."

They stood together and Nate Rosen extended his hand. "If you change your mind. . . ."

"Thanks, Dr. Rosen. I think not." Frank's voice was husky.

"Promise to contact me if you want a recommendation, then."

Frank nodded, released the principal's hand, and stepped quickly out of the office.

The whole process took only a week after the close of school. The furniture, he sold. Small possessions he couldn't bring himself to discard, he packed in cheap cardboard storage boxes and stored them in his sister's attic. Carrie's clothing was the most difficult decision. He finally packed it in a box and gave it to the Goodwill store. He crammed his remaining possessions into a used VW bus and headed north on the New England section of the Thruway.

He discovered that acquiring a boat was simple. Acquiring

the right boat was almost impossible. He wandered around his first boatyard in Mamaroneck. Then from yard to yard along the New England coast he queried owners, probed keels, and examined bilges. Everytime he examined a boat, he listed the information in a journal. Norwalk. Milford. Guilford. New London. Jamestown. Town by town he thrust the city farther behind him in his quest. He thought he had found his boat as he drove by a yard near Marblehead one Saturday evening. It sat high on props and had a hand-painted "For Sale" sign taped to the bow. He checked into a motel and patiently waited out the last of a three-day drizzle. He was at the gate on Monday morning when the yard owner appeared at seven to open. The boat had been sold just before closing the previous Saturday. The yard-hand had failed to remove the sign. Frank accepted the cup of coffee offered in apology, and examined two other boats in the yard. They didn't feel "right" to him, however, and he thanked the owner and left. He was in no hurry. He would enjoy the quest just as if Carrie were with him.

Avoiding the turnpikes, he worked his way along the narrow stretch of New Hampshire coastline and crossed the bridge over into Kittery, the open steel mesh buzzing like something alive beneath his tires. He continued north along the beach route and reached the outskirts of Colonie Town. At two in the afternoon, he stopped for gasoline.

"Fill 'er up?" The wiry, sharp-chinned proprietor squinted at his license plate.

"Yes. Please." Frank swung his feet out from under the steering wheel and slipped out of the bus. He stretched and squinted toward the pebbled beach on the opposite side of the road. "Hot as it is, surprised there aren't more people out there."

"Sandier off'n Back-Bay Road."

Frank reached for his map. "That's the one that stays along the shore here?" He pointed to a thin line on the map marked with the number "1a."

"Ayeah." The old man clipped the last syllable short and nodded toward the bay. "Connects to Shelterport up the road a piece. See it pretty good across the bay now."

Frank followed the old man's gaze to the point of land crawling seaward and blending blue in the afternoon haze. The tops of two smokestacks thrust assertively up from the lay of the land. Immediately off the point, a beacon winked its intermittent message.

Frank glanced at the map again. "Pretty fair-sized town."

"Ayeah." The man replaced the nozzle in its cradle and took the bill Frank handed him. "Pulp come back. Some shipping. Beacon there marks the west side of a safe harbor. Tourists. Lumber." Frank listened to the man's dialect, enjoying the shadings of sounds produced when "there" became "they-yuh" and "marks" became "ma'ks" with the "a" flat rather than broad.

"How about boatyards?"

The man glanced up as he counted the change into Frank's hand. "All kinds. Depends. Big or little, power or sail."

"Sail," Frank grinned. "Not one of these floating bleach bottles. Wood."

"Them's the sweetest kind." The old man's eyes gleamed, but he appeared disinclined to say more.

Frank climbed up into the bus and started the engine.

"Myron Eaker's."

He peered out the window. "What?"

"Myron Eaker's yard on Wharf Street. Go right at the anchor. Can't miss it."

Frank waved his thanks and left.

He discovered that Colonie Town and Shelterport lay at opposite ends of a large "C" with Shelterport at the upper extremity. Back Bay Road connected the two with seven miles of beaches and summer camps on the side toward the ocean. More substantial year-round residences and businesses peppered the landward frontage. Shelterport sprawled westward halfway around the bay. Familiar eyesores, the ragged, ugly edges common to so many towns and cities, appeared: a garish billboard advertised a local realtor; motels hunched one against another along the road's shoulder, each advertising its particular attraction: "Color TV in Every Room"—"Kitchenette Apartments"—"Ocean View"—"Air Conditioning"—"Best Rates"—"Vacancy." A battered black-on-white sign advertised "Landfill hours 7:00 a.m.-4:00 p.m." and pointed down a gravelled road branching inland.

Back Bay Road widened and became Bay Street, and with increasing frequency side streets intersected from the left. Along one block where a new shopping center neared completion, modern streetlights sprouted from cement sidewalks like stately stemmed border plants, their pod-tipped tops bent oceanward. Frank felt that spores rather than light would burst over the street when darkness came. Residences-turned businesses, vacant lots, corner gas stations, traffic lights, and finally, shabby two and three-story buildings thickened around him.

Bay Street ended in a traffic circle dominated by a granite obelisk—a miniature Washington's Monument. A massive iron anchor lay in front of it, one fluke half buried in the circular green. Bay Street exited on the other side of the circle, sweeping inland to the main business district. Wharf Street followed the bay. Following the station owner's directions, Frank swung right and looked for Myron Eaker's yard. He finally found his boat—and Tammi.

"H'ain't much to look at now," Myron's words escaped from his mouth as though words were rationed. "But she's sound and fair." He led Frank along a line of boats until they came to a wide-beamed, shallow-draft catboat propped and cradled with 2 x 4's. "Hull ain't hogged, neither," Myron added. "When we haul 'em out for the winter, we support 'em proper. We don't go stingy like some ya'ds do."

Weeks of crawling in and out of sailboats of all descriptions had trained Frank's eye. He stepped back several paces and stared at the graceful sweep of the wide hull, changed his viewpoint and stared again. He reached in his pocket for his penknife. "Hadn't really thought in terms of a catboat before." He stepped in closer and probed the length of the long keel. "But it's . . . beautiful."

"Needs ha'dware, paintin' and engine work," Myron added, his face expressionless. "Do it yourself, boat's a ba'gain. Pay to have it done, price is fair." Myron inclined his head toward the wooden ladder leaning against the hull. "Go 'board 'n take a look. I'll be back in the office."

Frank spent the remainder of the morning looking under hatches, examining paintwork, probing for dry rot, sniffing bilges and looking for mildew and corrosion. Just before lunchtime he stood on the cabin sole, and leaned comfortably against the slid-forward main hatch. It caught him just under the shoulder-blades and he had a clear view forward. Turning to face aft, he could see Wharf Street, its sidewalk and occasional passers-by clearly. To either side and toward the harbor, hulls of larger boats sprouted like surrealistic mushrooms, their gently rounded hulls ranging from pristine whites to mottlings nondescript hues. He grinned. Certainly not a live-aboard, but good enough to learn the skills. Do the work himself and sell it, wouldn't lose any money. He could buy the bigger boat later. He climbed out of the cockpit and down the ladder.

Myron had pushed aside the clutter on his desk to make room for his lettuce and tomato sandwich. He glanced up as Frank walked into the office, and pointed to a smudged manila file folder. "Boat papers are in that."

"Guess you figured I would buy it."

Myron glanced at an ancient railroad clock on the plank wall. "Like courtin' a gal. More time you spend with 'em, more serious you get." Only the momentary twinkle in his eye acknowledged his own joke.

Twenty minutes later Frank owned his boat. Two hours after that, he had located a rooming house in the oak-treed residential section bordered by Bay and Wharf streets. A week following, he had settled into a work-sleep rhythm that pushed the shards of his former life into a hard, dark lump carefully tucked into a forgotten corner of his mind.

Only when Myron Eaker's wife acted as if her feelings would be hurt if he didn't share their Founder's Day picnic with them, did he take a day off. He wore his old clothes until he had eaten his fill at the clambake, walked the short distance to his rooming house to get cleaned up and changed, and then stepped out again.

He wandered across the park to Bay Street where the Boy Scouts and American Legion paraded ahead of the Masonic Lodge and Rebecca floats depicting the town's patriotic contributions since its pre-Revolutionary War founding. He walked the short distance back near the baseball field to have a hot-dog and iced-tea with Myron and his wife. It struck him as curious that such sharp-featured angularity masked a jovial, but genuine, friendliness.

Towards evening he strolled through the residential area surrounding the old community church, coming again to Bay Street where the business district began. He stood for a few moments on the northeast corner of Bay and High streets before the War Memorial, a pink granite slab bearing a brass tablet engraved with the names of Shelterport's dead from both World Wars. An old artillery piece, painted black, stood slightly to one side, and a short patch of grass stretched to a knee-high concrete wall. Some civic-minded individual had leaned a floral wreath against the slab. The wreath, the quiet of the evening, and the memorial made his caged loneliness leap out at him, and he turned away quickly in the direction of his rooming house. He would go to bed early.

The rest of July, and on through August he labored on his boat, anxious to get it into the water for at least a short time before winter. The new sails arrived just after Labor Day, and he stowed them under the forward hatch. He had only to finish the engine, a task he had put off till last.

There was a slight edge on the late September air. Working late the night before, Frank had decided to sleep for a few hours aboard the boat, and then complete the engine the next morning. Myron, accustomed to his eccentricities, had given him a key so he could have access to bathrooms and telephone.

By the time his drugstore alarm clock half-rang, half-rattled its six o-clock summons, a cold wind had blown in a thick, steel-gray cloud cover that stole all the gold from the dawn. Frank awakened, shivering. He slipped into a second pair of trousers and a grease-smudged jacket, lit the alcohol stove and poured water from a plastic jug into a battered four-cup coffeepot. Sliding the hatch forward, he stood and stretched. The raw wind chilled him at first, but as sleep left, he warmed himself by alternately sipping from his coffee mug and wrapping his hands around it.

An occasional car broke the early morning silence, its tires humming or chattering as they slipped from the tar-patched surface to the turn-of-the-century stones with which Wharf Street had once been paved. Before the stones, Myron had told him, it was originally dirt.

Frank hunkered back down into the cabin and slid the hatch almost closed to trap the heat from the stove. He would spend the next couple of hours crammed in alongside the engine. If he had to accept discomfort, he at least would make no concession to cold.

157

He didn't have to look at his watch to know when eight o'clock came. Since the Tuesday after Labor Day, gaggles of elementary school children scuttled down the cracked slate sidewalk in front of the yard. They attended the Nathaniel Crockett Elementary School—named, according to Myron, for a great-grandfather on his mother's side who led a dory full of local citizens to capture a British ship anchored in Shelterport Harbor during the Revolution.

Through the slit in the hatch, the ebb and flow of shrill conversations, shouts, and petty quarrels seeped in. As usual, he concentrated harder on what he was doing to destroy the harmony set up between them and the cold black lump in his mind. As usual, he wasn't successful. He could as easily stop tuning to them as a piano could stop sounding in sympathy to a plucked string.

The wrench dropped off the nut with a clank as he shifted his attention to the noise outside.

"SCARFACE! SCARFACE! COME AND LET US SLAP YOUR FACE!" The cries were high-pitched, mocking, carried on the cold morning breeze.

The dark lump swelled and burst molten and white as he scratched and clawed, backing his way out of the engine compartment. "God! Not here!" he breathed. He heard his jacket rip and felt the sharp scrape of an engine mounting bolt as he ended up on his knees in the cabin. "Not here, too!"

He slammed the hatch forward, stood, and yanked the three boards from the entrance, all the while searching out the source of the chant. He saw them, coming down the sidewalk, not yet abreast of the stern. A skinny girl, auburn pigtails flying, reading book clasped with both arms to her breast, stumbled panic-stricken down the uneven slate sidewalk. A group of boys, larger and older than she, bore close on her heels. One drew in, caught a long braid on the fly, and jerked it taut. The girl screamed and, trying to wrestle free, grasped her braid above his hand.

Although he recalled the scene many times in future years, Frank could never once remember how he got out of the boat, down the ladder, through the gate Myron opened promptly at 7:30 each morning, and out onto the sidewalk; but the rough wooden ladder propped against the side of the boat planted long splinters deep in the fleshy parts of his hands.

However it happened, suddenly he was in front of them. The girl freed herself and ran blindly into him, and he felt her desperate, trembling form against his legs.

"What do you think you're doing!" he roared.

The boys fell over one another in their anxiety to stop before they came within arm's reach.

Without waiting for an answer, Frank quickly and gently swept the girl behind him and clamped his large hand around the upper arm of the boy who had just released her hair.

"Lemme go, Mister! Lemme go!" The boy's voice had changed suddenly to a screech as he dropped his books and papers on the sidewalk to scatter in the wind.

"Yes, I'll let you go!" Frank snarled, grasping the boy's other arm, lifting him clear of the sidewalk, and shaking him. The boy tried to raise his hands to dislodge Frank's grip, but he was powerless as a puppet with severed strings.

"Lemme go! I'll get my Dad."

Frank stopped shaking him and drew him up until their eyes were only inches apart. "You do that," Frank said in a low voice. "You bring him here. And then I'll tell him how much fun you had leading a gang, and chasing a little girl half your size down the street making fun of a scar she has on her face." He set the boy down on the sidewalk with a jolt, but kept his grip on him. "If I ever hear of you doing anything like this again—anything—the principal of your school will hear about it first. Then your parents—" his voice went to a whisper. "And you might even get sent to a reform school."

"Please, Mister, please lemme go." The boy started crying. "I won't do it again. Honest. I won't do it again."

From the corner of his eye, Frank had noticed the rest of the gang drifting closer. Grimly, he realized that he had made the leader of the gang a victim. In one grotesque moment he had turned from protector to just short of a predator. And yet he knew the brutal necessity of his role if the girl were not to be victimized again. The other children had to see their leader terrified and sobbing. It was done. He released the boy. "Get out of here." He propelled the boy toward his friends. "The rest of you—get out of here, too!"

They flew away from him, the only sound the scuffing of their shoes on the slates.

Aware of a pair of arms clasped around his waist from behind, Frank glanced down and back.

Beneath her braids, her face was red from exertion and weeping. A burn scar, shiny and white, wrinkled the skin over the left temple, and left a glossy unpigmented path across the cheek, back of the jaw and down onto the side of the neck. Her eyes were green. He learned later that in moments of calm they would turn hazel. Her lips were a child's natural rose, and her chin pointed and trembling as she hiccupped the last of her sobs. Grimy streaks from her tears and the dirt from Frank's jeans smudged each cheek.

"Well—" he pulled a patterned red kerchief from his pocket and stooped down to wipe her face, but the kerchief had grime of its own, and he succeeded only in creating new smears. Frank had forgotten how warm and alive another human being could be. A flow of sympathy for her hurt washed away the last of his anger. "They shouldn't bother you any more."

She said nothing, but stared silently at him with tragic green eyes. He put his kerchief back in his pocket.

"Are you all right now?"

She nodded her head and snuffled.

Frank glanced up and saw Myron leaning against the door-jamb of the yard office. He could see the twinkle in Myron's eye, even at that distance.

"Would you like to go in to Myron's here and wash your face?"

She nodded her head and snuffled again.

He took her hand. "My name's Frank—Frank Rawlings. Can you tell me yours?" They walked together toward the office.

"Tammi." Her throat was still thick from crying.

"Tammi. That's a pretty name. Tammi what?" His voice was gentle, but against that gentleness, the angry lump he had crammed down into a corner of a conscience he wished he could forget, swelled like rising bread dough, and refused to be thrust back again. "Please," another Frank down inside pleaded. "I don't want to care again. I don't want to feel again." But it was too late.

The outward Frank grinned at Myron. "Think we could help a lady in distress fix her face?"

"Wouldn't be a bit s'prised," Myron replied in his careful, expressionless twang. He disappeared and a moment later stepped to the door with a rough hand towel, wet on one end. He handed it to Frank. "Doin' all right so far," he grunted and went back inside.

Frank wiped away the tear streaks, and struggled against the glow in the solemn green eyes. Finally he stood. "Better get to school now," he said awkwardly, "you're late already."

She turned and started to walk away, her shoulders slumped forward, her legs moving under her as if they operated independently. She stopped, turned, and stared back at him.

"Springer," she said.

"Springer." She pointed back toward the direction from which she came. "My daddy's the minister at the church." She turned and ran silently toward school.

"Community church couple of blocks this side of Bay Street," Myron supplied, standing in the doorway again. "Come a month or so ago. Real nice feller, so people say."

Frank hadn't heard him return, but he noticed that the hardness in the old man's face seemed to soften for a moment as he followed Frank's gaze in the direction of the school.

Myron was long dead. "Want that little girl's father to bury me," he had said, even though he never attended that church or any other. After two years, Frank had given up the struggle against himself and had returned, first to teaching, and then to college for three summers to get his administrator's certificate. Three things had not changed. He had never sold the catboat for a larger, live-aboard; he was still desperately lonely; and Tammi was still a frightened little girl, and now, he was convinced, more in need of help than ever.

Frank thumbed through some cards in a small plastic box, and reached for the telephone.

17

Jerome drummed his fingers on his green desk blotter. The interview had gone well enough, but he couldn't understand the tense undercurrent Jael had generated.

162

"Well, sending her out to buy a new outfit for my installation service will cheer her up," he thought. "Was a time when she had to wear 'missionary barrel specials.'"

He compressed his lips as he remembered the first time his father used the term during one of their frequent arguments.

"A preacher! A missionary!" His father snorted. "How you going to live?" Then his voice lost its derisive note. "There are preachers coming out of the woodwork, Jerome, and their wives and children get their clothing from 'missionary barrel specials.'" His voice became calmer. "Your mother and I have built a business for you, Jerome. We dreamed better things for you!"

"A preacher!" He sipped his coffee and glanced across the table to Jerome's mother, white-faced and silent.

"My father was a preacher. You know what it got him?" His shaggy eyebrows held the question with their fierce arch as he paused to answer his own question. "A heart attack at thirty-nine, that's what!" His eyebrows knit together again into a straight resentful line across the bottom of his wide forehead. "Oh, they took a 'love offering,' so they called it." He laughed, the low quiet sound carrying the pain through his thin lips from someplace deep inside. "It hardly paid for the casket, and. . . ," he clenched his fists on either side of his dinner plate as if the anger, once released, suffused his whole body, "and a month later they asked us to leave our home so they could paint and wallpaper the house for the new pastor. Ten years we lived there, and they wouldn't even buy a roll of linoleum."

He bit viciously into a croissant and washed it down immediately with a large mouthful of coffee. "No pension. No insurance. They wouldn't even pay enough for my father to afford the dollar a month premium."

"I still believe it's God's will for me to be a minister." Jerome felt his hands trembling with the fear he always experienced when he displeased his father.

"God's will? And what's God's will? Where do you find that?" his father challenged.

"I just feel it. It seems right to do that kind of work."

"Pah! As much as my father was taken advantage of, he wasn't that soft headed." Ignoring Jerome's glare, he continued. "God's will deals a lot more with what you are than what you do!" He nodded his head for emphasis.

"All right, maybe so," Jerome countered. He could hear blood pounding in his ears from his stress. Never before had he opposed his father so openly. Suddenly he discovered the terror that had cowed him into submission before was gone. He heard his words coming freely, defiantly. "But it's a lot easier to be what you're supposed to be when you're doing what you're supposed to do."

"So! For twenty years I've built a chain of department stores known for honesty and value—something you can be proud of—something that will make the lifetime of work your mother and I gave mean something—and you say, 'Thanks, but no thanks'?" He matched Jerome's glare.

Jerome sat silent, staring down into his half-finished dessert. His mother, still having said nothing, wept silently into her napkin.

"Where are you going to school to be a preacher, may I ask?" his father asked quietly. Only his heavy breathing betrayed his agitation.

"I've already applied." Jerome's voice was surly. "The acceptance came today."

"To that place down in Delaware."

"Yes."

"You've got a university education that your mother and I have saved half our lives for, and you're turning it down."

"I believe God wants me to go to Bible college." The words came measured in even syllables.

"Your friends would give an arm and a leg to go to the university!" He was truly puzzled at Jerome's statement. "And you're turning that down for a . . . a Bible college?"

Jerome didn't answer.

"And what am I supposed to do with 'Springer's Department Stores?'" His father's voice was edged with sarcasm and deep with bitterness. "Find another young man by the name of 'Springer,' and spend years training him? Maybe I can find a thirteen-year-old and start him in the mail room after school like I did you."

Unable to argue, Jerome set his lips in a straight line and simply repeated, "I'm going to Bible college."

"And what do you use for money?" His father's voice had turned cold. It was the same tone he used when he dealt with a delinquent account.

Jerome sat stunned. "I . . . I thought the money set aside for the university. . . ."

His father's eyes pinned him to his seat. "That money was set aside for the university, nothing else. You want to be a preacher? Go to Bible college instead? Fine. You pay for it yourself." He paused for a moment. When he spoke again, his voice was softer, and more gentle than Jerome had heard it in years. "You might burn your bridges, Jerome, but we won't. If you find you have made a mistake, that money will be there. But if you are going to be a minister or a missionary, or whatever, you might as well find out what it's like to scratch for the next dollar."

They sat in silence for a few moments, Jerome, his father, and his mother.

She had stopped her silent weeping, and from habit, she picked up the silver coffeepot, added a little to each cup, and set it down again, soundlessly, on the linen tablecloth.

Jerome cleared his throat. "Excuse me, please."

His father nodded silently.

Jerome rose and started to walk from the room.

"One last thing, Jerome." His father's voice was weary.

Jerome stopped beneath the archway separating the dining area from the living-room and looked back at his father. Somehow, the man, once so imposing and hard, seemed to have withered inside his suit with Jerome's diminishing fear; the man he now saw was tired, beaten, fortyish, and prematurely gray. Even the lines dropping from his widely flared nostrils to the turned-down corners of his mouth seemed to have deepened during dinner.

"I hope, Jerome, that your children honor their father and their mother more than you have honored us this evening." He drew his breath in with an effort. "Maybe your children should hurt you as you have hurt us this night. Maybe then you'll see that to do God's will is not an excuse to dishonor your father and mother." He withered a little more, turned away and lifted his coffee cup to his lips.

Two weeks later, they drove him to the bus station in his father's gold-colored Cadillac.

"Remember, Jerome," his father had said, his voice soft and husky. "Your mother and I are not of the 'make your own bed and lie in it,' school." He grasped Jerome by the shoulders. "If it doesn't work out, you always have a home. Promise me you'll come home—if it doesn't work?" He embraced Jerome in an awkward, unpracticed hug.

Jerome stood stiffly, his hands at his sides, embarrassed at his father's embrace. He was careful to give no nod or affirmation of promise. He felt his father lessen his grip and then let go. His mother kissed him good-bye, and he returned her kiss dutifully. He did wave through the window as the bus rolled away from the gate.

He reached the campus twelve hours later. When he unpacked, he found an envelope packed among his shirts. It contained two hundred dollars. The note with the money read, "Jerome—keep for emergency. Leave enough to get home with." It was in his father's handwriting. His mother had added in her finely-shaped script, "We love you, Jerome." Jerome put the money in an envelope and mailed it home the next day. The money he had received from selling his car covered his initial costs. Part and full-time jobs each semester and during summers provided the rest.

His mother died the Christmas before his graduation. He and his father had tried awkwardly to comfort one another, but the distance had grown too great. His father's hurt and Jerome's resentment had been swept away, temporarily, by their mutual sadness, but neither found the strength to reach first toward the other.

Although Jael insisted they send an invitation, he didn't expect his father to come to the wedding.

"You are my son," he had said simply when he appeared the night of the rehearsal. When Jerome introduced him to Jael, dressed then in sweatshirt and jeans, his father grasped her by the shoulders and looked into her eyes for almost a minute. Jael had returned the gaze, her wide-set green eyes confident and unflinching. At last he broke the silence. "I suspect that my son has finally done something smart—and," he smiled, "he has an eye for beauty." He released his grasp upon her shoulders, but before he could drop his arms, she lifted hers and entwined them around his neck. She placed a kiss on his cheek.

"Thank you," she said. Then, so only he and Jerome, standing next to her could hear, she added, "I shall love him as you and his mother have loved him."

Jerome was puzzled by her comment, and by the depth of their shared gaze as his father returned her kiss.

When Tammi was born, his father had sent Jael a huge

arrangement of flowers. Once when he had returned home to Croughton's Corners from a week of gospel meetings, he found his father seated at the kitchen table playing Chinese checkers with Tammi. Jerome was surprised at the softness and the happiness in the man's aging face. Afterwards, as they stood between the pines out back and stared across the lake, his father had finally admitted, "Well, Jerome. I was wrong. It looks like this is where you were meant to be, . . . and what you were meant to be."

Jerome forced his eyes to keep staring across the lake, but he strained his peripheral vision to glimpse his father's profile. While he made no reply his mind roared exultantly. *"I did it! He finally had to admit it! He was wrong! I beat him!"* He had difficulty controlling his glee.

"I, too, was successful," his father continued. "I learned too late that the success I was after . . . well. . . . " In the gathering dusk, they had walked a short distance away from the house. He turned and looked back toward the kitchen window set in the back wall, a pine tree on either side. The light from the kitchen formed a framed portrait of Jael as she stood at the sink doing the supper dishes. The yellow light illuminated her hair slightly and formed a yellow and auburn crown. "I was wrong about success, too, Jerome. You helped me learn that. You can tell it's the wrong kind when it leaves you with loneliness." He glanced from Jael to Jerome and back again as they stepped toward the house. "Don't go after the same kind of success I did, Jerome."

At the end of that week, his father returned to the city. Jerome didn't quite understand his father's musings, but he had understood that his father had admitted to a mistake, that Jerome had been right. He had admitted that Jerome was successful. As he watched his father's Cadillac drive away from the house, Jerome determined that his father would have to admit even more how wrong he had been. There would be a larger church and a larger work. He would support his family. He didn't need his father's help; he didn't want his father's business.

In the evil time, when Benni died, private nurses had appeared for Jael and the baby. Although no one would say for certain, Jerome suspected his father had paid for them. He felt resentment. His father well knew that Jerome would have refused the help had he known for sure the source of the funds.

His father's gaze, deep with eternity, fixed on Jael. The eyes had grown sunken and hollow. The strong brows were just as straight and just as gray, but the anger and bitterness had been replaced with truth. Glancing weakly to Jerome, he motioned him closer. Jerome took his hand and bent down to hear his whisper. "Many years ago, I breathed an evil prayer for you." He smiled at the memory of the supper table. "I have taken it back a thousand times since."

Jerome frowned slightly, trying to grasp elusive memories of that night. What he himself had said still remained clear, but his father's utterances had languished, long unreviewed, in some corner of his mind.

"Treasure Jael and Tammi," he whispered. "Don't let your . . . desire for success . . . ashes . . . mine. . . ." He rested again for a few moments and then turned his eyes silently to Jael. Jerome stood and moved aside for her. She bent down, as he had, and his father whispered something unintelligible into her ear. She nodded, kissed him gently on the cheek, and sat holding his hand for a long time.

Later, they had to wait only a few minutes for the nurse to give them the large brown paper sack with his valuables. "I couldn't quite hear what he said to you, near the last," Jael said, her eyes red from tears.

"Something about success," Jerome replied, shaking his

head slowly from side to side. "Kept asking me to forgive him." He smiled, "I said 'yes,' though I'm not sure what for." He put his arm around Jael's shoulder.

He couldn't cry at the funeral, either.

The telephone's jangle jarred him out of his musings. As he reached for it, he smiled wryly. Three months from now, a secretary would screen his calls. If only his father could see him now.

"Pastor Springer speaking."

"Jerome?"

"Yes?"

"Frank Rawlings at school."

Jerome leaned back in his chair and smiled. "Well, hello." He put one foot up on his desk. "Say, Frank, I won't be able to take you up on sailing this Saturday. I. . . ."

"Not calling about that, Jer," Frank interrupted.

"Oh?" He fixed his gaze on the black-framed Bible college diploma hanging on what he jokingly called his "Wall of Fame." At first the dominant decoration on his study wall, it had since become lost amid the other plaques, pictures, and awards of appreciation.

"You sound serious. Is there a problem?"

"Well—yes."

Jerome leaned forward and reached for a pen and scratch-pad. "One of our young people?"

There was silence at Frank's end.

"Well, it *is* one of our young people you're calling me about." Jerome fixed his eyes on a black metal plate fastened to a richly-finished walnut silhouette of the state. He had received that for getting churches involved in a foster home program for troubled teens.

"Yes, Jerome." Frank paused again. "I . . . this isn't something we can discuss over the telephone. Can you come down right away?"

"You sound really upset, Frank. Is it one of the church kids?"

The telephone became silent again.

"Jerome, did Tammi stay home from school today?"

"No. Left the same as usual." Jerome narrowed his eyes. "Isn't she at school?"

"Missed her first two classes and didn't show up for her third."

"Be right there."

Jerome replaced the telephone slowly in its cradle and struggled to recall if Tammi had said anything about a dentist's or doctor's appointment. "Jael probably scheduled her in someplace and forgot to write a note," he grumbled. "Done that before often enough." He stood and slipped into his sportscoat. "Strange she didn't say anything this morning." Closing the study door behind him, he stepped across the foyer of the empty church and down the three wooden steps to the landing at the side entrance. The musty church-basement smell reminded him that he had to call a work-day two Saturdays from now for a painting party.

"People want a place to look and smell clean," he thought, unlocking the car. "It's 'the little foxes that spoil the vines.' People leave when a place looks and smells bad."

When Jerome arrived at school, the black hands of the wall clock above the counter in the main office indicated eleven forty-five. He waited for the secretary, several feet to his right, to finish listening to the mumble of a student complaint. Another secretary at a desk in back of the counter studiously avoided his eyes as she counted something resembling coupons.

Compressing his lips, Jerome suppressed a wry grin.

"Education's holy of holies," he thought. Instead of the

heavy odor of temple incense, institutional smells of paper, plastic, "wood product" panelling, and chalk pervaded the place. Even the teachers left conversation outside when entering this inner court.

"May I help you?" The measured businesslike irritation in the voice indicated that the question was a second invitation.

Jerome glanced to his right. The student had gone.

"I have an appointment with Mr. Rawlings." He stood, unbowing, irreverently refusing to drop his gaze.

She blinked her displeasure. "Yes, he's expecting you." Her lips tightened a little. "It's the third door on the right." She motioned to the self-closing gate at the end of the counter. "Go right in."

Jerome slipped through the gate and walked down to Frank's office. Entering, he saw Frank gazing through the office window, his large football-player silhouette blocking the view to the street.

"Morning, Frank."

Rawlings turned slowly. "Morning, Jerome." He motioned to a chair at the side of his desk. "Sit down."

Something in Rawlings' voice triggered alarm. Jerome sat slowly in the black vinyl chair. "All right." His lips tightened. He felt the rims of his ears turn cold and his stomach tighten. "Let's have it, Frank."

Rawlings removed his wire-rimmed glasses and placed them gently on his desk. He looked directly into Jerome's eyes. "We've been picking up some—well, some bad talk over the past few days."

Jerome sat carefully motionless, his hands studiously loose and relaxed in his lap. He heard his voice say, "Go ahead."

"Well. . . ." Frank's forehead beaded with an unprofessional perspiration. "I started checking around."

Jerome felt himself shrivelling. "What kind of talk, Frank?"

"Tammi and Ted." The voice was calm, controlled. "Bad talk. Really bad."

Jerome fought to keep his own voice even. "I can't believe that, Frank." He licked his suddenly dry lips. "I don't remember the last time they had a date."

"Tammi isn't at school today, Jerome." Frank's pale blue eyes glanced down at the folders in front of him. "And you told me she wasn't home."

"She might have had a dentist's appointment or some such thing. Let's not go jumping to conclusions, Frank." Jerome breathed heavily. "Who's doing all this talking anyway?" His voice was pitched higher than usual. "They're a couple of nice kids. People gossiping about them ought to be horsewhipped." He stood and walked stiff-legged to the window. Glancing through it, he stepped back to Frank's desk and leaned forward, resting his weight on his hands. "Who's spreading all this garbage around, anyway?"

Frank glanced at the manila folders on his blotter. "So far," he sighed and started again. "So far, we've had the stories coming from three sources."

"Yes?"

"They've all been traced back to Ted."

Jerome sank down into his chair.

"Ted?" He no longer spoke with the well-modulated tones of the trained preacher.

"He must know where she is. Haven't you sent for him?"

Frank looked up again and breathed deeply. "Sent for him first thing this morning. . . ."

"He gone too?" Jerome wiped his brow. His throat wanted to close over his words.

"No. He's in the detention hall," Frank replied quietly.

Jerome sat down deliberately. He swallowed, trying to moisten a suddenly dry throat, and he couldn't stop the ring-

ing in his ears. "I'd like to talk to him, Frank." His voice was
hoarse with anger.

18

Ted swung into the school parking lot and glimpsed Ron
Farmer's green van parked next to the gym. Dodging the
speed bumps on the black-topped lot, he zig-zagged across,
enjoying the grumble of the deep-toned exhaust system he
had just installed. Lurching to a stop beside the van, he grinned
at Ron and Harry Harden, who was seated in the passenger
seat.

"Hey, Poppa Tolleson, how you doin'?" Ron smirked.

Ted's grin disappeared. "Cool it, Ron," he snapped. "Told
you not to spread that around."

"What you so uptight for?" Harry interrupted. "So she can
get an abortion. Big deal."

"Yeah. One thing you guys didn't tell me when I bet that I
could score with her."

The boys in the van leered at him "What's that?"

"She has a religion hang-up. She won't get an abortion."

"That's her problem, then. You're not going to marry her."

"Hey—'I came! I saw! I conquered!'—but MARRY?" Ted
grew serious. "Sex is one thing. Marriage is another. At least,
that's what my Dad told me the last time."

"The last time?" Harry's eyes narrowed with the question.

"Yeah," Ted continued. His voice no longer carried a brag.
"Girl got pregnant back in Oceanside." His lips formed a thin

bitter line. "Wasn't my fault, either. Never even got close to her."

"She claim you were. . . ."

"She and her folks knew we had money. The guy who did it couldn't even afford the gas to get his jeep to the beach."

"So you got stuck."

"And how. Nobody'd believe me when I told them that I wasn't the guy. Not when she stood there pointing her finger at me."

"Man. You sure got a rotten deal."

"My father wouldn't believe me, either." Ted focused his gray eyes on a pebble embedded between the treads of the van's back tire. "He bought her parents off—paid for the abortion and a whole lot more."

"What happened then?"

"I was staying with my Mom. Only reason she kept me around was for what she could get from the trust fund—she managed it. But when the thing with that girl happened, guess she figured I was causing too much trouble. They sent me here to live with my uncle."

"Boy," Ron remarked, "you sure got a rotten deal."

"No more." Ted grinned bitterly. "Way I figure, I already got the blame for getting a girl pregnant. Seems like I paid in advance." He looked at his two friends. "So when you guys gave me the dare to score with the toughest girl in school, I figured I'd have the fun. I've already had the hassle." He stepped out of his truck and slammed the door. "Let's get to class."

"Well it's all over school that she's an easy take," Ron mumbled as they walked. "Is she?"

"Why don't you try?" Ted replied with a twisted smile. "I didn't have much of a problem."

"She try to make trouble for you?" Harry asked.

"Just moons around. Tries to get me after school to 'Talk.'"

He shifted his books to the other hand as he yanked open the door to the school hallway. "No, she hasn't made any trouble." They stopped in front of their lockers and spun the combinations.

"What if she does?" asked Ron.

"My dad'll do the same thing he did before—write a fat check, and that'll be the end of it. No big deal." Ted slammed shut his locker. "See you later."

Ted and Harry headed toward Mr. Carston's room.

"What if she doesn't want a check from your dad, Ted?" Harry asked. He stared straight ahead, frowning slightly.

"Are you kidding?" Ted retorted chuckling. "My dad's right about one thing—money talks. Her folks'll take it—how'd it look for a minister's daughter to have an illegitimate kid? They're going to need it to get her out of town—'Go visit an aunt,'" he sneered. They reached Mr. Carston's classroom. "My dad told me, 'Money always talks—it's just that some people's hearing improves with the size of the wad.'"

Harry stopped him at the doorway. "They're not like you think, Ted," he said quietly. "I never thought you'd go through with the dare. You're bigger than me and tougher than me, but man, . . ." his eyes narrowed as he hissed the remainder, "I feel cheap for being involved in the whole thing. And," he added, "I feel sorry for you, real sorry." He turned and walked into the room. Harry never even glanced over to him when Mr. Carston placed the pink office call slip on Ted's desk.

"Now," was all Mr. Carston had said.

And now Ted sat sullenly in the outer room adjoining Mr. Rawlings' office, "So this is what the guys call the 'Holding Tank,'" he thought. He stared at the wall opposite him and wondered if all schools purchased their "gas station rest-room green" paint at the same salvage sale.

"Ted?" Mr. Rawlings stood framed in the doorway leading to his office, "Would you come in please?"

176

19

Jael frowned slightly as the door swung open against the pressure of the key. "Jerome must think we're back in the mountains," she muttered. Stepping inside she kicked the door closed with her foot. "Jerome? Are you home?"

"In here." Jerome's voice seemed curiously subdued.

"The front door was open," Jael said, stepping into the living room and dropping her packages onto the couch. "I thought maybe—Jerome, what's wrong?"

He sat in the platform rocker near the window, both his feet flat on the floor, his hands lying limply in his lap. "Tammi's gone." His voice was flat.

"What?" Jael sank to the couch beside her packages.

"Didn't show up at school today. Frank Rawlings called." He gazed blankly at a thread on the carpet.

"That's not possible," Jael said, her voice low, puzzled. "She left on time this morn—." Her eyes widened. "You don't think someone's—she's—did you call the police?"

"No. She hasn't been hurt, not that way." He shifted his gaze from the carpet to his hands. "She's run away."

"Run away!" Jael whispered through the sudden clamping in her throat. "How do you know that? Why?" Her voice rose in pitch as she grew more excited.

"She's pregnant." The words fell dull and heavy from Jerome's mouth. He continued staring at his hands.

"Preg—" Jael stared at him. She swallowed. "Pregnant?" She gazed out the window at the scarred trunk of the apple tree and fumbled through her purse beside her for a handkerchief to wipe the tears from eyes suddenly filled. "How do you know?" The tears glistened on her cheeks as she dabbed at first one eye and then the other. "Ted?"

"Yes. It's all over school." His voice was still flat, helpless.

"Oh, no. Not Tammi." She started to sob now, short silent sobs that started deep in her abdomen and rippled up to burst through her throat. "Please, God, not Tammi."

They sat, Jerome's stare fixed on first one detail in the room and then another, Jael sobbing quietly, her handkerchief now soaked as she clutched it against her face. The imported German clock on the wall opposite the window dropped its sad, slow "click-clack" like large heavy drops slipping from a leaking faucet.

Jerome stood, walked slowly to the window and gazed at the May-green leaves on the trees bordering the street. "Where could she be?" He turned to face Jael. "How could she be so thoughtless and ungrateful?"

Jael, still clenching her handkerchief against her face, leaned back a little and stared at him with widened eyes.

"You know what she's done?" He spit the words out, "She's destroyed everything we've worked for. Gone!" He clenched his fist and hit the window frame with short, sharp controlled blows, again and again, absently following the dull rhythmic beat of the carved wooden clock, like another beat of another clenched hand upon a linen-covered table many years ago.

Jael removed the handkerchief from her face. Her lips formed a thin, bitter line.

"Is that all you can think about?" Tight with emotion, her voice was high-pitched but calm. "Everything *you've* worked for?" She flared her nostrils slightly and narrowed her eyes. "Yes, *you!* Not *we.*"

Stunned and silent, Jerome had turned his head at the beginning of her outburst to watch her. His frown deepened, and his lips turned down at the corners.

"Here Tammi is God knows where, and all you can think about is how it'll affect what *you've* worked for." Jael's eyes flashed green as the locked-up bitterness over their marriage poured from her, as evil as the serpentine contents of another vessel so long ago. "And it was you—you and your lust for success—not 'we'. I never wanted to come here!"

Jerome, his face a stone-like mask, turned to stare out of the window again.

"In Frank's office," he said, his voice vague, "I asked Ted if he knew where she might have gone." He turned to face her again. "He didn't know." He stared at the clock.

Jael sat, breathing rapidly after her outburst. Finally she asked, "Isn't there anyone else? Surely she must have told one of her girlfriends."

"One of her girlfriends?" Jerome laughed harshly. "I asked about that. Rawlings said as far as he could tell, she didn't have any—no one close enough to confide in, at any rate." He paced back to his chair and sank heavily into it. "Well she sure confided in somebody—with a vengeance," he said angrily.

"Well," Jael snapped, "that burn scar on the side of her face certainly doesn't attract people to her."

"Especially when her mother makes her conscious of it at every opportunity!"

"Conscious of it?" Jael hissed. "How can she *not* be conscious of it? All girls her age worry—even about a silly pimple. She has a scar that will mark her the rest of her life—all because you were too busy with 'God's work' to fix the handle on a pot!" She paused, panting for breath. "And now," she added, her voice almost a whisper, "she has another scar, worse than the one on her face, because you were too busy with 'God's work' to . . . to spit in her direction!"

"Jael!" Jerome heaved himself to his feet, his arms straight by his side, his fists clenched.

"It's true!" Eyes gleaming with the sudden release of her ten years' frustration and bitterness, she continued in a low, steely voice. "I'm beginning to wonder, Jerome, was it really God's work? Or was it Jerome's work? Is it God who keeps a father—

even if he is a minister—too busy doing 'God's work' to dig a hole for an apple tree?" She stared over his shoulder at the tree trunk outside the window. "Isn't planting a little girl's apple tree important to God?"

Jerome stared at her, confused. "Jael, we're talking about a sixteen-year-old girl who has committed fornication," Jerome said evenly. "I love that girl, Jael. I love her more than my own life." He paused. "I love you, too. More than anything else in the world. You knew when we married that being a pastor's wife—well—it's not the same as others."

"Doesn't God expect a pastor to show his love to his wife and daughter clearly enough to let them know they're important to him?" Jael retorted. "Or does a pastor get a special dispensation from God freeing him from paying at least as much attention to his wife and children as he does to his flock?"

Jerome turned to stare through the window again, his back toward her. "So it all comes out my fault." He laughed suddenly, humorlessly. "My father would sure love to be here now." He squeezed his eyes shut and drew his hand slowly across his face as if he were attempting to rip away the last several hours as one would rip out and discard a spoiled page from a diary. He opened his eyes again and focused on the windowpane. A bee, its buzzing punctuated with a faint "tic. . . . . . .tic" as it beat against the invisible windowpane barring its escape, seemed to fill the room with its sound.

"He always told me everything I did wrong. Too bad he's dead. He'd really enjoy himself today."

"Enjoy himself!" Jael laughed. "Jerome, he loved you! From the first day I met him, I could see that. Were you so intent in proving him wrong that you were blind to that, too?"

The silence stretched between them again, gathering tension from their anger and confusion.

The wooden clock whirred, clanged the hour, and resumed scattering its endless soft clicks through the room.

"All these years—you've blamed me for Tammi's burns."
Jael still clutched her handkerchief. She no longer cried.

"And for Benni's death, I suppose," Jerome sighed. A
heavy, accusing silence hung between them. "Tell me, Jael,"
Jerome continued quietly, "Why didn't you leave me?" He
turned to face her now.

She lifted her eyes to meet his. "I wanted to," she admitted,
and then looked down again. "I even packed my suitcase,
once—the day Tammi and I dug the hole for that tree."

"That long ago." He stared at her, trying to comprehend.
"What stopped you?"

"For better or for worse," Jael answered, her voice a half-
whisper.

"What?" Jerome cocked his head a little and frowned.

"For better or for worse," Jael repeated in a stronger voice.
"That was the promise, wasn't it? Wasn't that the commitment
I made at the altar?"

"The promise—duty—that's all that held you?"

"Tammi needed a place to grow up." She paused. "To
leave would have destroyed you as a pastor. I didn't see much
point in that."

Jerome drew his palm across his brow and down the side of
his face. "Destroy me as a pastor!" He laughed harshly. "And
you now tell me that what I thought was affection and love
these last ten years was a sham, a hypocrisy?"

"I don't know," Jael said, shaking her head from side to side
and refusing to meet his gaze. "I don't know. I try to love you,
Jerome. But I've been so empty for so long—it always came
back to doing what I have to do." She sat staring at the handkerchief wadded in her hand. "Sometimes, like now, it seems
like I should have left. Maybe Tammi wouldn't be pregnant
and a runaway."

"Do you still want to leave?"

Seated on the couch, she drew away from him a little as he
lifted his hand to stroke the top of her head.

"I don't know."

He looked slowly around the room. "Well," he sighed. "I doubt you'll have to worry much about destroying me as a pastor now." He smiled sadly. "And we certainly won't be staying in Shelterport, not after the church finds out." He walked back to the window. The bee no longer buzzed but lay on the sill, its wings battered, its legs barely supporting its weight. Jerome absently opened the window and watched the bee crawl across the painted wood to the outer sill. It rested a moment and then, erratically, flew from sight.

"You are free to leave, now, Jael, if you want to. There's no more duty involved." His voice was barely audible.

"Tammi needs us," she replied. "Together." The resignation to duty edged her tone.

"Yes, I suppose she does," Jerome sighed. "She has trouble enough. We need not add to it."

20

Jerome walked back to the platform rocker and sank down into it. "Well," he sighed, looking at Jael, seated on the couch, her purse still in her lap. "Guess I'd better call Sharkeys. Better they hear it from us." He picked up the phone and dialed.

Jael sat clenching and unclenching her fingers around her damp handkerchief.

"Hello?" Jerome's voice sounded mechanical and flat. All the energy seemed to have drained from it. "Bill? Jerome. Yes. Say, could you come over for a few minutes? Yes, she has . . . this morning sometime . . . yes . . . all day." He replaced the phone on its cradle and sat staring again. "Well," he sighed. "I wasn't fast enough. He's already heard."

More silence.

"When will he be coming?" Jael's soft voice was muffled by the tightness in her throat.

"Right away. Wife's coming, too."

"I'd better put some coffee on."

Jerome's puzzled gaze followed Jael as she stood, placed her purse deliberately on the couch, and plodded heavily out to the kitchen. "Duty," he muttered. "God. Have I killed everything in her except duty?"

Ten minutes later, Bill Sharkey swung his large Buick into the gravel driveway, slid out of the driver's door, slammed it shut, and then walked around the front of the car to wait for his wife to complete her emerging process. Jerome grunted in disgust with himself, trying to eradicate the incongruous similarity between Bettina Sharkey's plump form extricating itself from the Buick's doorframe and a cicada struggling to free itself from its glossy tan shell. The two stood for a moment, straightening clothing and hair, and then came up the walk toward him.

"Jerome." Bill's voice was soft and subdued, and his grasp firm and warm as he shook hands.

"Thanks for coming over so quickly, Bill, Bettina." He nodded in her direction.

"Jael in the kitchen?" Bettina's usually strident voice had softened with genuine concern.

"Yes." Jerome shook his head slowly. "Making coffee."

"Helps to keep one's hands busy," Bettina said as her large form forged down the hall toward the kitchen.

"No idea where Tammi went?" Bill asked, following Jerome into the living room. He glanced at Jael's brown patent purse lying on the couch and the damp, crumpled handkerchief between the straps. He sat at the opposite end of the couch.

"Not yet."

"Too soon to call the police," Bill commented after a short silence.

"They won't even accept a report until a full day has gone by."

"I know," Bill said sadly. "Went through the same thing when our Tom ran away."

"Oh?" Jerome raised his eyebrows at this new piece of information.

"Found out where he was pretty quickly," Bill continued. "Friend's house. Let him stay until he was ready to come home. Had a long talk. Aired some things out. Was better after that."

"Spent the morning calling all the friends we could think of—Frank Rawlings and I."

"Sure felt like a failure as a father when that happened," Bill continued, oblivious of Jerome's comment. "About destroyed Bettina." A moment later he added. "Seemed to change her, somehow. She started wanting things better than other people had." He glanced sadly toward the kitchen. "Always tried to find something wrong with everybody, after that. Wasn't always that way."

The two sat in the living room, each locked in his private pain. Bettina's gushing soprano and Jael's occasional muffled murmur ebbed and flowed from the kitchen.

"Huh. Here comes Frank," Jerome said, looking out the window at the car sliding up behind Bill's Buick. "Wonder if he's found anything out?"

"He's a good man," Bill added. "Even if he does spend more Sundays sailing than singing in the choir." He chuckled at his feeble attempt at a joke.

Jerome waited for Frank at the door. "Anything yet?" He held the door open and ushered him inside.

"Yes," Frank said. "Not much, but it's something." He

184

stepped in and closed the door behind himself. "Oh, hello, Bill—saw your car out there."

He walked slowly across the room and slouched into an easy chair across from Jerome.

"Called kids in all morning, Jerome. Finally got back to Ted again." He raised his eyebrow slightly at Jerome and shifted his eyes almost imperceptibly toward Bill.

"Go ahead," Jerome said numbly, following Frank's glance. "Go ahead. He has to know."

"Well, Ted said she went to a doctor on the other side of town. Didn't know his name." He paused. "That's when they found out for sure."

"How long ago was that?" Jerome glanced toward a sound in the hallway. Jael and Bettina stood listening solemnly.

"Little less than a month ago."

"A month ago!" Jerome gasped.

"And all I could do was to scold her for being so moody," Jael added, beginning to cry again.

Jerome shook his head sadly. "If she'd only said something. If she'd only trusted us."

"We weren't home much for her to talk if she wanted to," Jael snapped. "As I recall there were a lot of 'important' meetings this last month." She glared at Bill Sharkey.

Embarrassed, Jerome glanced at Bill, whose only reaction was a slight reddening of the ears. Jerome shifted his gaze back to Frank. "Nothing else?"

"Afraid not."

Jerome looked at the wooden clock clicking softly on the wall. "Too late to check doctors' offices now. It's past five." He glanced again at Bill, whose expression remained carefully blank.

"Coffee's ready," Bettina said quietly, putting her arm around Jael and steering her out toward the kitchen. "Make us all feel better." Her heavy steps receded, and the clink of cups and clatter of silverware from last-minute table-setting followed their departure.

"How Jael can even think to serve coffee—with all this—amazes me," Frank said, shaking his head.

"Always been like that," Jerome responded, standing. "Says it helps her sort things out better if she stays busy." He led the others into the kitchen.

The telephone rang as they sipped their third cup of coffee. Jerome set his mug down quickly, splashing a pale brown puddle around it, and hurried to the living room.

"Who? Yes. He's here." He raised his voice, "Frank—for you." He placed the receiver on the mahogany table and returned to the kitchen.

"Hello? Webb?" Frank's voice raised with expectation. The group in the kitchen sat silently, straining to hear.

"Great!" Frank's voice was calm, but there was a smile in it. "Listen, Webb, we really appreciate your taking your own time to poke around." He listened a moment more. "We'll get back to you if we can think of anything else." He hung up the phone and stepped back into the kitchen.

"Fellow I sail with works on the police force," Frank explained, returning to the table. "Gave him a copy of Tammi's picture from the school yearbook." He peered intently at them through his thick-lensed glasses. "Ticket agent at the bus station remembers someone looking like her buying a ticket sometime last week." He looked down at his cup and half-eaten chocolate-chip cookie.

"Does he remember where?" Jael's question hung heavy over the table.

"That's the bad part," Frank said quietly. "Could've been Boston or Portland, or even New York." He paused and then continued. "It was a busy time and better than a week ago. He tried, but he couldn't remember."

"Isn't there anything else we can do?" Bill Sharkey asked.

"Harry's going to go down to the bus station tomorrow and

show the picture around to the drivers who had routes today," Frank offered. "Actually, he's doing the same thing as if you had turned in a report." He added, nodding toward Jerome and Jael. "Good thing he had the day off."

"Looks like the Lord had his hand in that," Bill added, a little self-consciously.

"I've been screaming prayers from deep down inside ever since I found out she was missing," Jerome said, "But somehow, I still feel awfully"—he glanced at Jael—"empty."

"I've lived with that feeling a long time," Frank remarked. "In fact, I'm an expert on it."

The listeners at the table sat silently, waiting for him to continue.

"Carrie and I, we used to read the Scriptures a lot, even if we didn't go to church as often as we should have." He focused his sad eyes absently on the rose design on the sugarbowl. "After she died, I even stopped reading the Bible altogether, for a while." There was another silence. "But there's a lot of time to be alone on a little boat, and I've been doing a lot more reading and a lot more thinking." He reached into the breast pocket of his suitcoat and removed a thin, worn Testament. "I found something that helped with the emptiness." He opened the Testament to the back and began to read.

"O LORD, thou hast searched me, and known me.
Thou knowest my downsitting and mine uprising,
thou understandest my thought afar off.
Thou compassest my path and my lying down, and
art acquainted with all my ways.
For there is not a word in my tongue, but, lo, O
LORD, thou knowest it altogether.
Thou hast beset me behind and before, and laid
thine hand upon me.
Such knowledge is too wonderful for me; it is high, I
cannot attain unto it.

*Whither shall I go from thy spirit? or whither shall I
flee from thy presence?*

*If I ascend up into heaven, thou art there: if I make
my bed in hell, behold, thou art there.*

*If I take the wings of the morning, and dwell in the
uttermost parts of the sea; Even there shall thy hand
lead me, and thy right hand shall hold me.*

*If I say, Surely the darkness shall cover me; even the
night shall be light about me."*

Frank stopped reading, closed his Testament, and glanced
around.

Jael sat, confused, staring at him. She had shared with him
once, long ago, what she had felt at Benni's death; but she had
said nothing about the Psalm.

He had attended church off and on ever since she had
brought the chocolate-chip peace offering to the boatyard a
few days after his rescuing Tammi. Myron had directed her to
the boat hunched against the yard fence, warming itself in the
morning sun like a giant white housecat.

"Ahoy, there, Mr. Rawlings?" she had called from the foot of
the ladder, trying not to shiver in the chill air.

A moment later a large man with unruly brown hair and a
grease-smudged face emerged from the cabin and leaned
slightly to peer down at her as he wiped his hands on an
already greasy rag. He wore a long-sleeved blue work shirt and
a threadbare pair of jeans.

"Yes. Hello there." His voice was friendly enough, but a little
preoccupied.

"I'm Jael Springer, Mr. Rawlings. You became a knight in
shining armor to my daughter the other day."

The man laughed. "Just a moment," he said, and disappeared into the cabin again. He reappeared shortly with his

shirt buttoned and his hair partially combed. His hands were also much cleaner.

"Engines are filthy things aboard sailboats," he explained as he came down the ladder to stand in front of her.

"I'm very happy to meet you." His eyes crinkled at the corners with his smile. "I won't shake hands with you. Grease is contagious."

She accepted his explanation with a laugh. "I just want to thank you so much for coming to Tammi's rescue."

"Oh, I hear the kids come down the street quarreling once in a while," he smiled. "Usually I pay little attention to them. The other day was different, though. Figured I'd better do something about it."

"I guess it must be the teacher coming out in you," Jael laughed, then stopped abruptly as she saw the change in his expression. "My husband told me," she added lamely.

"Oh, yes, of course," he smiled. Had him aboard for a cup of hot chocolate yesterday."

"He didn't tell me," Jael replied. She extended a towel-covered plate heaped with chocolate-chip cookies. "Tammi wanted to give you something for being so nice."

Frank took the plate and peeked under the towel. "I don't know what elf told her these are my favorite kind. Thank you."

Jael laughed. "I've yet to see a man turn down chocolate chips."

He slipped a cookie out from beneath the towel and bit into it. "Ummm. Very good, Mrs. Springer."

"Thank you," she laughed. "I'll let Tammi know they passed the test."

They stood awkward in each other's presence.

"Pastor Springer tells me that you folks are about as new as I am to Shelterport."

"Yes. We came here a little more than a month ago."

"Well," he smiled and slipped the remnant of the cookie

into his mouth. "I guess I'll have to come to church Sunday, if for no other reason than to return this plate."

Jael laughed. "That's why I didn't give you a paper plate." Her face became serious. "Mr. Rawlings, thank you again. Jerome and I are very grateful."

Frank Rawlings returned her plate and towel the following Sunday, leaving them in a paper sack on the foyer table with a thank-you card bearing Tammi's name.

Over the next several years Frank attended infrequently enough to stand in no danger of being asked to join the church, but regularly enough to be respectable.

Occasionally when Jerome disappeared for hours at a time, especially on a rainy afternoon, Jael knew he would be with Frank Rawlings, chatting, reading, debating, or just listening to the rain on the cabin roof. Following such retreats Jerome would return home, not preoccupied with church business or community demands, but relaxed and cheerful, more able to share in hers and Tammi's world.

One Sunday following church she saw Frank standing alone in the old town graveyard adjoining the church on the side opposite the parsonage.

She stepped carefully along the gravelled walkways, careful to avoid the dingy patches of slush and mud common in late March. He didn't look around when she approached, but continued gazing at a pink granite headstone.

"Too bad Myron couldn't have been buried here too, next to his grandmother."

"I guess they had to make a decision someplace," she said quietly. "Still it is a shame. Jerome tried to get them to make an exception when he had the funeral last year."

"His grandmother was the last one buried here." It was her marker he stared at.

"Do you come here often?" she asked.

"Once in a while, when I want to do a little thinking."

"Oh." Jael stood for a moment gazing at the stone. "I'd better be going."

Frank turned his head quickly to glance at her. "Oh, please—that was clumsy of me. I wasn't hinting you should leave." He stepped beside her as she walked slowly back to the church. "You know, I lost my wife a few years ago." They stopped at another marker and read the inscription. "I'm having a hard time burying her." He tapped a finger against his temple. "Up here." They moved toward the church again.

"I understand," Jael replied. "I, that is Jerome and I, lost a child. I often have the same problem."

"How do you handle it?"

"I tell myself over and over again that it is God's will, that He is sovereign." She gulped, confused and upset that she was sharing something so intimate with him. "But deep down, mostly I don't handle it very well at all. Sometimes it just seems empty." They had reached the low stone cemetery fence and stood reading the state-shaped historical marker. "How do you handle it, Mr. Rawlings?"

He grinned. "I tried running from it, packing my day so full with things to do that I have no time to think. Going back to teaching to try to work it out of my system, walking in graveyards—you name it. I even think sometimes that my sailboat has become a sort of womb for me, a return to a time when I had no sense of emptiness. It doesn't work. Like you, I mostly don't." He grinned self-consciously. "Say, this conversation has certainly gotten a little on the heavy side. I'm sorry."

"Don't apologize, please." They stepped outside the entrance and walked toward the church entrance where Jerome had just completed an after-service meeting with the Board of Deacons. "It was good for me finally to say these things." She smiled. "I really came to tell you how much I appreciate your being a friend to Jerome. He keeps himself very busy, but there are few he can talk to as friend—who enjoy him for himself alone, and let him be himself."

Frank grinned. "He's mentioned that. I guess I'm a safe harbor." He glanced up the stairs to the small group of men surrounding the pastor. "Why don't you try to get him free the last Saturday of next month for first sail of the year. I'll supply the boat, you and Tammi and Jerome can supply the food."

"That would be fine," Jael replied. They started to shake hands, but each pulled back before their fingers touched.

"Good-bye, Mrs. Springer," he said. "I hope you can fill that empty place."

"And I you," she replied.

Following dinner that Sunday, she and Tammi did the dishes and then she sat for a few moments as Tammi and Jerome napped. She picked up her worn Bible and read aimlessly for a few minutes. Suddenly she caught her breath as her heart pounded in her throat. Her hands felt suddenly cold as she read the passage, at first quickly, and then more thoughtfully. When she finished, she sat for a long time and looked through the window beside the easy chair.

Jerome and Tammi sailed with Frank the next month. For herself, Jael arranged an essential appointment. She would see to it that there would always be such appointments. After that Sunday, whenever they spoke, she always called him, "Mr. Rawlings." Somehow, she knew that he had understood. While he remained a friend to Jerome, he came to church just a little less frequently and almost never approached her except for necessary conversation.

She wondered if he had found the same Scripture she had that afternoon:

"Drink waters out of thine own cistern, and running waters out of thine own well."

Frank Rawlings sat and stared at the closed Testament in

192

front of him, his face reddening at the surprised silence around the table. "Oh, I'm not a total pagan," he added. "Just since Carrie died, I—well, it seemed like God was far away." Frank continued, "But I'm beginning to learn . . . that something a wise old Jewish man taught me long ago is true." He paused again. "None of us have a shelter from evil—not you, Bill, or I, or Jerome, or you, Jael, or Tammi. Not while we're in this world." Suddenly, his expression started to change as if a series of switches were being closed one after another in his mind. "But He does fill the emptiness." A smile started across his face as he repeated the phrase again, drawing out the third word. "But He *does* fill the emptiness." His smile contracted a little as he said more thoughtfully, looking squarely at Jael, "He does fill the emptiness. There is no empty place with God." He smiled again. "He surrounds us with Himself when we have to go through the evil."

They looked at him, all puzzled except Jael.

"You see it, don't you?" He stared intently at first one and then another. "A child, Tammi, runs away when things seem empty. When God—and her parents—seem far away."

They all sat for a moment, the silence broken only by the soft "clink" of silverware and the quiet wooden tick of the clock in the living-room.

"I'm not much at praying," Frank continued, "but when I was courting Carrie, and went to her house, the whole family used to pray together. They'd join hands and they'd really ask God to do something special."

Jerome cleared his throat softly. "I don't think we could ask anything more special, Frank, than for God to fill up the emptiness—Tammi's and ours—and surround us in the evil places."

A little self-consciously they joined hands for the first of several times that evening. When Jerome prayed in his turn, Jael detected a hint of a broken spirit too long absent, and felt the spiritual trickle of something cool and sweet in a well too long dry.

21

Jerome sighed, rolled over on the bed, squinted at the softly glowing face of the clock beside him, sighed again, and lay staring at the ceiling still black in the 2:00 A.M. darkness. He moved closer to Jael lying beside him, but she stiffened at his touch and drew away slightly. Imperceptibly, he pulled back toward his side of the bed and lay lonely and empty, despite their prayers earlier in the evening.

Jael stirred, sat up, and turned on her small reading lamp. "I'm going back to Tammi's room to look again. Maybe I missed something." She stood, pushed her hair back from her face, and smoothed her rumpled clothing.

Jerome sat up. "At least we got a little rest." He stood, rubbed his burning eyes, and nodded toward the clock. "Be light soon." He turned to face her, but Jael was already gone.

He slipped on his shoes, trudged to the bathroom, soaked a washcloth with cold water and spread it across his face, holding it against his temples with both his hands. He dropped the cloth in the sink and repeated the action, trying to ease the dry, burning sensation in his eyes. Wringing the cloth out, he replaced it on the rack, dried himself with a rough towel, slipped out into the hall, and crept down the stairs.

The night air chilled him as he stepped out the back door and into the yard.

Only a few stars penetrated the night mist. He started across the yard to the church, but his restlessness forced his steps out into the street and he found himself standing on the sidewalk facing the front of the house and Tammi's apple tree. He stared at its black branches softened with new foliage against an even blacker sky. The tree had been identified with Tammi for so long, he felt that, if he could speak its language, it could tell him where Tammi was. He turned and walked toward Wharf Street.

"God—" As he prayed, the night wrapped the sound of his footsteps in its dampness. "You promised to be in the empty places, but I can't find You!"

A voice long silent whispered from the empty place inside.

Just as Tammi and Jael couldn't find you. God's will was for you to fill their empty places. You left them desolate.

"But God called me to serve Him."

God called you to obey Him.

"I did what God called me to do."

God called you to become. A fragment flicked across his imagination, a man newly withered, with shaggy eyebrows.

"But I've won men to Christ! God honored my ministry!"

The Truth won them. God honors Truth.

Jerome walked faster, unconsciously keeping pace with the argument raging inside. He reached the end of Wharf Street and turned left into a park at the base of the jetty stretching seawards from the west side of the harbor entrance.

"God has honored me." The image of the study wall formed in his mind.

It was not God who honored you. Yes, look at the wall, Jerome, and see truth. Look beyond the wall, also.

And Jerome looked. From the empty pictures emerged fragments long repressed or forgotten.

195

He had wandered beyond the seaward perimeter of the park and worked his way out along the stony comb of the jetty. Choosing his footing as much by feel as by dim sight, he stepped from one large faceted granite slab to another where they lay tumbled in the misty moonlight.

Emptiness threaded the pictures together. In a long-ago dining-room, eyes under bar-straight gray brows, empty of a father's hope. Two seats empty at his graduation. The cold emptiness of a clapboard house on a Vermont mountain, the day following Jael's fall. The emptiness of Jael's body after she had filled a grave with a lost life. The empty expression in Tammi's eyes the first time she glimpsed her burn scar in the mirror. An empty upstairs bedroom, the neatly folded apple-blossom counterpane and a wooden chest, its once-bright colors now grayed and darkened, its hinges and antique padlock, now rust-spotted. The room's furnishings accented rather than filled the emptiness.

He had been an observer of others' emptiness—Jael's, Tammi's, Frank's. He had even glimpsed Bill Sharkey's. His mind reached forward to gaze, at last, into his own abyss.

He had reached the end of the jetty. The sea swells sighed a low-tide weariness against the rocks.

"And me? What is truth about me?"

Only the surge of the sea answered him, endless swells, products of some faraway upheaval, frothing darkly along the jetty.

"What's truth about me?" He cried into the darkness and the sound of the swell swallowed the sound of his voice. "Oh, God, what's true about me?"

Only the sea answered with its endless parade of evenly spaced swells surging from some place invisible to hump their shoulders against the jetty.

"God, I've failed! Help me." The dialogue ended. He was left only with the image of the wall in his mind and the surge of the sea in his ears.

In the east, the sky had grayed a little. Jerome shivered, pulled his jacket closer about himself, and felt his way back toward the shore.

When Jerome reached the side yard between the church and the kitchen, the sun had smeared a purplish red streak in the east. He pulled a ring of keys from his pocket, held it up to catch the light spilling from the kitchen window, found the key to the church and let himself in through the side entrance. He flipped the old rotary switch behind the door, and went up the stairs to his study.

He sat at his desk and stared at the plaques covering the wall opposite him.

"The truth is in the wall," something had said.

He opened the upper right drawer and reached for the study Bible he always kept there. "Ecclesiastes," he mumbled. "Ecclesiastes. The book for empty people." He chuckled bitterly as the thin pages rattled under his fingers. He read, trying to let the Scriptures push his fragmented attention into some sort of focus. His eyes skimmed words, verses, chapters, pages. The thoughts, charged in fine black print, crackled into his mind.

"What profit hath a man of all his labor which he taketh under the sun?"

Jerome looked up at the plaques, their brass and walnut mocking him in the reflected glare of his desk lamp. He dropped his eyes to the page again.

"All things are full of labour; man cannot utter it; the

197

eye is not satisfied with seeing, nor the ear filled with hearing."

He gazed again at the wall. "Is that it, Lord?" The plaques gazed back at him, silent, mocking. "The more I succeed, the more I crave to succeed?"

Jerome stood and moved to the wall as if something drew him to it. He reached out his hand and traced his fingers lightly over one token after another, like a blind man trying to sense through his fingers what his eyes could not tell him. "It's true," he thought. "The more I achieved, the more I craved to achieve. There was always something else. It's always been, 'The Work.'" He closed his eyes. "I wonder whose work it was?"

He wandered trance-like back to his desk and continued reading. His mind, now channeled towards a different problem, guided his eyes as they swept from one verse to another.

"Then I looked on all the works that my hands had wrought, and on the labour that I had laboured to do; and, behold, all was vanity and vexation of spirit, and there was no profit under the sun."

"Success." The word slipped out of his mouth like a serpent's hiss. "Success."

He read the portion over and over again. Again and again the question throbbed at his temples: "God's work? My work? Whose work?"

He stared at the plaques a long time. "Who benefited from the recognition?" he asked himself. "Who got the praise?" He asked again, "Who got the glory?" Etched testimony to his own name repeated the answer on every plaque and framed certificate. His "Wall of Fame," as he jokingly had called it, had become now a wall of condemnation, each achievement a theft from God. He had stolen God's glory for himself and built an elaborate rationalization to cloak his own lust for success

198

with the respectable mantle of "achieving great things for God." The truth was on the wall.

Jerome placed his hands on the desk and slouched back against the impersonal leather of his chair. The prayer tumbled through his mind behind compressed lips. "Lord, is it all gone? My father? My wife? My daughter? My ministry?" He chuckled bitterly. "I can't even stop saying, 'My ministry!' Have I destroyed everything because of my own vain ambition?"

He stepped from behind the desk, his feet noiseless on the thick carpet, and stood before the wall. He removed the most recently acquired plaque—an outline of the state, recognition for heading a committee for a self-help young-people's employment cooperative. He glanced sadly at it for a moment, stepped over to the plastic waste basket, and placed it gently in the bottom. He brought the basket back with him to the wall.

One by one he removed the plaques from the wall. As he glanced briefly at one and then at another, verses from Ecclesiastes haunted him:

"There is no remembrance of former things." "A time to cast away, and a time to gather."

Hardening his face, he dropped the plaques one after another, more and more rapidly into the basket. "Like throwing away the years of my life," he thought. The years of his life, following one after another like the swells on a night-quiet sea.

He reached for the last token, the black-framed parchment diploma that once had been the wall's only occupant. Over the years, however, it had been crowded high and to the left as more recent and more attractive symbols of achievement took its place. In the thick formality of gothic letters it announced that "JEROME RICHARD SPRINGER" had been awarded the degree of "Bachelor of Arts in Applied Religion," after having completed "all the necessary prerequisites," of "Pleasant Valley Bible College." He remembered how proud he had felt when he had finally walked across the platform and grasped the parchment, attractively bound in a blue cardboard cover.

"Even Jael was proud of me that day," he said to himself sadly. Not even his seminary diploma, prominently displayed on another wall, had satisfied him more.

He reached up and removed the diploma from the wall. He had been so convinced God wanted him to go to Bible college. He had sacrificed everything to that end. University. Inheritance. His father's blessing.

He remembered the silent dark swells. He had called for truth. God had given him only the sound of the waves.

He had sacrificed his father's blessing. Jerome turned and stepped back to his desk. Gently he set the black-framed diploma just outside the circle of light falling upon his Bible, and sank into his chair. He had begged of God the truth about himself, and he had been answered with an image of the wall—and the sea.

He glanced back at the diploma.

His father hadn't wanted him to go to Bible college. He couldn't have followed God's call without going. He had to disobey his father. There was no other choice, not if he were to follow God.

Suddenly, Jerome knew the truth.

So had his father.

He had said it that night at the dinner table. "To do God's will is not an excuse to dishonor your father and mother."

God doesn't contradict one command with another to get His will done.

God's will wasn't a feeling. His father had been right in that, too.

The truth. He had just read it in the Bible open between his elbows.

"Let us hear the conclusion of the whole matter:
Fear God, and keep his commandments: for this is the
whole duty of man.

For God shall bring every work into judgment, with
every secret thing, whether it be good, or whether it be
evil."

Leaning against the chair's heavily padded back, Jerome closed his eyes, and shook his head sadly. He had drawn God into his lie, playing an elaborate charade of serving Him while seeking his own self-esteem. God's judgment was not immediate, but, had he been looking, he would have seen it.

In the beginning, it had been a green and gold spring afternoon. Now, it was a bleak, dark predawn May morning.

In the beginning, he had been surrounded with friends. Now few, other than Frank Rawlings, cared enough to know him well.

In the beginning, eager to begin their future together, Jael had sat close beside him during the dedication service before graduation. Savoring that memory, he closed his eyes, and recalled her softness and her strength as, smelling of talcum and sweet perfume, she had slipped her shoulder slightly behind his and pressed against him, blending her strength with his.

She had been persuaded that he wished to serve God.

Jerome's eyes widened as he saw the truth. He had defrauded her. He had wanted to serve success. She had known, and had remained despite that knowledge. And now she searched an empty room from which sixteen years of her life had disappeared. His defrauding had withered her affection into duty, and her sweetness into pungent bitterness.

In the beginning, Jael had taken his hand as they lay together beneath her grandmother's wedding quilt, and placed it against her abdomen so he might feel Tammi's first faint kicks. "Like a butterfly," Jael had smiled." Now there was no more butterfly. Overnight, their lives had become empty co-coons from which life had departed.

Jerome opened his eyes and gazed again at the wall. The light from the desk lamp was barely sufficient to disclose the lighter patches left by the plaques.

"Honor thy father and thy mother." The words bubbled up out of the dark empty place, the darkness where long ago he had made the choice to disobey. The swells of that disobe-dience had touched, through a sea of years, and in ever-widening circles, everyone close to him.

He had asked for the truth about himself.

The sea had answered. He simply hadn't understood.

His tight-reined control snapped someplace deep down in-side. Slowly leaning forward over the polished mahogany desk, he placed his hands, fists clenched, over each temple. The gasps came first, deep, man-sobs. Then tears ran in un-controlled streams, neither diminishing nor increasing with the sobs, following the strong line of his chin, and gathering at the cleft to drop sporadically upon the desk. "Oh God, have I destroyed us all?" he gasped. "Is everything gone? My father? Jael? Tammi? You?" Each sob seemed to come from some-place deeper than the previous one, until he sat with no more tears and no more cries. His breath came with fewer gasps, and despite the chill in his study, sweat drenched his shirt.

He hadn't heard her enter. He simply felt her cool, soft hand upon his head, comforting him. Finally, he slid his elbows from the desk and slouched back in the chair. He saw her gazing sadly at the wall.

"Getting gray with morning," she said. "Come to the house. I've fixed something to eat."

Two hours later the telephone rang. It was Ira.

22

Tammi became more restless with every mile closer to Shelterport. She fidgeted in the vinyl-upholstered seat, rummaged through her day pack, and peered out the window to spot familiar landmarks. She finally forced herself to tilt the seat as far back as it would go and closed her eyes, hoping sleep would blot out her fear; but the shrill voice of a twelve-year-old boy across the aisle kept her awake. Then the loudspeaker at the front of the bus clicked alive with the driver's voice.

"NEXT STOP—COLONIE TOWN, FOLKS, COLONIE TOWN."

She felt the bus sway as it left the main highway for the winding Macadam Road along the edge of the bay.

The soprano voice of the twelve-year-old carried clearly across to her as he read from a travel brochure.

"Colonie Town, a suburb of Shelterport, on the south side of the bay. . . ."

The bus swung left along Front Street. Tammi gazed intently across the bay to the east shore. She glimpsed Shelterport's early evening lights winking through the haze over the water. Another twenty minutes after Colonie Town, and she would be there.

The boy continued reading as if the travel brochure were a litany. "Shops and homes have been recon—reconstructed to reproduce a typical seafront of the days of the great clipper ships. Visit the 'Flying Spray,' a four-masted trading ship of the tea trade. Colonie Town also is a yachting center, featuring many completely-stocked ship's chandlers. . . ."

Tammi triggered her seat forward. *Ted works in his uncle's marine-supply store across from the yacht basin!* The thoughts raced through her mind. *Mom and I brought him there one Saturday when his truck was broken down.*

The sign announcing the Colonie Town city limits swept by her window.

Ted would certainly know she had run away by now. "He'll certainly feel bad about the way he's been treating me," she tried to convince herself. "He said he'd do whatever was necessary. If he would face my parents with me—"

Gears clunked someplace deep inside the bus as the driver slowed in the evening traffic.

"He told me himself, I'm the only one he has, I'm the only one he really cares for."

The bus whirred to a stop beside the magazine store serving as a depot, and the door thudded open. Tammi fumbled for her day pack and hurried down the aisle after the twelve-year-old boy and his parents. She glanced at her watch. If she hurried, she could walk the two blocks before Ted left work. Ted drove fast. They could get to the main terminal almost as quickly as the bus.

Daylight had slipped toward darkness by the time Tammi reached the parking lot, but the streetlights had not yet blinked on. She hurried by a neatly restored, nostalgic structure of a bygone, more innocent era, and slipped down the alley alongside it.

She found Ted's truck in the corner of a gravel parking lot at the rear of the store. The doors were unlocked. She slipped her day pack inside the camper, opened the passenger door, and slipped inside.

The building's dingy hindquarters contrasted with the cleanly scrubbed and painted façade the public saw. "But most people don't come back here anyway," she thought.

Near the top of the building, power and telephone lines stretched black against the heavy gray sky like strands of a coarse spider web. Brown and gray scabs of window fans and air-conditioners covered the lower halves of unwashed windows. Gas and water meters hunched (at eye-level) like rusted gray roaches sipping what nourishment they could from grey pipes springing up to them from the gravel. In the corner of the lot opposite Ted's truck, a steel trash container lounged in stolid indifference. Pieces of cardboard, old newspapers, and crushed styrofoam cups lay forlornly in cracks and crevices. Low spots in the hard-packed dirt and gravel contained greasy muck from a morning shower. The back door of the shop opened, and Ted emerged.

In the gloom he didn't see her until he had almost reached the hood. He stopped abruptly, scowled, continued to the driver's seat door and yanked it open. "What're you doing here? Haven't you got me into enough trouble?" he snarled. He threw himself in the driver's seat and slammed the door.

"Ted, I'm in trouble, too," Tammi gasped, stunned at his vehemence.

"Then you take care of it. I already had mine with old man Rawlings and your father." He tapped the steering wheel in agitation.

"But you . . . you said you'd help me," Tammi insisted. "You said you'd do whatever you could! Ted, all I want is for us to go together to face my folks at the bus station." The words tumbled out like blocks spilling from a child's toy box.

"I tried to help you, Miss Goodie-Goodie," Ted sneered. "Where do you think the money for the doctor came from? I told you I'd pay for the abortion."

"I can't kill a baby, Ted."

"Well, it's your problem now," he said, his voice cold and even. "That's all the help you're going to get from me!"

"Ted—I'm not asking for money!" Tammi begged. "Just go to my folks with me! I can't face them alone!"

"Forget it!" he laughed. "You're not going to use me again. No one's going to use me again!"

"Use you!" she whimpered. "Ted I never—"

"Like heck you didn't," he lashed back. "Before I dated you, there wasn't a boy in school who'd look twice at you. You didn't give the girls the brush-off either—even though they made friends with you to make me notice 'em. I didn't see you turning down any of the attention."

Tammi sat speechless, pressing herself against the corner of the truck door as Ted continued.

"Well, you had your fun and I had my thrill." He gazed at her in silence for a moment. "Y'know, everybody told me that Christian girls 'didn't.' " He leered as he continued. "I just wanted to find out for myself. Who knows? I might have become a Christian if you hadn't been such a phony!"

Tammi groped for words. "Ted, Ted—I'm so sorry . . . I just . . . Oh, Ted, I'm sorry."

"Nothing to be sorry about," Ted said matter-of-factly. "Fact is, we both know how easy you are." He laughed. "Now that it's all over school, you really ought to use it—"

"Please, Ted. Don't say that," Tammi sobbed. "I can't believe you'd say that." She shook her head slowly in disbelief. "You're not like this. You can't be like this."

"Like what?" He looked at her with mock innocence. "Just being honest. A Christian girl went all the way. Just told the guys about it. How else do you think I persuaded your new lab partner to take my place? It certainly wasn't your pretty looks." He reached over and ran his finger roughly down the scarred tissue on the side of her face. Then, reaching further to open the door, he attempted to caress her with a mock tenderness. "You're close enough to find your own way home."

Tammi slipped numbly from the truck and stood unsteadily beside it. Ted slammed the door, started the engine, and throwing gravel with his back wheels, skidded out of the parking lot.

Hands at her sides, Tammi stared after him. So many of her emotions had been violated that she felt only a numbing, dark emptiness. Her mind roared confusion and self-accusation. Finally, she stumbled to the wall of the building and sank down beside the back door. "Oh, God . . . Oh, God! What'll I do?" It was Ted who had started the stories about her. "No one will believe me—they'll all be whispering behind my back. They'll make fun of all the other Christian girls. They'll all hate me. What have I done? Oh God, what'll I do?"

When she finally calmed herself, it was well after dark. "Well—" She whispered to herself to help sort her thoughts, "I'll never be able to go home now. Can't go back to Aunt Bea and Uncle Ira, either. Nobody'll want me now. Nobody. Might as well keep going."

She reached down for her pack and suddenly remembered she had left it in the back under the camper shell. Her eyes widened, and she lost the shards of calmness she had so carefully pieced together. She sat in panic and beyond tears. "Oh, no! Oh, God! Why do You hate me? Why? Oh, God, oh, no!"

She huddled down against the wall and shivered in the blackness. Despair paralyzed and numbed her so that she was only vaguely aware of the pair of headlights probing the alley and sweeping the parking lot. They flooded the back wall of the building with their colorless glare and fixed on Tammi. An engine stopped and doors opened.

"Tammi! Tammi!" From the darkness, her mother rushed into the glare and, kneeling beside her, pulled Tammi into her arms. "Tammi! Oh, my Tammi," she cried over and over again. "It's all right. We're here now. It's all right."

Then her father came, helped them to stand and embraced them both together. In the glare of the headlights, Tammi saw and felt and tasted his tears for the first time in her life.

23

Jael poured coffee first into Jerome's cup and then into hers. "She's still asleep."

"After what she's been through, she'll probably sleep the clock around." He clasped both hands around his cup, lifted it to his lips, and sipped it slowly, savoring the taste and the aroma, and watched Jael butter the toast. "Was just God's mercy that the bus driver remembered her getting off at Colonie Town. Said he wouldn't have noticed her but for that blue day pack."

Jael glanced up and wrapped his gaze in hers, "Good thing she left it in Ted's truck, or God alone knows where she'd be now."

"When she wakes up—when she gets up," Jerome began uncertainly, "what do we say to her? What do I say to her?"

"I don't know," Jael said gently. "What we feel—you and I." She placed his toast in front of him. "She'll have the same problem."

He stared at the butter melting into the toast. "Never had the time just to sit and talk with her before." He picked up a half slice of toast and held it poised in the air. "No, that's not the truth. Never *took* the time to learn to talk to her." He tore the toast apart, placed a chunk in his mouth and chewed thoughtfully. He reached across the table and covered Jael's hand lightly with his. About to get up again for something, Jael sat back in her chair.

"Buttery fingers and all," he said, attempting a smile, but not quite succeeding. "Jael, I—I got confused about a lot of things. I'm not sure any more what, or even who I am." She sat silent, drinking him in through large eyes. The two small creases between her brows from her habitual half-frown eased, and seemed to absorb the years with their softening.

"I'm confused about what we're going to do next." He kept her gaze, his own eyes troubled. "It will be different . . . for you . . . and for Tammi . . . and for me." He squeezed her hand and released it.

Almost shyly, they smiled at each other. Jerome wiped the butter from his fingers with his napkin and gulped a mouthful of coffee.

Jael left the table and stepped to the counter, her back to Jerome. She reached into a lower cabinet for a tray. "It'll be all right," she said quietly. There was a catch in her voice. "If God can bring Tammi home the way He did, He can take care of the rest." Her hands worked in quick nervous movements as she placed silverware and dishes on the tray to take to Tammi. She checked the pancakes on the griddle, poured a mugful of coffee and sat down opposite him again. "Maybe if I hadn't brooded in my own emptiness . . . ," she said quietly. She sipped her coffee and stared at a smear of jam on the toast plate. "All of this. . . ," she set her cup down and groped for her words, choosing each as if it were a single plank to build a bridge. "Frank said it the other night when he read the Psalm, about God being in the empty places. Suddenly I realized that He is the only one who can be there. I tried to fill my empty places with anger and resentment, and the emptiness simply swallowed them and grew larger." She smiled.

Her voice was low, but it carried an intensity which had been absent for many years. "While you were gone the other night, I couldn't think, or look, or anything. I couldn't even pray. I just lay on Tammi's bed, and I saw my emptiness."

"Then I came into the study and saw you sitting in front of that wall. That empty, bleak wall." She squeezed her hands gently. "Can you forgive me? I blamed you for filling your emptiness with work, and I was doing the same thing, only with resentment."

They sat silent for a moment and then Jael stood. "Better turn Tammi's pancakes."

Jerome remained seated watching Jael move about the kitchen. She looked different this morning. At first, he couldn't place what it was. Suddenly, he saw it. It was the robe. She wasn't wearing the tasteless, shapeless robe Mrs. Sharkey had pressed upon her. It was an older one of a soft yellow material that flowed with her figure and brought back memories of carefree mornings pungent with the scent of pine and wood fires.

Jerome drew his hand slowly across the stubble on his chin. "I didn't see, until the other night, that I had become so obsessed with proving I could be a success, nothing else mattered." He slipped his arm around Jael's waist as she refilled his coffee cup. Setting the pot down, she turned slightly towards him and drew his head gently against her body with her free hand.

"Thank you for not leaving me." His voice was muffled as he pillowed the side of his face into the softness between her hip and ribs. She reached up with the other hand and traced her fingers along the line of his chin. How warm his head felt against her! She smiled as she at last understood what Bea had told her long ago, "Woman's softness gives a man strength. God made us softest when our men are weakest." She looked down at his thinning sandy hair. They would start over again. She would help him to be strong.

He loosened his grip and drew away slightly to look up at her. "All those pieces of wood and brass and glass, just to prove my father wrong." He let her slip free to tend to Tammi's pancakes, slowly charring themselves black on the stove. "If my father were here now, how I would ask his forgiveness! How I would deeply beg his pardon!"

210

"You wouldn't have to." Jael did not turn around as she scraped the last pancake from the griddle.

There was a puzzled silence. Then, "What do you mean?"

"He told me the night he died, to tell you." She filled a small pitcher with hot maple syrup, picked up Tammi's tray, and turned to face him. "He told me to tell you, when you were ready to understand, that he forgave you."

Suddenly silent, Jerome stared at her. "He forgave me?"

"Yes." Her voice was very soft. "That's what he whispered to me that night in the hospital just before he died."

Jerome shook his head slowly. "And it's taken me all these years."

Upstairs, a door opened and then closed. The sound of Tammi's retching carried faintly down to them.

Jael smiled. "Sounds like *someone*—woke her up." She glanced down at the tray. "Well, my mother always told me that burnt toast and burnt pancakes helped settle the stomach."

"Fine," Jerome chuckled, and then continued more seriously. "She'll talk to you more easily than to me." He added almost as an afterthought, "She's going to have to decide what to do with that new 'someone' pretty quickly."

"We'll get to that when she's ready," Jael said simply and climbed the stairs to Tammi's room.

Balancing the tray in one hand, she knocked on the door. "Tammi? Can I come in?"

There was a short silence. Then a muffled voice called, "Yes." Jael opened the door and stepped inside.

"Heard you in the bathroom," she said, placing the tray on the desk and closing the door. "Brought you some pancakes and maple syrup. Something sweet—and burnt—," she smiled wryly, "always helped me feel better when . . . when I had bad mornings," she finished, carefully cheerful.

Tammi lay unmoving. Turned to the wall, she had covered

her head with the apple-blossom quilt. "I'll eat it later, Mom," she sighed, trying to push herself further into the nest formed by her bed and the wall.

Jael sat on the edge of the bed, leaned over and grasped Tammi's shoulder, gently, but insistently. "Tammi, look at me," she commanded softly.

Tammi didn't move.

"Tammi. Turn over and look at me," her mother commanded again.

This time Tammi rolled over reluctantly and buried her face against her mother. "Oh, Mom," she whimpered, "I don't deserve to feel better. After what I've done, you and Daddy can't love me anymore. God can't love me anymore." She was silent for a moment. "I deserve to be hated." She forced the words out.

Jael pulled Tammi closer against her side and caressed her hand. "Tammi, 'deserving' has nothing to do with Daddy and me loving you." She swallowed in an effort to control her voice and then continued, almost as if she were a third person comforting herself as well as her daughter. "If God treated us according to what we 'deserved,' Tammi, there'd be no forgiveness, or love, or hope."

Tammi gazed up at her mother. "But how can God forgive me? I was supposed to be such a great Christian! Now everybody's calling all the Christians at school 'hypocrites' because of me!" She pulled the quilt closely around her. "Ted told me he would have become a Christian if I hadn't let him. . . ." Her voice trailed off as she huddled miserably against her mother. "Oh, Mom, he said such horrible things!" She started to sniffle. "Said he was just trying to find out if a Christian girl would . . . would . . . and then he said I was a phony. . . ." She stopped talking and brought her tears under control. "Then he laughed as he drove away. A horrible laugh." She was silent again. Finally Tammi rolled back to look into her mother's face. "It's my fault if he never accepts Christ, Mom.—It's my fault."

Jael looked away, concealing the anger in her face from Tammi. Her eyes narrowed slightly as if she were peering into a place beyond the room, searching for something half-hidden. Then her face softened a little as she looked down again.

"Tammi," she spoke deliberately, clearly, "Ted never had any intention of accepting Christ."

Listening intently, Tammi huddled more tightly against her mother.

"When God starts to attract someone to Himself," Jael continued, "He doesn't ask anyone involved in the transaction to do wrong things." She paused. "Not anyone—not you—not Ted—not anyone." Jael reached to the nightstand where Tammi's Bible lay, the one left there in despair two mornings before. Opening it toward the back, she thumbed through several pages until she found what she was looking for. She propped it up a little on the bed so Tammi could see it and placed her finger beside a verse. "Can you read this, Tammi?"

With a muffled, tired voice, Tammi read hesitantly, "Let no man say, when he is tempted, I am tempted of God: for God cannot be tempted with evil, neither tempteth He any man.'" Tammi lay her head back again on the bed and looked at her mother with wide eyes as Jael continued to comfort her.

"If Ted rejects Christ, Tammi, it will be that he chose to do so, not from something you did or for something you refused to do." She smoothed Tammi's hair with her hand. "When Ted encouraged you to do something wrong, that wasn't God working in his heart." Jael's eyes gleamed intently as she tried to pierce Tammi's conscience with Scripture. "God will never tempt you to sin." She said it again, slowly, deliberately, "God will never tempt you to sin."

Tammi straightened her legs and rolled onto her back. With

her fists clenched around its edge, she still held the quilt up under her chin. "Ted said all those things to hurt me? To make fun of God?" She frowned. "Why? Why would he want to hurt me?"

Jael leaned back a little and smiled as she perceived the new turn in the conversation. "For the same reason those boys chased you and called you names the day you met Mr. Rawlings," Jael explained. "Unless God changes us we have cruel natures, Tammi."

"And I—I never saw what was happening." She turned her head so she could see her mother. "I'm so dumb!" She looked away again. "I wanted all the kids to like me. More than anything else, I wanted that. And I wanted Ted to love me. And I thought if I could get the kids at school to like me. . . ," she took a deep breath as she opened the door on her own emptiness, "you . . . you and Daddy wouldn't be so ashamed of me because of the scar on my face."

Jael clasped her daughter more tightly against her. "Oh, Tammi! Daddy and I were never ashamed of you, not for the scar on your face, not for anything."

Tammi lifted her face and looked into Jael's face. "Not even now?"

Jael heard her heart in her ears. "*God, help me to give the right answer, now!*" she prayed, the words coursing silently across her mind.

"Daddy and I are ashamed that we became so preoccupied with our own problems that we . . . we forgot about yours."

"I thought Daddy never had time to do anything with me, or go any place with me, because he was ashamed of the way I looked."

"No, Tammi. Oh, if we had only known . . ."

Tammi lay with her eyes closed for a moment, but when she opened them, the uncertainty was still there.

"Am I going to hell?"

214

Jael flinched at the unexpected question. She looked down at Tammi and shook her head slowly. "Of course not!" All she could think to do was to hold her daughter closer and to stroke her long hair with light, comforting, fingers.

"But after what I did," Tammi insisted, "God certainly wouldn't want me anymore."

"Tammi," Jael's voice was very gentle, "do you remember that day in the church basement when you were a little girl, you asked God to make you 'family'?"

"Yes, I went down there the morning I was sure I was pregnant." Her eyes met Jael's, and the dark circles beneath them from too much weeping and too little sleep seemed to increase their greenness. "But it didn't help."

Jael frowned slightly, concentrating on her words. "You didn't feel like God's family then, did you?"

"No."

"When you ran away, did you feel the same way about Daddy and me, like you didn't belong anymore, like we hated you?"

Tammi nodded her head.

"When you came back, Tammi, did we still love you? Were you still our daughter?"

Tammi nodded her head again.

"Tammi, there's a lot of hurt and heartbreak. There'll be more, especially as you have to deal with consequences—and a baby is a pretty drastic one. We can't keep you from those consequences, but we can love you through them, and help you."

As Jael spoke, Tammi's face gradually became more peaceful.

"Now, Tammi, answer a question for me." Jael's voice became firm and businesslike.

Tammi opened her eyes, and frowned slightly, bewildered at the change in tone.

"Do you actually believe that Daddy and I can out-love God?"

Tammi thought for a moment. "No. No, I guess not." She struggled with the idea.

"While you were gone, did you ever stop being our daughter?"

"No."

"Tammi," Jael looked into Tammi's eyes, struggling to help her understand, "We go to heaven or we go to hell because of what we are, not because of what we do. You're 'family'— God's, and ours. There is always forgiveness with family."

Tammi sat up slowly, letting the apple-blossom quilt fall, and clung to her mother. They sat entwined and silent, each finding a woman's strength in the other's embrace. Then Tammi whispered. "Will you forgive me, Mom? I'm so sorry. Oh, God, forgive me. I'm so sorry I hated You." They sat together, mother and daughter, rocking gently back and forth, reaching deeply into one another's heart.

24

Jerome pulled back the bedroom curtain and, squinting a little in the golden splash of Saturday morning sunlight, peered toward the church parking lot.

"Harry Simpson's here—that's all of them," he grunted. He

picked up an envelope from the small corner desk and turned to Jael. "Sure you want to be there? I have no idea what's going to happen."

"We've endured too many painful things apart," she said, glancing at the black-framed picture of the Croughton's Corner's church, its whole congregation posed in two wide-spaced rows across the front.

"How do you like my suit?" She stepped away from him and turned around to show it off.

Jerome tilted his head critically, placed a finger beside his nose and peered through half-closed eyes in mock concentration. "It's a suit worthy of a. . . a District Superintendent's wife." Their laughter eased the tension. He looked at his watch again. "We'd better get it over with."

Entering the fellowship hall through the back doorway, they saw that the board members had seated themselves behind three long folding tables, set in a sort of semicircle. Jerome and Jael approached a fourth table, set up to face the other three. The men greeted them as they came.

"Mornin' Jerome, Jael," Bill smiled solemnly and shook hands. The other men followed suit.

"Good morning, Bill." Jerome nodded to the others in turn.

"We really hadn't planned on Jael being here," Bill said, uncertainty edging his voice.

"That's all right," Jerome smiled with more confidence than he felt. "I'll get her that chair over there." He stepped over to another table pushed against the wainscoted wall, and returned with a steel folding chair.

They seated themselves and faced the board members.

The men had placed themselves with Bill directly in the center of their line. Four elders sat to his right, four deacons to his left. It reminded Jerome of old woodcuts he had seen in a book about the Spanish Inquisition.

"Sam, would you open in prayer?" Bill nodded toward one of the elders.

Sam stood hesitantly, began with, "Let us pray," and cleared his throat self-consciously. "Be with us now in this meeting. Whatever we do and say, help us to glorify and honor You. In Jesus' name, Amen."

Silence hung heavy over the group.

At last, Bill Sharkey cleared his throat. He looked nervously at Jerome and then at Jael.

"There's no easy way to say it, Jerome." He glanced down at his hands as if the words he was looking for had been lost between the sheets of paper he shuffled.

Jerome waited for him to continue, his gaze fixed on Bill's face. Finally, he completed the chairman's statement for him. "You're telling me that you want my resignation, effective immediately," Jerome said simply.

The board members sat silent. "That was Dr. Soberman's counsel," Bill admitted. "But—"

"I understand," Jerome interrupted. He stared at a faded print on the wall behind the chairman, a faded print of a shepherd rescuing a lamb from a narrow ledge of a rocky cliff.

He hurried on with his prepared speech while he still trusted his voice.

"A pastor cannot fail with his family, if he's going to keep his credibility."

"Jerome . . ." Bill tried to break in again.

". . . or the church he serves loses its credibility in the community. You are right in asking for my resignation."

He gazed intently upon one and then another of the board members as he finished.

They returned his gaze. Nine pairs of eyes. Brown, gray, blue. Some set in hardened faces that had seen more of life than they wished, and others in smooth-skinned, optimistic

218

faces, not yet betraying their accumulated pain. None of the eyes flashed condemnation or rejection.

Jerome reached into his breast pocket, removed the envelope containing his resignation, and laid it on the plastic veneered table.

"We're not asking for your resignation, Jerome."

Jerome's eyebrows lifted. "I don't understand."

"You just told me. . . . Dr. Soberman . . ."

"We choose not to follow his advice."

"Why?" Jerome almost whispered the question. He and Jael held each other's hands tightly.

Cal Henry, seated at the end of the table to Jerome's left, answered his question. "Because being a pastor doesn't excuse you from the human race, Jerome." He paused for a moment and then continued, "I've disagreed with you sharply on many things." He smiled as he paused again, "but whatever you may have believed before, being a pastor does not exclude you—or your family—from the faults, and the pains of being a human being." He looked directly at Jerome and Jael. "We're satisfied with a human being for our pastor. A plaster saint can't understand pain." He smiled again.

Silence hung suspended over the group.

Conquering his initial confusion, Jerome asked, "How . . . does the congregation feel about . . . keeping me on?"

"We had a congregational meeting while you were absent last Sunday," Bill replied. "They want you to stay."

"All of them?"

There was a short silence. "Most of them. Their major care was for Tammi. They thought maybe she could keep a sort of 'low profile,' until. . . ."

Jael, silent until now, and having shared Jerome's confusion, suddenly laughed.

"Low profile!'" Jael burst out in exasperation and amusement. "How can a pastor with a pregnant, unmarried daughter, keep a 'low profile'? Especially the daughter! If they're around three months from now, I'll show them a 'low profile!'"

Startled, the men waited until she finished speaking, and then chuckled at the ludicrous impossibility of their own comment.

They sat silent again.

"What about those who want me to leave?"

"The majority want you to stay."

Joe Perkins, seated on the elders' side, spoke up. "Probably a few will leave, Jerome. But as a board and congregation, we've decided we want you. There aren't many willing to 'cast the first stone,' so to speak."

"This could split the church," Jerome said, his face thoughtful.

"Well, Pastor Springer," Sam Johnson snapped, "it seems to me, if a church splits in a matter of mercy, they're far better off after than before." His seamed fisherman's face seemed not to move as he spoke.

Jerome sat stunned, his eyes fixed upon the picture on the wall behind Bill.

"Why don't you reconsider giving us this for a while," Bill suggested, pointing to the envelope on the table.

There was another silence.

Finally, Jerome asked, "Before I take this back for reconsideration," he motioned toward the envelope, "may I share something with you?"

The men sat silent, listening.

"I've pastored this church for almost ten years. In that time, I became so caught up in programs, and buildings, and seminars, and Sunday schools, and special meetings, and rescue missions, and social and neighborhood improvement, and in being a professional, successful pastor, that I forgot the people. I forgot the individuals who were the real reason for my being here. I forgot my own family."

He looked into each somber face again. "What I felt was 'success' has been nothing more than abject failure in God's eyes, because it was a drive for success that motivated the efforts, not God."

He fixed his gaze upon one and then another of the board members. "From the very first, when I came, I saw this church as no more than a stepping stone to something more." He sighed. "From the very beginning, I've defrauded you as a pastor."

"Well, if that's the case, Pastor Springer, it certainly isn't true any more. Seems to me that you simply heard, maybe for the first time, some of your own sermons." The men chuckled at Sam Johnson's observation. "Can't help but be the better for us, far's I can tell."

Jerome reached out and removed the envelope containing his resignation from the table. "I certainly didn't expect a response like this," he remarked, looking at Jael, "not like this."

"We've invited Dr. Soberman to speak again next Sunday, Jerome," Bill said, his voice serious. "Why don't you think about it for awhile and give us your answer next week?"

"I shall," Jerome said, his voice husky. They stood to leave. Starting at Cal Henry, Jerome looked each man in the face and shook hands. It wasn't the "preacher's hearty handshake" they all used to joke about. It was the historic handshake of antiquity, human beings face to face, declaring with strong, clasped right hands, "I have set aside weapons with which to harm you."

Jerome and Jael squinted in the bright sunlight as they stepped out the side door of the church and walked together back toward the house. They saw Tammi watching at the kitchen window, and smiled at her.

When she opened the door for them, they could see the tension on her face.

"I thought maybe you'd like a cup of coffee."

"You're right," Jerome grinned. "Didn't feel much like eating before we left."

"Did. . . . were. . . ?"

"No, Tammi," Jael smiled, as they seated themselves. "They asked us to stay."

Tammi poured their coffee and her own, placed the pot back on the stove and sat down slowly. "Oh, I was so worried!"

They sat silent for a moment, knowing it was not the time for small-talk, but not knowing what else to say. Finally, Tammi broke the silence.

"Before I forget to tell you—Aunt Bea called. Wanted to know how we were."

Jael smiled, picturing the cheerful, buxom woman in her mind. "Anything else?"

"Yes. Said Uncle Ira thought we might be wanting a vacation soon." Her voice trailed off with sudden self-consciousness. "Said we'd be welcome to spend some time with them in the mountains, if we'd like."

Jerome and Jael looked at each other for a moment and smiled "We'll call him back this evening," Jael said.

Tammi continued, her voice more matter-of fact. "I called Mr. Rawlings while you were . . ." she inclined her head toward the church. "I can take my exams in his office next week." She looked at them, her chin high, and made no attempt to shrink from their gaze. "I figured since this whole mess was my fault, I'd better start to do something to try to help . . . somewhere." The words tumbled out one after another and then stopped abruptly.

Jerome took a muffin from a plate and buttered it. His eyes narrowed a little, as they always did when he concentrated on a problem. He placed the knife on his plate, took a sip of coffee and a bite from the muffin. "Um. Just made these, huh?"

"Yes. Put them on before you went."

"Smelled good when we came in the door," Jael added.

"Tammi," Jerome spoke quietly, in a matter-of-fact voice. "I don't think you caused this at all." He followed his comment with another mouthful of muffin as he watched the expression on Tammi's face.

She was not convinced.

"Do you know what a 'catalyst' is, Tammi?"

She looked a little puzzled. "Yes. Had it in chemistry. It's something that makes things happen, or makes things happen faster." She grinned. "Just went over it." The animation bubbled momentarily to the surface and submerged again.

"This may be hard for you to understand now, but what your mother and I had to face this last couple of weeks, Tammi, was my own doing. You didn't cause it." He grinned. "You simply made it happen, well, more abruptly than it would have on its own."

Tammi frowned slightly, trying to understand.

Jerome sighed, "I guess God isn't going to let me off the hook until I come right out and say it." He shifted his glance from Tammi to Jael and back again. "Many years ago, I wanted to serve God. At the same time, I carried a terrible bitterness toward my father. It was easy to combine the two and form a self-righteous excuse to disobey him." He looked sadly at Jael. "That was the pebble in the pond. The ripples circling out from that put the circumstances in my life, your mother's life, and your life, all out of adjustment. Even the good things couldn't work right."

Tammi looked at him, her eyes round with the beginning of understanding. "Will they ever work right—for any of us?"

"Yes. But you and I need to do something first for that to happen."

Tammi looked from one parent to another. "If only I could. I'd do anything. If only I could."

"Forgiveness, Tammi. I'm asking your forgiveness for neglecting you for so long. Will you forgive me?"

A few moments later, Jael shook her head and stood to clear the table. Tammi wouldn't be much help. She didn't seem to want to leave her father's arms.

When Tammi finally stepped to the sink to help with the dishes, Jael glanced back over her shoulder to make certain Jerome had left the room.

"Tammi?"

"Hmm?" She couldn't seem to stop grinning.

Jael watched carefully from the corner of her eye as she asked the question. "Have you forgiven Ted?"

The smile disappeared. Tammi continued replacing the dishes in the cupboard with slow, deliberate movements. She didn't answer Jael's question.

Jael continued speaking quietly while she wiped the sink and faucets with a cloth.

"Your father was right about things being out of adjustment." She paused and turned to face her daughter. She caressed with tender, light fingers, the whitened scar on Tammi's face. "I blamed your father, the night of the storm. Your getting burned. . . losing the baby." She paused for a moment. "I blamed God for making my life so empty. I didn't stop to think that blaming your father made it impossible for God to fill the emptiness in all our lives." She dropped her hand from Tammi's face, turned away, and folded the cloth she had been using.

"Ted needs your forgiveness—for his sake, and yours."

Tammi said nothing, but slipped her arm around her mother's waist for a moment, turned, stepped from the kitchen, and climbed the stairs to her room.

25

"Daddy, I'm scared." Tammi murmured as her father stopped the car in front of the school office.

"I know, Tammi," her father answered. "It's all right to be scared, remember?"

"How can I forget?" she replied, trying to smile. "Mom's been telling me that at least once a day for the last two weeks."

"That's because we feel scared ourselves so often."

They laughed and sat for a moment, staring through the windshield.

"You'll be all right?"

"Yeah. I'll be all right."

"Don't want me to walk in with you?"

"I'm going to have to face them sooner or later," Tammi said. "Besides, it's class time now. There won't be too many around."

"Just do your best." He squeezed her hand. "Mom and I will be praying for you."

Tammi sighed, leaned over and gave her father a peck on the cheek. "I should be finished a little after school's out."

Tammi slipped uncertainly from the front seat of the car and closed the door.

She watched her father drive away, then turned up the sidewalk to the main entrance. The hollow sound of her hard heels on the pavement reminded her of the slow-motion dreams.

As in her dreams, her senses were remarkably acute, responding to the heavy green scent of approaching summer, the soft chatter of the tractor-driven mower shaving wide swaths along the side fence, and the glare of sunlight bouncing from stainless steel and glass as she reached the double door and pulled it open.

As she walked down the empty hallway, disembodied voices seeping through closed classroom doors added to a peculiar sense of detachment. She felt as if everything were happening around her and she was severed from any cause-effect relationship. It was like returning as a ghost to a world once known, but now no longer a part of her.

A wide floor-to-ceiling window separated the main office from the hallway. Tammi pushed open the steel-framed door and stepped in front of the walnut-veneered counter.

From her stronghold at her desk, Miss Kallus, Mr. Rawlings' secretary, peered up over straight-topped glasses. "Yes?" Then she raised her chin to look directly through her glasses. "Oh, yes, Tammi." She stood and walked to the counter. "It's good to see you," she said kindly, "I'm sorry to . . ." she glanced down at Tammi's figure, and then reddened slightly as she felt Tammi's eyes on her. She cleared her throat delicately. "Mr. Rawlings has your tests in his office." She motioned to the end of the counter.

"You must be a very special person," she added as Tammi slipped through the spring-loaded half door separating the waiting area from the offices. "He's never done this before for anyone else."

Mr. Rawlings looked up and smiled as she entered his office.

"Hi, Tammi. I'm glad you came."

She swallowed, and stood awkwardly just inside his doorway. "I . . . I don't deserve this, Mr. Rawlings. Thank you. I've caused you a lot of trouble."

"My job is to help with trouble," he smiled. "Besides, you were my first 'client' when you were in third grade." He motioned her to a seat in front of his desk.

"Yes, I remember," Tammi relaxed a little. "You were working on your boat on Wharf Street." She glanced at him behind his large glass-topped desk. His graying hair was combed neatly, and he wore a sportscoat and tie. "You scared them so much, running and shouting from your boat, grease all over your face and hands and your work clothes—" she giggled. "They never called me . . . never bothered me again." She sat silent remembering the chant from long ago. "SCARFACE, SCARFACE," piping voices lilting with the cruelty only children can imagine, "COME AND LET US SLAP YOUR FACE!"

"We've set a desk up for you in the 'tank.'" Mr. Rawlings smiled, using the students' term for the detention room adjoining his office. "Thought it would be the best place." He continued with a joking tone as he let her walk first through the doorway. "We've arranged for the rest of the students to behave themselves today and tomorrow, so you'll be able to take your exams without interruption."

An electronic tone sounded over the public address system.

"Speaking about interruptions," Mr. Rawlings smiled. "Guess we'll have to wait for another minute or two."

"May I have your attention for announcements please." The principal, his voice distorted by an electronic buzz, cleared his throat and began to read.

"Student Council will meet immediately following school in room 13." There was a shuffling of papers and a pause. "Extra practice for the orchestra this afternoon in the auditorium for graduation." There was an irritated pause. Then the voice continued. "Student Council meeting has the priority."

As the principal droned on with the endless list of class activities, Tammi suddenly realized that she was indeed changed.

"Buy your flowers for the Junior-Senior Prom . . . ."

There had been a transmutation, and she no longer shared the same world with other sixteen-year-olds.

"Graduation announcements must be picked up by Friday . . . Wildcat track squad trounced . . . Newspaper will be distributed . . . . He closed finally with, "That's all the announcements for today. Thank-you." The speaker clicked off.

She sat silently for a moment as the counselor placed a packet of test papers in front of her. "Mr. Rawlings?"

"Yes, Tammi?"

She couldn't look at him. "It will never really be the same again. I'll never really be just a high-schooler again."

Mr. Rawlings grasped a student desk, turned it to face Tammi, and crammed himself into it. He brought his eyes down to Tammi's eye-level before he spoke.

"No, Tammi." The heartiness had left his voice. "That's one of the problems of growing up." He paused and scratched an eyebrow with the tip of his little finger. "You can never go back again."

"That's awfully scary."

"Yes. It is."

"My folks told me you came over when I was—gone."

He leaned back in his chair and looked absently at the pale green wall. "They've been good friends to me over the years, Tammi," he chuckled. "Even if I came to church only occasionally." He glanced down and then up again, grinning. "Besides, I don't like to see my friend, Tammi, hurt."

He blinked his eyes and opened a manila file folder. "I've got your English test." He cleared his throat of a sudden huskiness. "We might as well start with that." He reached over and placed it in front of her.

"Take as long as you need, Tammi," Mr. Rawlings said. "Don't worry about having to finish when the other students leave." He extricated himself from the student desk and walked through the doorway separating the detention room from his office.

When she heard the intercom buzz in Mr. Rawlings' office, she had completed two tests. "Yes, Miss Kallus." His voice

228

seemed to jump through the door to the room where Tammi sat and bounce off the green walls.

"Pastor Springer is here."

Mr. Rawlings came to the door and smiled. "How're you doing?"

"Just been stalling," she admitted.

He winked and returned to his desk. "She'll be right out." The intercom clicked off.

Tammi placed the exam papers together and stood to stretch. She glanced at the clock. It was a little after three-thirty, and she had heard most of the students surge home-ward through the hallway and out of the parking lot fifteen minutes before.

"Two down, two to go," Mr. Rawlings said, slipping her history exam from the desk. "Be here tomorrow?"

"Yes," she said. Then she lifted her chin a little. "At eight o'clock, when school starts." She picked up her purse. "I'd like to go out this way." She stepped to the door leading to the corridor rather than the one leading through Mr. Rawlings' office. She stopped in the half-opened door for a moment and turned slightly toward him. "Mr. Rawlings?"

"Yes?" He looked over to her from the doorway leading to his office.

"Thank you."

She forced herself to face the hallway, and whatever students might be coming by, alone. She breathed a sigh of relief at finding it deserted. She turned to walk the few steps to the hall entrance of the main office, then heard Sandi Beech's low, but loud, voice. "Well, how's Tammi?" Tammi stopped and turned to face the cheerleader who had just turned the corner from a locker area. "Hello, Sandi." Her voice was weak and she had trouble catching her breath. She was surprised, how-ever, that she felt no anger.

Head tilted a little to one side, eyes narrowed, Sandi surveyed her from head to toe. "Sorry you got hurt," she said with a slight sneer, "but you can't say I didn't warn you."

"That's right, Sandi, you did," Tammi replied softly. "I should have taken your advice."

Sandi blinked a little and dropped some of the façade. "I really am sorry, Tammi." There was a carefully hidden pain behind Sandi's reply.

"Sandi?"

"Yes?"

"Being popular—you found out it isn't worth it, too?"

They stared at one another. Someone far down another corridor dropped a book and the noise bounced hollowly off walls and terra-cotta floors, making both of them start as if it had been a shot. Sandi dropped her gaze for a moment and then looked up again. "No, it isn't," she replied. "But then I've never found anything that was." There was silence again for a moment. "I was hoping you had."

Replacing her mask with the wrinkling of her nose in a momentary, carefully-practiced half-squint, she smiled and turned away. "See ya, Tam."

Tammi watched her as she wandered aimlessly down the empty hallway. "Oh, God," she prayed, "she wanted to see You in me, and I failed her, too." She watched as Sandi pushed open the double door at the end of the corridor and disappeared.

"Please, don't let me do that again. Please." She took a deep breath, masked her own face with a smile and stepped to the large-windowed office area.

Her father stood in front of the long counter, his back to the hallway, waiting for her to appear from Mr. Rawlings' office. Tammi tapped on the window, and made a face at him as he turned around.

As he stepped out into the hallway, he seemed both surprised and pleased. "Figured you'd get your feet wet?"

"Yes."

They said nothing more until they got into the car.

"Mom was right."

"Hmm?"

"Mom was right. I used to hate Sandi Beech. She was always so mean to me." She was silent for a moment as her father pulled out into traffic. "I think we really could have been friends if I had been . . . different."

Tammi continued. "I let her down. She didn't see something in me she was looking for, and she was—well, sad. That's worse than being hated, Dad—to have someone disappointed in you."

"Yes, Tammi," her father replied quietly. "Much worse."

He opened the door for her and added in a lighter tone of voice, "Mom wants us to hurry home. We have a surprise."

"Oh? It's not fair to get me curious!" She laughed and hoped the surprise wasn't something greasy.

They had finished supper, except for their dessert. Her mother and father sat looking at her, their expressions seemed more relaxed and happy than she had seen in a long time.

"I have a feeling I'm going to find out what the surprise is," she said cautiously, shifting her gaze from first one and then to the other.

Her father and mother exchanged glances, and she saw her mother's nod.

"Yes. I guess so," her father sighed. He slouched back in his chair and stared intently at the ice cream in his dish as he spoke.

"I had to give an answer to the church today, Tammi."

Tammi set the spoon beside the mound of ice cream in her

dish and placed her hands in her lap to hide their shaking. From the way her father spoke, she wasn't sure she would like the surprise.

"Your mother and I have talked it over, but we want to know how you feel before we do anything final."

By now, Tammi was certain that she wasn't going to like the surprise.

"When we take a wrong turn it's impossible to go back and start in a new direction," her father continued. "But we can stop and take a good look around, if we are not sure, and maybe stop going in a wrong direction—if it is wrong."

"You're going to resign," Tammi heard herself say. "Because of me, you're going to resign from the church."

Her mother reached over and clasped one of her hands, now trembling, as she knew it would. "No, Tammi, not because of you, but because we want to be sure that what we do next is what God wants."

"Why can't we stay here until . . . you know."

"I've been known to confuse God's will with mine," her father reminded her with a grin.

"Where will we go?" Her mother's hand felt warm and strong, and she clung to it.

"We're going to stay at Uncle Ira's, at least for a while, until I can find—," her father hesitated, "—another position."

The silence was broken only by the soft wooden click of the German clock in the living room.

Tammi quelled the urge to squeal with delight. There were more important considerations now, and she had another world to deal with.

She gathered her courage and asked the question which had been gnawing at her since that day her parents had met with the board. "Will you still be a minister?"

Deep inside, she prayed, "Oh, please, God, please."

Her father peered over the edge of his dish of ice-cream.

"Tammi, a minister is someone who loves the people God gives him." He lowered the dish and smiled at her. "I've learned these last weeks that it has little to do with the way one makes a living."

26

When he heard they were moving, he had tried to avoid her house, but something had drawn him. He had parked his truck around the corner and had strolled casually down the uneven gray slate sidewalk on the opposite side of the street from the parsonage. He stopped and leaned against one of the oaks that painted the sidewalk with its dark summer shade. With the tree trunk partly shielding him, he was close enough to see, but far away enough to remain unobserved. For almost an hour he watched Tammi's father and some other men carry boxes and furniture from the house to a truck parked at the curb.

"Hello, Ted." The voice came from behind him.

Angry that she had found him there, he cursed under his breath.

"Hello." Keeping his back to her, he made no move to turn around.

She said nothing more, but he could sense she was still there.

Finally he heard her draw in her breath. "I saw you coming down the street from my bedroom window."

He made no reply, but cursed mentally again. She knew how long he had been there.

"I went out the back and walked around the block," she continued calmly, "because I have to say something to you." There was a pause. "And I can't outrun a truck." He expected her voice to be sarcastic, but it wasn't.

He sighed, decided to let her have her say, and get it over with.

Ted turned to face her. "It's a free country. Talk all you want." His tone was light and a little mocking. The half-smile mask he had cultivated so carefully over the last few years was fitted carefully into place.

"Ted." Her voice was no longer the nervous trill of an uncertain high-school girl, but she did hesitate a moment.

"Thanks for putting my day pack on the porch."

He twisted his mouth in a half smile. If that was all she wanted, he would have to say something to win.

"Forget it."

He turned his back on her again and looked vacantly across the street. For him to win, she would have to leave first. She didn't. He sensed she had no intention of leaving.

"There's something else, Ted." She waited for him to turn. He decided not to give her the satisfaction of an answer. His lips turned up slightly at the corners. That's what he used to do with his parents. His father, especially. Merritt J. Tolleson, Attorney-at-Law, would become so angry, he'd stamp out of the room.

"I didn't come to give you any trouble, or to have a tantrum, or try to hold anything over you, Ted."

He disciplined himself to remain unmoving, silent. That always bothered people. It had sure bothered her father. With those big green eyes, she would have to stare at his back.

"Ted."

Let her talk.

"I want you to forgive me."

234

He blinked, clenched his teeth to swallow the "What!" trying to burst from his throat, and continued his contest.

Moment, by moment, by moment, like flesh turned statues, they maintained their stances.

No one could take that for long. She would leave soon.

But she didn't.

"Ted, we've wronged each other. Will you forgive me?" He could hear her shallow, rapid breathing.

For him to walk away would admit defeat.

For him to talk would admit defeat.

For him to say, "No," would admit defeat.

Only losers admitted defeat.

He'd hold out. She'd have to give up.

"You said I . . . I used you."

He repressed a smile. He was winning. She'd cry in a minute. She always cried.

She remained silent a moment. When she continued, her voice was calm and firm.

"You were right, Ted. I used you. I didn't know that's what I was doing. I just wanted someone to want me, someone who would accept me, scar and all." Unconsciously, her fingers went up to that side of her face. "And I did what I did that night because I thought those things were love."

He listened, disgusted. She was just trying to get him to feel sorry for her. Same trick all losers pulled. Let her talk to his back. Sooner or later she'd realize how stupid she looked.

"And now," she continued rapidly, "I'm going to have a child I have no right to have . . . ."

Here it comes. The money pitch. Just like the other time.

"You should have had the right to have your child with someone who really loved you, and . . . and who you really loved."

Love. Love. It didn't exist.

"Ted, tell me you forgive me—please!"

She was weakening. Just a little bit longer. He could feel a film of sweat on his face.

"Ted, I've had to feel a lot of guilt because of this. Please forgive me."

Forgiveness? Nothing is ever forgiven. Her father preached all that stuff—sounded great in church. But he sure didn't have much that day in Mr. Rawlings' office. Then her father telling his uncle! Forgive her! She had to be kidding. His uncle fired him and told him to leave the day after graduation. Forgive!

"Please, Ted."

He felt her fingers rest gently on the back of his shoulder. Carefully, he kept the muscles relaxed. The fingers fell away. He heard her draw in her breath and then release it with a sort of a raspy sound. She always sounded that way when she was ready to cry. He should know. That's all she seemed to do the last few times he saw her. A moment later, her footsteps started away from him.

He had won.

He turned carelessly and took a step toward his truck.

The sound of her footsteps stopped.

"Ted."

This time he didn't bother turning.

"I forgive you, Ted."

He could feel her gaze until he turned the corner.

What a loser!

But his own emptiness had swelled larger with the win.

He had already packed, and it would be a matter of only a few minutes to throw his belongings under the camper shell over the truck bed.

He checked his wallet. His driver's license and a charge card with his own name and a California address. He had figured he wouldn't be around this place long enough to bother with changing the addresses. He had plenty of money. The severance pay his uncle had given him, plus what was left of the check he had received from the trust fund upon his graduation, would get him to California with plenty left over. He would be gone before his uncle closed the store.

Someplace between Lincoln and Denver, his air conditioner failed. He drove throughout the afternoon. Sweat coursed from his forehead, gathered in his eyebrows and slipped, stinging, into his eyes. Repeatedly he wiped his face with a handkerchief already soaked in his own sweat. The hot, humid swirl of air beating in through the open windows refused to cool and dry him, and sweat saturated his shirt and the top of his trousers. As the sun set outside of Sterling, he could see lightning playing back and forth among a phalanx of developing thunderstorms, but there was no rain.

He reached Denver and found a motel on East Colfax. Since leaving Shelterport three days before, he had stopped only for gasoline and an occasional two to three hours' sleep in rest areas.

It was almost sundown when he awakened. He showered, shaved, dressed, and packed. Not wanting to waste time looking for a restaurant, he ate in the motel dining room. While he waited for the waitress to bring his steak, he studied the road map. He could go the northern route through Grand Junction or the southern route through Trinidad to Santa Fe. Local drivers told him of another route through the mountains over Wolf Creek Pass. He found it on the map. It ran roughly like the hypotenuse of a triangle between the two other routes and would bring him through Cortez and the Four Corners. He would go that way.

The sun was well down before he had slipped over the first pass and dropped between the ranges toward Fairplay. There

237

would be two more passes before Monte Vista where he'd turn right and start the climb through Wolf-Creek.

The air in the high valley was crisp and chilled, and for the first time he lost the oppression which had soured the whole trip. The stars glittered so brightly he almost expected to hear them "clink" like a glass chandelier. Blue moonlight splashed the valley so brightly that he could easily see details in the fields and slopes clear back to the stands of forest furring the mountainsides.

Just like another night last winter.

He cursed and beat his fist on the steering wheel.

He pressed harder on the accelerator, and narrowed his concentration to the splash of colorless light pushing the blackness away from in front of him.

There was little traffic on the road, and he saw no patrolman. He slowed considerably on the uphill side of Wolf Creek, but once he reached the summit, the truck ran easily again.

The speed signs before each switchback on the downgrade swung unto the glare of his headlights more and more rapidly. The truck stuck to the curves like a marble in a groove. He would sleep in Flagstaff. One more day's driving and he would be home.

Home.

What home?

By now his father and his mother knew.

They would have little to do with him.

Who cared? He'd get enough from the trust fund to have his own apartment.

Only losers had to be "wanted."

Like Tammi.

And the baby. A loser before it was born.

A square speed sign capped by a diamond-shaped warning marker flicked by. He glanced at the "25 mph" message and the curve symbol.

Forgiveness! What a hypocrite. She knew he should have been the one to ask that.

The tires squealed as he entered the curve wide and drifted to the inside of the arc around the switchback. The squeal grew louder and then softened as he came out at the other end. He smiled. The control was positive, firm. Should take the next curve even faster.

She always tried to make him feel guilty. It wouldn't work.

Another yellow warning sign flashed past in the momentary glare from his headlights. "FALLING ROCKS" registered briefly, and was gone.

No one would ever make him feel guilty again.

Another rectangular speed sign. Another diamond warning. Switchback left.

Not his father. Not his mother. Not Tammi. Not even God, if there was one.

The road slipped off to the left, and he entered the curve wide, as before, but five miles an hour faster. The radial tires scrubbed and screeched on the blacktop, but held well as he took the whole road's width.

The rock loomed grayish-tan in his headlights and disappeared. The thud beneath the front end was muffled. For a moment time, light, truck, thought, hung suspended in some horror of an empty universe. Then the road, the mountain, and the night, disintegrated around him in an explosion of breaking glass, tearing metal, burning rubber, and the hollow, impersonal death sounds of a vehicle turning once and again, and again, until it wedged against a dark granite outthrusting.

The engine roared into the night for a few moments and then died. Ted tried to turn off the ignition, but his right hand wouldn't work. He worked his other arm out from underneath himself and reached around the steering column until finally he could reach the key.

The truck lay on its left side, partly inverted. One headlight still probed the night, its lone beam slanting upwards through the blackness. He smelled and tasted the grit and dust that had shaken loose in the wreck and begun to settle in the silence. He tried to move, but something heavy held his legs. He reached down and felt the jagged edge of the instrument panel where it had sliced into his right leg just above the knee, and he knew the warm liquid coursing out from the wound under his fingers was blood.

There was less pain than he expected, and more regret than he could have imagined.

He smelled raw gasoline and closed his eyes.

Winners don't die like this.

"Oh, hell." There was no anger, only a deep, surprised, empty disappointment.

He wondered—would she ever tell it who he was?

27

"Don't know why that telephone has to ring just as we're getting set down to our Fourth of July picnic," Bea fumed. She placed the dish of beet greens on the table with an impatient clatter and huffed into the parlor.

"Even if we are having it inside because of the rain," Jerome joked.

"Who?" Bea's voice carried clearly.

"And supper rather than lunch," Ira added with a chuckle.

"Mister MacIntosh?" Bea chuckled. "Yes. Yes. MISTER MacIntosh is here. Hang on."

Leaving the table at the first "Mister," Ira had disappeared

240

into the parlor after Bea. A moment later, Bea bustled out through the same doorway, leaving him behind with his mumble of conversation.

"Can't be anyone around here," she said. "Mister, indeed." She looked around the table to Jerome and Tammi. "Hope he isn't too long," she continued, her voice lower. "Shame for these greens to get cold."

They heard Ira hang up the phone. He returned to the table and sat down slowly. "A lady—Mrs. Wagoner—" he said, placing his hands deliberately beside his plate, his fists loosely clenched. "They've got a woman out there in the county hospital, other side of Burlington," he took a deep breath, ". . . claims she's Sissie." He fixed his eyes on the butter melting over the mound of beet greens. "Wants me to come."

The before-dinner chatter suddenly ceased, and sounds of water hissing on the stove, and rain dripping from the eaves dominated the room.

"After all these years." Bea gazed sadly at Ira, her round face tender with his pain. "After all these years."

"She's dying," Ira said quietly.

"When do you have to go?" Jerome asked.

"Soon's I can."

"Like some company?"

"Not of a mind to turn it down."

"Might as well take our car."

"Be obliged." Ira glanced around the table. "We'll eat when we get home, Bea." Their chairs scraped on the kitchen floor as they stood.

Ira and Jerome pulled into the parking area of the hospital a little under two hours later.

"Made good time," Ira grunted.

"Used to do it once a week when I had the program," Jerome replied, making small talk as they trudged toward the entrance. "Two hours was about average in good weather."

His voice trailed off as if he were lost in the tangles of his own thoughts.

They entered the lobby and approached a tired-looking telephone operator seated at an ancient switchboard. She finished a call, lifted a plug from its place at the bottom of the board and jammed it into a hole below a light winking its impatience. "May I help you?" The voice was nasal and condescending.

"You have an Amanda Murray here?" Ira asked.

"It's after visiting hours, you know."

"Mrs. Wagoner called," Jerome interrupted gently. "She—" He hesitated. "I'm a minister. It's all right for us to see her."

"Let me check with the floor nurse," the operator insisted, her voice heavy with authority. She plugged another cable into a hole and dialed a number.

"Head nurse, please." She drummed her fingers irritably on the black half-desk of the switchboard. "Miss Percy? Someone here to visit an Amanda Murray."

She sounded disappointed as she yanked the plug out of the board. She didn't bother to turn to face them.

"Fifth floor. Take the elevator at the end of the hall and turn left after you get off. Room 542." She picked up a lurid-covered paperback lying face down by her purse and started reading.

Leaving the elevator at the fifth floor, they stood in the hallway for a moment, adjusting to contradictory smells of disinfectant, alcohol, stale food, soiled linen, and poverty.

"Rather be sick in my barn," Ira grunted, his face grim.

"Lot of sick people, not much help, and less money," Jerome replied. "This place is not as bad as some, cleaner than most."

"Just the same, hate to think of family being here," Ira answered.

242

They found room 542 and stopped beside the open door. "You go in," Jerome said. "I'll stay out here for awhile."

Ira stepped over into the doorway and slipped quietly into the room. It was a four-bed ward, and according to the pink cardboard tag slipped into the brass clip on the door, Amanda Murray lay in bed "5-d", in the far corner, near the window. Ira shuffled over and stood by the bed, looking down at her face.

"Sissie?" His voice was little above a whisper, and he turned his battered red and black hunting cap around and around in his rough, farmer's hands.

She turned her face toward his voice and struggled to focus her eyes, large and hollow with pain.

One of the attendants had combed her thinning gray hair and had placed a brave red ribbon in it.

"Ira? Ah, Ira. Is it really you, Ira?" She reached her thin fingers to touch the sleeve of his blue work shirt.

"Ayep, Sissie, it's me," he whispered hoarsely. "Few more wrinkles than when I was seventeen, but it's me." He lifted a hand from his hat and placed it gently over hers plucking at his sleeve. Not trusting himself to talk more, or to move, he gazed, awe-struck, down at her.

He recognized only vaguely the sister he had lost so long ago. There was still the trace of brown in the tufted gray hair, parted in the middle as she used to do. Her warm, widely set brown eyes peered up at him as if they were looking from a place forty years deep. Pain and disappointment had shadowed the area below the eyebrows a bluish black, as if the things she had seen had bruised her with the viewing.

"I missed you, Sissie," he finally managed to say. "Still have your room. One up over the kitchen."

She glanced briefly around the ward and then back into his eyes. "Funny." She frowned a little, and then smiled. "Wanted to come back almost soon as I left. Pretty scared of Pa, though. Afraid he'd beat me." She lay resting for a moment, her eyes fixed upon him as if she were drinking his image detail by detail.

"Ira?"

"Carl, is he still . . . ?"

"Yes." He was careful to keep his voice without expression. "Never left his farm."

"Poor Carl."

Ira's lips twitched in displeasure.

"Wasn't Carl's fault, Ira."

"What do you mean, Sissie?" He leaned forward to catch her words.

"He wanted to marry me, especially when he knew I was carrying his child." Her smile made her face seem more transparent. "Said he wanted a big family anyhow—" She closed her eyes and continued. "Told him I wasn't going to be 'breedin' stock'. 'Sissie MacIntosh ain't goin' to spend her life havin' babies to be slave to some run-down farm,' I said. 'I'll fix it up. I'll make it a good farm,' he said. 'Marry me,' he said. 'Our farm'll be the best in the county—I'll do it for you,' he said. 'You'll see,' he said."

She lay resting again. The other patients, settled for the night, lay breathing gently, or snoring. Somewhere on the opposite side of the room, oxygen bubbled through a jar of water.

"I laughed at him. 'No farm for me,' I said. 'I'm goin' to New York, and I found a man to take me.'"

Her breath came more shallowly now. She rested longer between sentences, lying silently, squeezing Ira's hand now and again.

"Man from the mill, it was. Joe Murray. 'Drive you to Albany,' he said. 'Easy to find work, someone like you,' he said."

When she turned to look at Ira, her eyes gleamed. "You can imagine the work he had in mind. I couldn't go back to Pa;

with the baby coming, wasn't even good for that. Lived with him same's if we were married. Used his name ever since. He run away though, less'n six months. Carl only one who loved me . . . ." Her voice trailed off again.

"We'd of had you back, Bea and me," Ira tried awkwardly to comfort her.

"War was on by then. Not Pa, he'd a never had me back. Only right thing I ever did for my baby. They give him a good home . . . ."

She looked back at him. "Of them all, Carl was the only one who loved me. His was the only child I had. . . it's all ruined . . . poor Carl . . . ." She rested a long time, her breathing light and irregular.

She mumbled something. Ira bent closer to hear. "Letter in the drawer," she whispered. "Maybe he won't hate me, Ira. Do you think maybe he won't hate me any more? Even for my stealing a son from him?"

"No, Sissie." Ira ignored the unaccustomed tears spilling down his cheeks. "We're gettin' too far along, you and me and Carl, to go on with this hatin' foolishness."

"Take him the letter. Make him read it, Ira. Make him read it. He'll hate me and throw it away. Make him read it first."

"He won't be throwin' it away. He'll be right back here with it to see you, I reckon."

"No," she breathed. "I'll be with Someone I used to hate. Wish I hadn't waited so long to start believing He loved me. Only one besides Carl."

She died a half-hour later, clasping Ira's hand, her dark, deep eyes drinking in his image. "Good-bye, Ira," was all she said at the last. "Tell Carl I'm sorry." She squeezed his hand gently and died.

It took two hours to take care of the details. She had few possessions. The doctor signed the death certificate. A call to the mortician arranged for someone to pick up the body from the morgue down in the basement. The telephone operator was still behind her desk as they walked out, carrying Sissie's cheap cardboard suitcase. Ira noticed she had only the last few pages to complete of the paperback lying face down beside her purse.

A cool after-rain breeze sighed through the night-darkened parking lot. It seemed to banish the stench of sickness, of poverty, of death stuffed into every crevice of the hospital.

"Ayep," Ira breathed.

"What?" Jerome looked across the roof of the car at Ira's face, dim in the glow from the hospital entrance.

"Ayep," he repeated. "Never figured it out before." He slipped into the car beside Jerome.

"What's that?"

"Only two things ever really ours. An' one of 'em's a bad bargain."

Jerome started the car, and, listening for Ira to continue, headed toward the street.

"Ayep. Love and hate. One of 'em just ain't worth the price."

28

Ira shook his head as he turned down the dirt road leading to Carl's farm. "Haven't really spoke to 'im since before Pearl Harbor, not since I thought it was his fault 'bout Sissie."

"That's a long time not to talk to someone," Jerome smiled.

"Nothin' to it," Ira said grimly. "Just reckon him dead." He dodged a pothole. "Hate's as good as a bullet."

"I came to see him once when I was a pastor here. Lost a leg in the war."

Ira shifted gears as he topped a steep grade. "Hear tell, that and more. Never married."

They coasted down a short incline and swung into a weed-clogged farm road leading to the house. "Didn't come to me till the other night," Ira continued, "at Sissie's bedside, that I'd done about the same as if I'd shot him with the deer rifle."

Ira pulled his old Dodge around to the back of Carl's house, and backed down close to the porch where the winter wood was stacked.

Carl sat on a rusting metal lawn chair, his crutches propped, just within reach, against the shiplapped wall.

"Afternoon, Ira," he said in a flat, non-committal voice. His hard blue eyes narrowed as he took in Jerome, the truck, and its load. "Don't know what yer got there. Be obliged if ye took it away again."

Ira looked into Carl's eyes for a moment and drew the letter from his shirt pocket.

"For you," he said simply, climbing the rickety steps to the porch.

Carl sat, still unmoving. "You the mailman, now, Ira?" There was no humor in his cracked voice.

"From Sissie. She wanted to be sure you got it."

"Sissie?" Carl's shock and bitterness carried in his low voice. "Sissie, you say?" He scratched a mosquito bite beside his nose with a deliberate index finger. "No reason her writin' me, leastwise through you," Carl snapped, but Ira could sense the curiosity around the edges.

"County hospital called night before last." Ira watched Carl's face closely. "We stayed till she died, little after midnight." He placed the envelope on a cluttered table beside Carl's chair.

"Take it or not, as you will," Ira challenged. "I've got some

247

work needs doin'." He stalked away from the one-legged man, stepped off the porch, and sauntered to the truck.

Carl glared at Ira's retreating figure and then picked up the envelope. He turned it over and over in his twisted hands, examining it. "Looks like it's been around a while."

Ignoring the remark, Ira busied himself with freeing the tailgate. It slammed down spilling several chunks of stovewood on the dirt driveway.

"What you doin' there?" Carl bobbed his head at the truck.

"Gotta thin out on the mountain this summer. Got stacks from five year back. Lot more'n Bea and I need."

"Don't need no charity, Ira," Carl snapped. "Ain't so crippled but that I can get my own wood just fine."

"Charity ain't my long suit, Carl," Ira returned. "But no point in waste." He turned and started handing stove-sized chunks to Jerome for stacking.

Carl stuffed the letter in the torn pocket of his shirt and reached behind him for his crutches. He cursed as one fell with a clatter.

From the corner of his eye, Ira watched Carl use the second crutch as a tool to retrieve the fallen one, place both in front of him, and heave himself to his feet. The screen door slammed behind him as he clumped into the house. Ira looked at Jerome, grinned, and tossed a chunk of wood to him.

"Ira," Jerome spoke in a low voice, between gasps as he caught and stacked the wood. "If Carl lost his leg in the war, how come they didn't give him an artificial one?"

"From what I hear tell, he has one," Ira replied. "Hear he said once, after he come back, 'no wife'd want half a man one way, 'n half a man 't other.'" He tossed another chunk to Jerome. "So he never wore the leg," he continued. "Just give up, I guess."

Carl appeared in the shadows behind the screen door.

"Ira?" He watched as Ira straightened from his stooped posture atop the load of wood and looked toward him. "Whyn't you let your man unload that wood for a spell." He stared at Ira silently for a moment and then disappeared into the shadow of the room. Ira dusted his hands on his overalls and climbed deliberately down from the truck. He stepped onto the porch and into the house.

To Ira, the kitchen appeared as if Carl's mother had been the last to clean it the day before she died, fifteen years ago. The heavy window curtains allowed only slivers of the after-breakfast sun to slip around the sides and through the narrow slits where the curtains lacked an inch of meeting at the center. The wallpaper's thirty-year-old print had long since retreated under a generation of soot and smoke from countless suppers fried in the grease-encrusted cast iron skillet on the stove. Flies buzzed familiarly around the round oak table where Carl had pushed aside his cracked coffee mug and old restaurant-style plate.

He had already seated himself, the letter in a cleared space in front of him, when Ira entered.

"Cup o' coffee?" He nodded toward the gray-enamelled pot on the stove.

"Hot already this morning," Ira grunted. "Get a taste of water in a bit from your pump." He leaned back on the old kitchen chair and folded his hands behind his neck.

"I'd of married her, Ira." He smoothed the letter on the table. "Told her so." He looked up at Ira, his eyes empty of everything except pain.

"She told me," Ira said. He hesitated. "What happened— weren't your fault."

"You read the letter?"

"Nope." Ira lowered his arms and folded them across his chest. "Not mine to read."

"I've got a son . . . someplace."

"Sissie told me." Ira's voice was gentle as he saw Carl's eyes glow.

"Never know him, even if he were to walk in that door." He motioned to the screen door where the sounds of Jerome stacking the wood sifted through. "But someplace . . . someplace there's a man walkin' around with my blood in his veins. Somewhere I have a son." He peered through the screen door, fixing his gaze on the hill behind. "I ain't goin' to die, now. Now that I have a son."

Carl sat back in his chair and swept his eyes slowly around the cluttered kitchen as if he were seeing it for the first time. "Lot's gone to waste, Ira," he said sadly. "Lot's gone to waste."

"Not all," Ira said thoughtfully. "Something's saved."

Carl sat staring at the letter again. "Yep," he said finally, still staring at the letter. "More important that somethin's saved of it than that I be able to tell who he is." He fixed his eyes upon the wall where an old calendar print of a Hudson River steamer hung, but Ira could tell he was looking far beyond.

"Sorry she never did get somethin' better than I could've give 'er." He tapped the letter. "She deserved better." He ran his finger tenderly over the page. "She deserved better."

Ira stepped out to the back porch to get a cup of spring water from the pump and to let Carl have a moment. He gazed across the farmyard and up the hill. Although the fallen trunks which had concealed him those many years ago had long been swallowed in the encroaching brush, the tall lopsided pine still stood, as it did then, just to the right of where he had held Carl in his sights.

Carrying the filled cup carefully, he entered the house again and set it on the table.

"Never did feel proud about the way I talked about her, Ira."

Ira watched him and sipped his water. "Not proud myself about what I thought of you, Carl."

Carl pushed himself up from his chair, balanced himself for

a moment on his one leg, and placed his crutches under his shoulders. "Folks say my bees make the best honey anywhere's around," he puffed a little as he worked his way into his pantry and back out again. He had placed two small jars of honey in a one gallon paint can, and carried it by grasping the bail against the handle of one crutch. He chuckled. "Tough to carry things when both hands are full of crutches. Little paint can sort of handy."

He placed the can on the table and removed the two amber-colored jars.

"Take that other jar o' honey for that other feller's wife," he said quietly. "Know I seen him before, but can't remember where."

"Used to be the preacher here, few years back—when the big storm came."

"Wife lost her baby? Buried down in the old cemetery?"

"Same one." Ira paused. "Be buryin' Sissie there, day after tomorrow." He looked at Carl sadly. "Know she'd rather have you sayin' good-bye to her than most anyone else."

Carl reached out his hand. "Thanks, Ira."

Carrying the two jars of honey, Ira stepped off the porch and started toward the truck.

"Ira?"

He looked back at the man on the porch. "Ayeah?"

"That the fellow goin' to do the buryin'?"

"Ayup."

"Comin' back as preacher?"

"Hasn't said."

With Jerome seated beside him, Ira drove away from the old Hartley place. As they slipped around the curve on the rutted farm road, Jerome glanced back at the incomplete figure seated on the old lawn chair on the porch. There was a flutter of something white in Carl's hands, and then he was hidden from view.

"Lot o' years wasted hatin'," Ira commented as they bounced onto the county road. "Lot o' years wasted hatin'."

29

"Don't remember it being so hot the last summer I spent here," Tammi exclaimed, placing the paring knife on the counter and pulling the curtains aside from the screened window over the sink. She leaned forward clumsily to feel more of the elusive August breeze.

"You weren't carrying a passenger last summer you were here," Bea chuckled. "Sakes alive, 'fore long you won't have to do up the dishes. Way that tyke's growing, you won't be able to reach the sink."

She turned a little to Jael. "You folks figure what to do, when the time comes, with the baby?"

Tammi could feel their eyes on her. The silence lengthened.

"That's something—something Tammi's still struggling with," her mother said gently. "There aren't any easy answers to that one, Bea." She moved over to Tammi and gave her a little hug around the waist. Then she lifted a colander of rhubarb Tammi had just filled. "I forgot how much you have to cut, just to get a little sauce." She slipped the contents into the large pan simmering at the back of the stove and placed the colander back in front of Tammi.

Tammi concentrated on slicing the endless supply of rhubarb stalks into inch-long pieces.

"Some girls keep 'em," Bea continued, ignoring the hint. "The Dixon girl, down Croughton's Corners. She kept hers."

252

She stirred the sauce. "Decided to stay with her folks a spell. Ended up turnin' gloves for the factory till the state wouldn't let her anymore." She snorted derisively. "Said the factory was 'exploitin' her,' so they took away the only way she had o' makin' money. Who's exploitin' who is what I want to know! Be on the county now!"

The telephone rang a short and a long.

Tammi sighed, and breathed a prayer of thanks for the escape from Bea's endless stream of well-meant chatter. Her mother's eye caught hers and they smiled at each other as Bea turned away from the stove to dry her hands on a dish-towel.

"Wonder who that is this time in the afternoon," Bea remarked, disappearing into the parlor.

Tammi couldn't hear the conversation over the sound of the water running in the sink, but Bea's chubby form popped back into the kitchen a few minutes later with the report.

"Feel like taking your baby for a walk?" she asked.

Tammi turned away from the sink. "I suppose so. Where?"

"Down to the pond." She looked at Jael and grinned. "Big boss down at the mill wants to put some men on buildin' trusses for summer camps. Heard Jerome was back. Imagine him remembering Jerome working for him way back when he was pastor here!" She picked up the paring knife Tammi had abandoned and stood slicing rhubarb into the colander. "Anyhow, wants him to call before quittin' time."

Tammi untied her apron and wiped her hands dry. "I'll go get him."

As she let the screen door slap closed behind her, her mother and Bea continued talking. "That would be good if Jerome could get that. This vacation's got to come to an end pretty soon." The women's voices grew fainter, "baby . . . hospital . . . work . . . ." The slight breeze, and the locusts' long-drawn cries drowned out their voices as she stepped along the parallel ruts of the dirt farm road circling up from the house to the apple orchard beyond. The hill crested and the road flattened and then dipped generally downward as it bordered the orchard. She stopped for a moment where, years ago, Ira had lifted her out of the truck to stand when he had dug out her apple tree. It seemed so long ago. She smiled at the memory and continued through the orchard, pulling a half-ripened apple from its branch and biting into it.

"Ugh! Still too sour!" she spit the words out with the mouthful of apple and flipped the remainder, softball style, into the weeds bordering the road. "Should have known better," she thought, licking her lips to dilute the bitterness. "Not their season yet."

She saw them as she crested the hill overlooking the pond, two men in overalls, one steadying a fencepost while the other, wearing a billed cap, hammered against it. She stopped for a moment, watching the hammer land out of time with the hollow "thock . . . thock . . . thock" sound rolling lazily up toward her on the summer heat.

Her father looked up as she walked down the slope toward them. "Can't be calling us for supper already."

"No," Tammi smiled. "Man from the mill called. Wants you to call him back before five."

Ira stopped hammering and straightened up. "That'll hold for awhile." He looked from Jerome to Tammi and back again, and then pulled a large watch from the bib pocket of his overalls. "Make it a little after four," he observed, replacing the watch. "Whyn't you take the truck." He glanced at Tammi again. "S'pose you can still hold a post steady."

Tammi held her hands straight in front of her. "My arms still reach farther than the rest of me." They smiled at one another. As she had grown larger with child, she had, over the weeks, grown less self-conscious about her shape, at least with her parents and Ira and Bea.

254

"You go ahead and take the truck," Ira said to her father. "Tammi and me will come back through the orchard."

While she steadied the old fencepost, Ira hammered fast the bottom strand of wire and stood again.

"That'll hold it, least for another year." He chuckled. "Don't know why I keep fixin' that fence. No more cows. Because it's there, I guess." He slipped the hammer into a loop just ahead of his back pocket.

They walked together to the edge of the pond and watched for a few moments as the slight breeze rippled the water.

"I remember the last time we were down here together," Tammi said.

"Ayep, young one. Day we got your apple tree."

"I was crying because I didn't want to leave." She continued gazing at the surface of the pond. The breeze stilled, and the pond became a dark-green mirror.

"Uncle Ira," she looked at him, her eyes dark and troubled. "Can't things ever be as good again, once they've been—changed?"

Ira gazed out over the pond and the meadow beyond. The crow's feet deepened at the corners of his eyes as he squinted slightly in the afternoon sunlight. He bent for a moment, dug several small stones from the mud at his feet, and stood, weighing them in his hand.

"Lotta things hidden in that pond there," he said quietly. "Used to have an old rowboat. Sank fishin' one day for bullheads. Lost a good rod and a Sears-Roebuck reel." He chuckled. "Never did tell my Pa what happened to it." He drew his arm back, and threw the stones deliberately, one after the other, towards the center of the pond.

The splashes came in order, raising saucers of water glinting transparent in the summer sunlight. The heavier stones sent an abrupt "puh-lunk" back to their ears as the pond swallowed them. The lighter ones disappeared with an almost silent "chuff."

"Young 'un, it's like everybody has a pond." He spoke slowly, and his words hung in the afternoon air. "Things we do, like those stones I just threw in, make sounds—loud or soft.

"Make ripples too—reach out and, sooner or later, everybody round us feels 'em."

Together they watched the concentric rings from the stones spread and intersect on the surface of the water.

"Once they start, no way to get 'em stopped."

The ripples flattened out and grew gentler as they spread, finally reaching the shore in a gentle, almost imperceptible undulation.

"Pretty upsetting at the beginning, just like those first ripples were pretty sharp. After a while, they get gentler. Not many people to see the hurt—'less they know how to look."

"Will it always hurt, Uncle Ira?"

"Hurt gets gentler, as time goes by. It'll keep poppin' up though, from time to time. You'll see the ripples. Always be a little bit of it there."

He stared across the meadow beyond the pond where long ago, rifle in hand, he had tread the path toward Carl's farm. "Forgivin'," he said, almost to himself. "Forgivin's the honey in it."

Tammi looked down at her swelled abdomen. "I guess, what I do with the baby, whatever I do, it'll always hurt."

The pond lay flat again, riffled here and there only with the gentle fingers of the afternoon breeze.

EPILOGUE

He looked up from the letter he was typing and straightened his back to ease the cramp. He heard the rain pelt upon the cabin roof and wondered how long it had been coming down.

He had cleaned the old-fashioned coal stove earlier and, despite the evening chill, had decided not to build another fire for only an hour or so. He had brewed a pot of coffee on the old Primus instead, and the cabin had grown snug with its heat.

It had been a good boat. He was glad he hadn't sold it for something larger. He leaned back and let his gaze wander around the cabin. The brass portlights gleamed yellow in the light of the kerosene lamps. Set in pairs into the mahogany sides and front of the trunk cabin, the circular ports had been green with corrosion when he first bought the boat. Now the wood brightwork glowed from years of meticulous care, the charts were current, the gear in good repair and functional, and he had finished yesterday preparing the engine for the winter.

There really had been nothing else to do this evening. He had simply wanted to spend one last evening with his boat, enjoy one last whiff of varnished wood, one last pot of fragrant, fresh coffee. He propped himself against the main cabin bulkhead and proofread the letter while he sipped from his mug.

Dear Dr. Rosen,

This is simply a personal note thanking you for keeping in touch with me these last ten years and reminding me of your interest in my career.

257

You told me a long time ago, that there is no shelter from evil, that the best a teacher can hope for is to try to help a few cope with the evil surrounding them.

I attempted to flee that, and, as you prophesied, it failed to work.

You were right. As a teacher, I wasn't called to shelter, but rather to do the living that has to be done.

My application for a position with you is already in the mail.

Respectfully,
Frank Rawlings

He finished reading the letter, folded it carefully and slipped it into the already-addressed envelope which had lost its crispness in the humid cabin atmosphere. He sealed it and slipped it into an inside pocket.

He slid the cabin hatch forward, and stood in the opening as he had done countless times before, wrapping his cup with his hands to keep the chill from his fingers. The rain had stopped, and the night wrapped itself black around him except for the wet pavement on Wharf Street reflecting the streetlights.

He drained the cup, placed it with his few remaining possessions into a cardboard box, set the box outside, and emerged from the cabin's protection to stand in the cockpit. Sliding the hatch closed, he slipped the padlock together with a soft "click," balanced the box awkwardly on his shoulder and backed down the ladder to the ground.

He lifted a hammer, nail, and "FOR SALE" sign from the box and fastened the sign to one of the supports cradling the boat for the winter.

Unlocking the yard gate, he drove his car into the street and stepped back into the yard to slip the keys into the drop-box beside the office door. He stood in the entrance to gaze at his boat for the last time.

Carrie had told him not to be afraid.

At last he understood.

He locked the gate and walked slowly to his car.

He would do the living that had to be done.

ACKNOWLEDGMENTS

Many people encourage, help, and invest their time, energies, hope, and encouragement in an author. I hope this book is worthy of the many who believed in it.

A grateful thanks to my mentors:

Jim Johnson, whose class at the 1979 Decision School of Christian Writing gave me the "nuts and bolts" to get the story started.

Stan Reilly, who saw promise in my first crude scribblings, and whose enthusiasm made me believe I could do the job.

My high school English class, who had the courage to tell me when they didn't like something.

Barb Francken, who gathered valuable material for me by proxy.

Dr. Allan Clemenger, who let me see a portion of the story through his eyes.

Charette Barta Kvernsteon, who was still able to smile despite a broken leg, a writers' school full of students, and an author who wanted to contact "just one more editor."

My wife, Joyce, who put up with a mountain of chores undone and encouraged me to finish the book.

Del Woods and Carolyn Welch, who critiqued and proofed repeatedly.

Dr. Penelope Stokes, whose copy-editing skills saved me many an embarrassing slip 'twixt the pen and the press.

Judith Markham, an editor who drew from me more than I knew was there.

Finally, a special thanks to Sheldon Vanauken, who encouraged a stranger a generation and two thousand miles away with the following:

> *Each of us must sound his own unique note in the orchestra of the music of the "Great Dance," for if that note is never sounded, the music will be the less rich.*